FIVES ACADEMY

L. Wood

Copyright © 2026 by L. Wood

All rights reserved.

No part of this publication may be reproduced, distributed, or transmitted in any form or by any means, including photocopying, recording, or other electronic or mechanical methods, without the prior written permission of the publisher, except as permitted by U.S. copyright law. For permission requests, contact L. Wood at author.lwood@gmail.com.

The story, all names, characters, and incidents portrayed in this production are fictitious. No identification with actual persons (living or deceased), places, buildings, and products is intended or should be inferred.

Book Cover by Atra Luna Design

Map Illustration by @shah_alom1

Edited by West of Mars

ISBN: 979-8-9944464-1-6 (Paperback)

ISBN: 979-8-9944464-2-3 (Hardcover)

First edition 2026

To my beautiful girls. Without you, this book would have been published two years ago. Without you, I would be missing two very special and important pieces of myself.

—I love you, more!

Contents

Glossary	IX
Fives Academy Map	XI
1. Chapter One	1
2. Chapter Two	5
3. Chapter Three	10
4. Chapter Four	19
5. Chapter Five	26
6. Chapter Six	31
7. Chapter Seven	37
8. Chapter Eight	41
9. Chapter Nine	46
10. Chapter Ten	50
11. Chapter Eleven	57
12. Chapter Twelve	63
13. Chapter Thirteen	70
14. Chapter Fourteen	76

15.	Chapter Fifteen	80
16.	Chapter Sixteen	86
17.	Chapter Seventeen	95
18.	Chapter Eighteen	99
19.	Chapter Nineteen	102
20.	Chapter Twenty	108
21.	Chapter Twenty-One	113
22.	Chapter Twenty-Two	118
23.	Chapter Twenty-Three	125
24.	Chapter Twenty-Four	133
25.	Chapter Twenty-Five	138
26.	Chapter Twenty-Six	146
27.	Chapter Twenty-Seven	152
28.	Chapter Twenty-Eight	159
29.	Chapter Twenty-Nine	167
30.	Chapter Thirty	174
31.	Chapter Thirty-One	181
32.	Chapter Thirty-Two	188
33.	Chapter Thirty-Three	193
34.	Chapter Thirty-Four	199
35.	Chapter Thirty-Five	206
36.	Chapter Thirty-Six	209

37.	Chapter Thirty-Seven	214
38.	Chapter Thirty-Eight	218
39.	Chapter Thirty-Nine	222
40.	Chapter Forty	229
41.	Chapter Forty-One	233
42.	Chapter Forty-Two	239
43.	Chapter Forty-Three	245
44.	Chapter Forty-Four	251
45.	Chapter Forty-Five	258
46.	Chapter Forty-Six	261
47.	Chapter Forty-Seven	265
48.	Chapter Forty-Eight	269
49.	Chapter Forty-Nine	274
50.	Chapter Fifty	281
51.	Chapter Fifty-One	285
52.	Chapter Fifty-Two	290
53.	Chapter Fifty-Three	297
54.	Chapter Fifty-Four	305
55.	Chapter Fifty-Five	314
56.	Chapter Fifty-Six	318
57.	Chapter Fifty-Seven	323
	Acknowledgments	327

Also by L. Wood

Glossary

Creatures: A short-lived sentient being created from an element and an enchantment.

Dark Mage: A mage who uses dark magic, giving them the ability to manipulate all four elements. To become a dark mage, they must kill an innocent, and they feed off ether mages. The more powerful the dark mage, the more they can control all four elements. Dark mages can only be killed by incineration or decapitation.

Elemental: A mage who can manipulate an element(s). *Same as a mage.*

Elixirs: A healing remedy created with herbs and/or plants and an enchantment/spell.

Enchantment: Powerful form of magic involving casting or infusing a spoken spell onto an object or element, creating or conjuring, with short to long lasting effects.

Familiars: A companion animal with a magical bond with its human, the human giving it part of their soul. Only level fours and fives can create a familiar, and the process can be caustic and deadly.

Mage: A magic user who can manipulated an element(s). *All mages are elementals.*

Spell: Magical words, actions, or ingredients to bring about a desired outcome, often a part of an enchantment.

Tonic: Helps prevent illness and other ailments, often created using spells.

Mage Levels 1-5:
1. Marginally manipulate their element but cannot create it.
2. Can manipulate and create small amounts of their element in its raw form.
3. Manipulate their element well and create it. Can create small elemental creatures with extensive practice.
4. Fully in tune with their element and can create large creatures. Their magic can be used through any part of their skin, not solely through their hands.
5. High and rare. Full capabilities unknown.

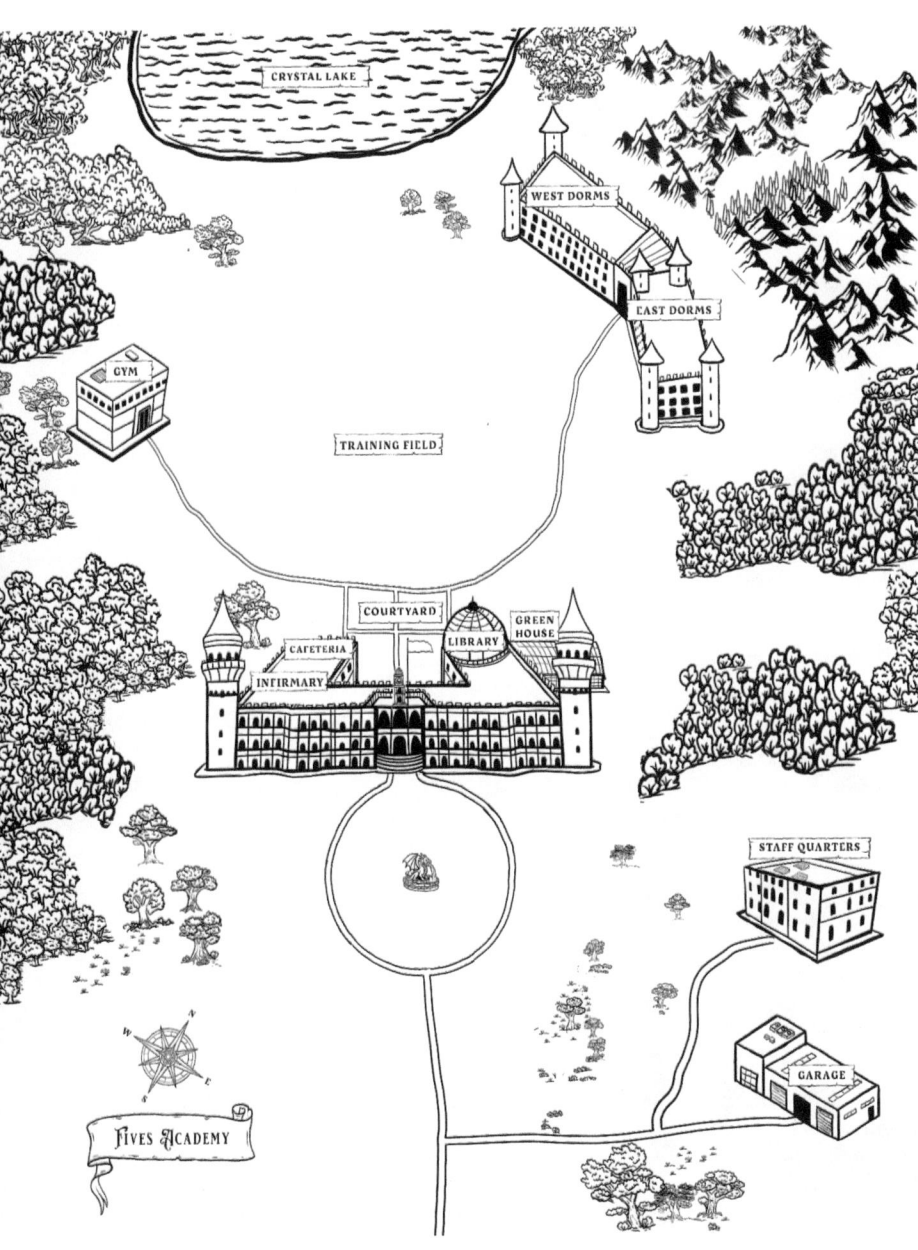

Chapter One
Selene

"Do you think this safe house has Oreos?" My sister began searching through the old wooden kitchen cabinets as if the only thing that mattered was her Oreo addiction and there weren't people trying to kill us.

"You're worried about cookies? Right now?" I asked, my clipped tone making me sound like Mom. I winced. Mom was murdered two days ago and we had just arrived at the safe house.

"Not just any cookie." She shut the cabinet door with a clank, the noise causing me to cringe. "The best chocolate cream-filled cookie to ever exist. But you already know that."

I traced my finger along the bland wooden framework on the interior wall of the quaint cabin, ignoring the sting in my chest. Mom always had Oreos for us—mostly because Vivian had a deep, profound love for them.

"They're even still delicious long after their eight-month shelf life," my sister continued. She had her own way of mourning: hiding behind jokes, reciting futile information, and occasional sarcasm.

I stopped tracing the woodwork and examined my finger, which lacked dust despite no one setting foot in the cabin for months. Mom would take the trip once or twice a year to make sure the safe house was still *safe* and stocked. Any mediocre air mage—a magic user who manipulated the element of air—could create a spell to prevent dust from settling. Mom had been anything but mediocre.

A dull scent of smoke began to seep into the cabin, and I scrunched my nose at the invasion.

Then realization hit.

"Vivian! Quiet!" I ordered my sister in a hushed tone.

Viv twirled around to face me, openly offended and taken aback at the use of her full name. Her lips parted, likely intent to argue, but she didn't get the chance as I yanked her to the ground. I motioned for her to stay quiet and follow.

We crawled across the Aztec rug until we were behind the countertop that divides the living room from the kitchen and pressed our backs against the wood paneling.

Rain pelted against the metal roof, masking any noise. Peering over the counter, I grabbed the monitor and pressed the side power button, but a black screen greeted me.

"You said you plugged it in hours ago when I was starting the generator," I whisper-yelled at Viv.

"The cord must've fallen out." She shrugged.

So help me... My sister was brilliant—when she wanted to be. I crawled to the wall where the charger was and connected it, gripping the edges of the small black monitor.

"Did you hear something?" Viv leaned over my shoulder, her silky black hair sprawling over the screen. "I don't hear anything."

"Smoke." I brushed her hair off the monitor and pointed to my nose.

Viv lifted her chin, taking a big whiff. "It could be anything. People camp, and they usually have campfires. We *are* in the middle of the woods."

"You think there are campers all the way out here in the middle of the Venezuelan jungle, while it's pouring, with a fire that is close enough we can smell it?" My lips pressed flat, letting my skepticism seep into my expression.

She must've finally understood because her eyes widened and she sucked in her lips. The monitor lit, displaying different camera views set around the perimeter of the cabin, but nothing could be seen. Smoke blanketed the grounds. It easily differed from fog, rising unnaturally in the rain.

"Shouldn't the alarms have gone off?" Viv asked, eyeing the monitor.

"Should've." The thought was unsettling. Even if the monitor was off, there were sensors throughout the grounds that would set off an alarm long before anyone got close. We had been careful getting to the cabin, just like Mom had showed us. After traveling by ferry from Dominica to the mainland, we journeyed the rest of the way during the dark and hid in an abandoned building during the day. Sighing, I set the useless monitor down. "Grab your pack. We'll sneak out the basement."

Viv crept down the hall. There was a good chance we were surrounded, but it was our only option. There was no way we could defeat the mage who killed Mom.

My throat clamped shut and my mouth went dry at the memory.

I grabbed my escape pack, which leaned against the back of the green couch, wincing slightly as the strap made contact with a small cut on my palm I had received from a piece of glass during the attack. The pack was our lifeline—not just clothes, but also passports and cash ... lots of cash.

"Got it," Viv whispered nonchalantly as she emerged from the hallway holding her pack, but the sweat on her brow told me she was just as frightened as me. The mage who had killed Mom was a water mage—or at least was a water mage before they went dark—and they bore a dark, inky circle on their palm. But if a dark mage was powerful enough, they could use all elements, just like the widely known, and extinct, ether mages. The more powerful the dark mage was, the farther the mage had slipped into the darkness, being eaten by an obscuring madness.

I gave our clothes a quick once-over, noting Viv's deep blue T-shirt and black pants, and my army green T-shirt and black pants. We were still dressed for cover. The edge of the Aztec rug lifted easily, revealing a handle. Taking a breath, I lifted the hatch to the closet-sized basement that led to a narrow passageway. An old underground wine cellar waited on the other end.

"We have to be prepared, like they know about the tunnel and as if they're expecting us to use it." I tucked a loose strand of my medium-length brown hair behind my ear and looked back at my sister. "And Viv?"

"Yeah?" She raised a brow.

"Let's not make it easy on them."

Chapter Two
Selene

THE TUNNEL FROM THE house to this old, musty wine cellar was the perfect escape—probably part of the reason Mom had chosen the place. I cracked open the cellar hatch leading to the backyard and my eyes began to immediately burn from the smoke. Across the unkempt yard, the cabin sat quiet and dimly lit, just as we had left it.

I scanned the rest of our surroundings and heaved open the reinforced iron hatch the remainder of the way, rain dampening my hair. Mud and weeds squashed between my fingers as I hoisted myself out. Viv climbed the ladder behind me and I lent a hand, pulling her out onto the overgrown lawn. The forest line to our right had tall trees with thick, broad leaves, creating the perfect cover.

I started toward our escape with Viv right behind me but only made it a few steps before shadows emerged in our path. I held out my arm, stopping Viv in her tracks.

Figures stepped out of the woods around us. They stopped advancing, but the ones directly in front of us slowly lessened the distance between us. Viv and I crept backward, like prey being herded into the center of a circle. My heart raced as I attempted to formulate an escape plan.

"I don't think we're sneaking away," Viv whispered, her retreat in step with mine until we halted.

"No." My jaw clenched. "We aren't."

My breathing slowed as I told my muscles to relax, preparing for a fight. I wasn't going to let them take my sister. Although she was only a year younger than me, it was my job to keep her safe. She only had me, and she was all I had.

"Selene Thomas." The voice sounded mature, influential even, but I couldn't see through the haze to make out who it belonged to.

One of the obscured figures took another step, the smoke separating to reveal a tall, lean man with dusted-grey blond hair. I assessed his dress shoes to his khakis and all the way to his collared shirt. It was in the seventies and about to get a lot hotter with the rising sun—who would wear dress shoes in the jungle?

A beautiful white fox slinked out of the shadows behind the man's legs. It plopped its small rump down next to the man's foot, its black eyes staring directly at me, the smoky grey tips of its ears twitching.

"Vivian Thomas." The man spoke, and I looked up. The man nodded at my sister, his shoulders set with the same confidence his tone held.

"What do you want from us?" I stepped in front of my sister.

Off to the man's side, an older woman called attention to herself by twitching her hand, and I bent my knees, bracing for an attack. Then the smoke dissipated. *Fire mage.* She wasn't preparing to attack; she was shutting off her magic. Still, I held my defensive position as a dark scarlet lizard hunkered down on her shoulder, its bold blue tail draping down her upper arm.

I didn't like being trapped.

"My deepest condolences regarding your mother." The man held out his hands as if he were submitting, and the hair on my neck rose.

Mom had trained me to trust no one, and that *feeling* was a part of me.

I stayed silent, not wanting to give anything away. How had he known she was dead? Had they followed us here from our home in Dominica?

"We're with Fives Academy. These are its guards"—the man pointed around the circle—"and I am Headmaster John Sanders, also a member of the Mage Council."

Great.

"We aren't orphans," I stated. I'd heard of the council sending academy guards instead of agents to track mage orphans. Orphans posed too much of a threat to the human world if not *tamed* or taught how to use their magic.

The Too-Put-Together-Headmaster didn't reply, only offering a slight dip of his head, displaying the pity he took on us.

"We. Aren't. Orphans."

"Whoever killed your mother is coming after both of you. You will be safest at the academy," the headmaster said.

"How did you know where to find us, John?" I asked, ignoring any formalities, and glanced at the guards surrounding us. Sewn on their jackets under their left collarbone was a gold insignia of all four elements—earth, fire, wind, water—lined a circle and dappled with a couple of stars in the center.

"It's my job." John's lips pursed. Dark mages were ruthless. It wouldn't have surprised me if they had caused destruction and death prior to finding us, which would have led John and the guards to Mom. "I promise we are only here to help. You're sixteen, and your sister is fifteen." He nodded at my sister, as if pointing out our age solidified his reasoning. It only made it creepier, though it wasn't entirely shocking. Mom had gone through great lengths to keep us hidden, but the mage council was notorious for being thorough with their records. "Fives Academy has the strongest protective wards of all other academies or places in the world, Selene."

"It's Sal," I corrected. I rarely went by Selene.

At least mages had high regards for the security of their children, doing anything to protect them. Other mages were not the only threat. While little knowledge of elementals existed in the human world, we were known to some—or rather, to folklore. The Mage Council helped protect our secrets and existence, but they couldn't keep it from trickling out. It was thought by the non-magic population that our capabilities only consisted of mere magic tricks, and we were referred to as witches. They surely did not know about dark mages. There would have been mass panic.

"That's why the council sent academy guards all the way from Alaska?" I glanced at the fox at his feet, its little mouth opening in a wide yawn. *Was it bored?* It had a teal to purple gradient collar with a small charm. It had to be his familiar—a companion animal with a magical bond with its human—given the way it practically sat on his feet, but I'd never seen a familiar until tonight. Now I'd seen two, assuming the lizard belonged to the fire mage. "How do we know you are who you say you are?"

"You don't." John stayed where he was, no longer advancing.

Viv and I could fight—Mom had made sure of that—but we were outnumbered and had no clue of their levels of magic. He was right. Viv would be safest there.

Mom had taught us about Fives Academy. She had said it was not only the most prestigious academy for training but also the most secure. She knew because she had gone there. It was one of the few elemental academies in the world that recognized fighting as a required skill.

I couldn't win a fight against the dark mage who killed Mom, but a dark mage would have a hard time crossing the academy's wards. If this group wanted to harm us, they already would have tried.

"Okay." I nodded. "We'll come."

"What?" Viv grabbed my arm. "You can't be serious. We can't trust them."

"No. We can't." I lowered my voice. "But if they're telling the truth, it's our best option. We've already been found once. That dark mage, Viv. If it found us instead ..."

Viv blanched. She took a deep breath and nodded. "Let's go to school."

She deserved to have a normal high school life.

I didn't.

Chapter Three

Selene

By five o'clock later that day—which was essentially our midnight—we were driving through Fives Academy's massive iron gates, its name intricately swirling across the top like metal vines and bending to create symbols that acted as a ward. A few of the pickets below the name were bent to form the same insignia the guards wore on their jackets.

Just five minutes ago, there had been a blinding desert of snow, but once we had crossed an invisible threshold, the massive manor-style academy appeared inside a clear dome, the other end not visible. Woods bordered the buildings while luscious green grass with tall trees rolled over the hills and surrounded the stone buildings. Some of the leaves were painted red and orange, a sign that fall had arrived.

"The academy is cloaked from the outside world. Only when a mage crosses its border is it seen," John said from the passenger seat of the Jeep, the fox sleeping soundly in his lap. If he had brought his cute familiar to seem more trusting, it wasn't going to work. "But the mage must be what we call *invited* to be allowed through. If humans were to wander out here, they'd become disoriented and simply pass by as if there was nothing and, after the matter, forget they'd even been disoriented."

"Like the Bermuda Triangle?" In the seat next to me, my sister practically smooshed her nose against the car window.

While the academy's beauty was evident, I saw nothing but trouble.

"In a way." John was facing the front, but there was amusement in his voice. "It's a mix of elemental magic and enchantments. Earth combined with air magic creates an invisible barrier—manipulating temperature and air density—and air pressurizes the surrounding area to disorient any unwanted visitors with an added complex spell."

"How does it differentiate humans and elementals?" I asked, wondering how that could be so easily detected. Dark mages were able to sense other nearby elementals, which helped draw them to powerful mages so they could siphon their magic. Other elementals could sense others by smell, but it wasn't always easy to pick up on, and magic could be used to block scents.

"It's similar to testing for elemental magic mixed with complex spells, which will be a part of your senior year." John glanced over his shoulder at me.

"And we were specifically invited?" If he was going to share, I would attempt to get as much information about this place as I could.

"Yes," John said in finality.

Okay. I guess he wasn't going to share everything.

"What about animals?" Vivian asked as a bird flew overhead.

"Animals can come and go, apart from those that carry magic. It helps the ecosystem, as the academy grounds extend through the forest and mountains." John pointed out the window. "The main entrance."

The gravel driveway perfectly circled a stone dragon fountain in the front, except the fountain shot out fiery flames from the center of the dragon's mouth instead of water. The dragon's body was entangled with vines and deep violet flowers that were almost black. Dragons symbolized strength, power, and courage. They were a natural enemy to dark mages due to their resistance to them, but the dark mages had eliminated dragons a long time ago for that reason.

Once the Jeep stopped, I hopped out, wanting to be out of a confined space. The air was filled with wood scents, flowers, and a hint of burnt pine—nothing like the salty breeze of what had been home. Loose strands of my hair swirled in the wind. It was styled in two French braids that led into two low buns—just like Mom had always done for me.

My heart ached, but I straightened my shoulders. I needed to be aware.

I spared a glance at my sister as she came to the front of the Jeep. She gaped, her lips curled up and her brown eyes wide. She had Mom's eyes but must have had Dad's black hair—whoever he had been. Mom had never talked about him, only mentioned that he had a kind heart and was gone.

The main building's shadow fell over us as a black flag at the top flapped in the wind, the sun glinting off gold symbols that matched the guards' insignia. It had to be five stories high, but the windows said it had three above-ground floors, and at the top was a parapet and three towers at the front, one in the middle, and one at each corner. A bell hung in the middle tower, and its smooth black exterior managed to glint in the lowering sun.

The academy's exterior resembled a castle in the style of an old, large manor with a sprawling estate straight out of a fancy magazine.

"Follow me." John waved us forward, but I hesitated and watched as the guards unloaded our packs, which still had our passports and money. I wasn't sure if the guards would go through our stuff, and I didn't want them confiscating our belongings.

"They'll bring them to your rooms," John said, following my gaze but continuing forward, the white fox in pursuit. I cracked the first knuckle on my pointer finger with my thumb, releasing tension, and turned to follow.

John led us through massive double stone doors, the surface etched like shale with a glossy black hue. I recognized the material. Tungsten—the strongest natural metal on earth. Powerful earth mages struggled to manipulate it, and no known mage had been able to create it. This place had been created to be a fortress. *Maybe we will be safe here.*

The foyer was just as extravagant with magic-lit candles, trees merging into the stone walls, and roots weaving into the black cobblestone floor. Off to the left, a wooden staircase climbed toward the vaulted ceiling, ivy crawling on its spindles. It was as if a princess fairy tale and a dark romance novel had converged.

If I had been brought here a week ago, before Mom died, I probably would have been allured by its magnificence and magical foundation. Now, it just made me want to run.

John's office wasn't far, and it matched the academy entrance and hallway vibes. The door was made of dark wood with elegant carvings, and inside, a large black chair sat on the far side of a substantial stone-slabbed desk with two tan chairs on the opposing side. The sturdy stone was held up by thick ebony wood pillars on either side, the subtle aroma of the smoky, sweet wood still present. A beige couch lined one wall and filing cabinets the other, and plants rooted in white ceramic pots hung from the tall ceiling.

A small wooden cart was made into a mini coffee bar, complete with a French Press coffee maker. I was going to avoid that deliciously painful liquid for a while. Mom had a French Press, and we loved adding cinnamon bark and vanilla to our cups.

Great. Every little thing—such as coffee—was going to remind me of her.

Candles lit the room from the walls to the glass jars on the shelves, and I couldn't help but wonder if they were enchanted to stay lit and keep the flames contained. A single mage light protruded from the ceiling, similar to the ones in the hallway. The warm glowing quartz added to the cozy, natural atmosphere.

"We aren't sure why this dark mage targeted your mother, but we will figure it out." John waved at the two chairs for Viv and me to sit, slight wrinkles at the creases of his eyes. "I am so very sorry."

"And how did you find out about her and find us?" I asked, wanting to hear more than just *it's my job*.

"Three dark mages were reported in the area." John rubbed his forehead as Viv took a seat. "They had a conflict with a couple humans near your home. It led to your house, and our guards figured out the rest. We were able to track you and your sister. The dark mages will be after both of you next."

I thought I had covered our tracks well. Clearly, I was wrong—and clearly, I had some practice to do.

"I didn't see the other dark mages' palms, but the one that killed Mom had a black circle. Does that mean anything to you?" I slowly sat, and once I did, so did John.

"It does not sound familiar, but it could be their clan mark," he said.

"And what makes you think they're after us?" I asked.

The fox jumped onto the long desk, causing me to flinch as its feet landed quietly on the stone. It glanced at me with its brown eyes—which I swore had been black—and then went to what appeared to be its cleared, dedicated spot and curled up into a ball. The little creature did not seem to care about my presence in its master's office.

"This is Aura." John rubbed the fox's chin. It closed its eyes and flicked its grey-tipped ear in approval. "Did you see the dark mages?" he asked.

"Not clearly."

"But you still saw them." John sighed. "Dark mages are merciless, and they don't leave survivors. Do you know anything about why your mother might have been targeted? It's doubtful three dark mages would attack a level-three air mage, as they can't siphon their magic."

I shook my head, unbothered by his classification of my mom, which he most likely read from the small folder in front of him.

"Nothing at all?" he pressed.

"No." I glanced at my sister, who was letting me do the talking, thankfully. As much as I hated to admit that I—sometimes—loved her babbling, she could accidentally say more than we wanted.

"Your mother's file did not contain much past high school. No address. No job. No phone records. Just that Anna Thomas had two children, Selene and Vivian Thomas—age sixteen and fifteen. Father unknown. The cabin we found you at had heavy surveillance." John rubbed his chin. "Perhaps there was something else?"

After a few more attempts and realizing I wasn't going to say any more, nor would Viv, he went through the entire welcome speech, initiation, handed us a map of the campus, and then explained that our classes wouldn't start until next week, giving us time to settle in. We would have roommates in the same grade as us—Viv a sophomore, and me a junior—and a student was on their way to give us a tour of the academy.

The headmaster also said Mom's ashes would be delivered in the following weeks. Due to the severity of the dark mage's magic, her body would need to be cremated. I bit back tears and held down the bile rising in my throat. I hadn't been sure of what was going to come of her, and it was comforting to hear she'd be back with us and not left to decay in our ruined home.

My plan had been for Viv and me to still be in Venezuela, hiding. Instead, we were hiding at a teenage introvert's worst nightmare—high school. My mom's death and her name were not going to be public knowledge, leaving our reason for being here undisclosed, and hopefully making our task at hiding easier.

April—our overly chipper tour guide and Viv's new roommate—led us down the hall toward the exit. We stepped outside, in the direction of the dorms. Far back by the trees, I could make out an enormous, glistening pond. Its size could easily classify it as a small lake. I scanned the map and saw the body of water was named Crystal Lake. *How pretty.*

April had wanted to give a grand tour, but I couldn't take more of her squealing laughs after the first three in less than five minutes. I asked her to show me where Viv's room would be and then mine. She could show Viv—who couldn't hide her own excitement—the rest of the academy. Viv could handle herself, but I had a feeling it was going to be hard for her to be discreet.

"Why aren't there hallways to the dorms? What if it's snowing or raining?" Viv walked ahead of us on the path.

April gave her a quick, curious glance, as if Viv's question was odd, before she neutralized her expression.

"It's typically seventy-two and clear skies—well, inside the dome." She pointed toward the invisible dome in the sky, her flower crown staying in her short, curly red hair as she looked up. "If it's cloudy outside the dome, we have cloudy days but aren't affected by the temperature. It's mostly sunny in this part of Alaska anyway, just frigid. But the short days that lack sun don't last too long! We have scheduled days when it will rain and snow. Right now, the leaves are mostly green with some red until they fall during our snow period. The flora is natural and has adjusted to our weather. Amazing, right? The rainy and snowy days will be on the calendar in our room. You'll also find rain and winter attire in your closets. We don't have school uniforms, but the academy provides casual slacks and shirts, which are strongly suggested but not mandated as long as the dress code is followed. The majority of the students choose their own clothing or match the school colors, black and gold."

FIVES ACADEMY

I eyed April's floral maxi skirt and white blouse—most likely *not* the clothing provided by the academy—and quietly sighed in relief at the mention of no uniforms. The paperwork we had just filled out asked for clothing and shoe size. I had been dreading the thought of wearing some preppy pleated skirt and stiff-collared dress shirt with long socks as a finishing touch.

"The teachers and guards have a separate dorm area with apartments closer to the front of the academy," April continued and waved toward the side of the academy. "The garage is also that way."

"The leaves are changing, and it's always seventy-two degrees out," I dryly commented. That was not a thing, but I guess it was inside the prison of Fives Academy.

"Yes!" April perked up. "We still have seasons, but the temperature is a little different and ..."

The words kept flowing from April's mouth, but I tuned them out. I hadn't meant to comment out loud. Magic didn't need an explanation.

A smaller building—but still massive with two wings—sat off to the side behind the main building and rose three stories high with a parapet and four towers, one in each corner. Pillars surrounded the front and between the two buildings, creating a terrace. The student dorms. *They went all-out.*

"The east wing houses freshmen and sophomores, while the west houses juniors and seniors. We're sophomores, Viv, so we'll be in East." April waved a hand over her hair, and her flower crown grew a small vine, snagging a straggler that blew in the wind. *Earth mage.* "The third floor is for seniors and is coed. The first floor is for boys and the second is for girls. The east wing also has boys on the first and girls on the second—the third depends on how many are enrolled. But don't worry; there are floor monitors to keep things in check."

Let me guess: she was one of these *monitors*.

When we finally arrived at my room, I was relieved to see my pack next to what appeared to be a welcome basket on one of the beds and to find the room empty. Dark wood floors and even darker vaulted wood ceilings made the room look more spacious than it was. A circular chandelier and two large sliding windows provided plenty of light, and the white walls contrasted with the dark floor and ceiling. There was an open door off to the side, and I was pleased to see there was a private bathroom.

"Oh, and Selene?" April asked.

"Sal."

"Sal." April nodded. "You might find your roommate gone at night sometimes, but I assure you she is cool and one of the nicest people."

Odd. But ... whatever. I gave April a short nod. I'd be perfectly fine if my roommate was never around. Viv and I shared a room, but that was different.

Before they left, I shot a warning glance at Viv, a look she knew well.

Be careful.

Chapter Four
Selene

"**Your sister's coming tonight**, right?" April's green eyes gleamed with hope as she looked at me, then back at Viv. "It's Friday night."

"She sure is." Viv grinned at me with a mouth full of burger.

"*She's* right here," I said, not hiding the displeasure in my voice that they were talking about me as if I wasn't sitting next to them.

"You are going? It's going to be great!" The blue eyes of my roommate, Sydney, gleamed with joy, but I suppressed a glare. Sydney happened to be a part of April's friend group, and I wasn't looking forward to frequently seeing her both in our room and outside the dorms.

I narrowed my eyes at Viv. Since our arrival four days ago, she begged me daily to eat dinner with her, which dreadfully involved sitting with her new roommate and her roommate's friends. Dinner was the only time I had stayed in public and near people. I had spent my time inside my room, avoiding conversation with Sydney, running in the evening, and doing recon of the academy at night. If we needed to escape or hide, I needed to know where we were and where to go.

"Parties aren't my thing." I plopped a French fry in my mouth, not giving in to Sydney's hopeful stare. She was kind, like April had said, but she was also around more often than I thought she'd be.

"It's Halloween weekend. The entire academy will be there." April smiled.

"Do you think Ender will go this time?" one of April's friends asked, her eyebrows waggling like little caterpillars.

"Seriously?" a guy with short black hair across from the girl asked.

Their names were Denise and Joseph, or at least I thought they were. I didn't try very hard to remember everyone's names. What was the point?

"What?" the girl asked innocently. "He's cold, dangerous, and gorgeous. Who doesn't want that at a Halloween party?"

"You'd just stand there all night hoping he would approach you," he quipped, causing a scowl from the girl.

"Yeah, yeah." Sydney waved a hand at her and rolled her eyes. "He's a total heartthrob."

"It doesn't matter if he or his friends go." April brought the attention back to me. "You have to—" She was about to say more but stopped and put her hand in the air, flagging someone over. "There's David!"

All eyes went to the handsome blond boy who'd just finished going through the food line. It wasn't just our table whose attention he had caught but practically the entire cafeteria, and since it was dinner, there was an abundance of the student body present. He waved one black-gloved hand while the other gripped a food tray, and he started making his way toward us, his boots clanking on the walnut floor.

Newbies caught attention, like my sister and me, but thankfully he overshadowed our spotlight. David had arrived yesterday—the seventeen-year-old boy who killed his parents because he couldn't control his fire magic and was shipped off to Fives Academy, or so the rumors said. On the contrary, April had mentioned the council had sent him. He was an orphan.

No one knew the real reason why Viv and I had suddenly appeared at the academy—and I planned to keep it that way.

David reached our table and I sank lower in my wooden chair, not liking the attention he brought. April had to be *so* friendly. It's not like David would've had trouble finding friends—he could've started his own table. *Why did I sit here?* He was easy on the eyes, had beautiful dimples, and his magic was apparently strong. Elementals liked power. People liked good-looking people. In books, schools were about popularity wars, and unfortunately, reality turned out to be the same way.

I spared a glance at the *popular* table of the strongest students, mostly seniors: Ivy Jade, Gwen Campbell, Nick Hughes, and Ender Hart. April had discussed their skills—and appalling attitude—at dinner yesterday. My breath hitched when my gaze met Ender's bright, hazel eyes. He was the only one at that table that wasn't gawking at David—but was staring directly at me. I looked away, an unfamiliar, unnerving feeling settling in my stomach.

David wasn't the only one with rumors about them.

The cardboard water bottle was something I hadn't seen before. It was environmentally friendly, but its thick walls were deteriorating thanks to my anxious fiddling. Add in a dash of extra magical flair, and the party seemed like a typical teenage Halloween party in the middle of the woods, but I much preferred celebrating Halloween at home with Mom and Viv.

Floating lanterns lit the area, using a mix of fire and air enchantments. A student must have taken a sound bubble spell from class to prevent any guards or teachers from hearing the blaring music and teenage babbling. Food, drinks, and cutlery were stacked on foldable tables next to a line of trees. Where they had obtained all the non-age-appropriate drinks while residing in a dome in the middle of Alaska was beyond me.

No one had paid much attention to me besides my roommate. I only slightly felt bad for her and her failed attempts to get me to talk. The only reason for my presence was for Viv's pleasure.

"I'm going to get some food." Sydney nodded toward the bowls and snacks. "Do you want anything?"

"I'm good," I said, not wanting to move from the shadow of a tree I stood next to.

Sydney nodded and headed over to the chips, loading a plate with an orange creamy dip.

"Hey." David walked my way, a red paper cup in his hand. "It's quite the scene, huh?"

"Yeah." I glanced at everyone's costumes and then at Sydney's. She had chosen to be a dragon, which suited her fire magic. "You didn't want to dress up?"

"This isn't dressing up?" David waved at his jeans and buttoned-up shirt, which were nicer than my workout clothes, then held up his nearly full cup. "Would you like me to get you something to drink?"

"Not a chance," I said without holding back my disgust at drinking random liquid from who knows where. He frowned, and I realized how my social awkwardness had struck. While Vivian was a natural extrovert, I wasn't. "Sorry. I don't mean it like that."

"Nah. It's okay." David laughed and scrunched his forehead, glancing at his drink and making a repulsed expression. "This *is* completely horrid."

I smiled, then looked toward the fire where Viv sat with April and her friends. She hadn't smiled this much since we were kids making castles on a sandy beach. With her soon-to-be-classmates, she was happy. In private, when we were alone, she showed her grief. It was brief and consisted of some tears, but it was there.

"April informed me that there are no sports at the academy, since finding a nearby school to play would be difficult." David nodded in her direction. "So these parties, training sessions, and the occasional events the academy holds are the main source of excitement for students."

"Doesn't seem too exciting to me," I commented and David laughed, his blue eyes brightening.

Nearby chuckling caught my attention, and I looked over to see a group of girls, all with cups in their hands, giggling and pointing at David.

Uh-oh. I'd better make my exit before they bring their ogling eyes over here.

David's gaze caught what I was looking at, and he frowned. The three girls made their way toward us, as if his seeing them was an open invitation.

"That's my cue." I winked at David. "Enjoy your delicious drink."

David grinned—his dimples at full force—and went to say something, but the girls had already started to surround him. I secretly thanked them for saving me from small talk and made my way over to the chip table, where Sydney was. I'd already been at the party for an hour, and I couldn't suffer any longer.

"I'm going to take off," I told her.

"What?" Sydney spun around, her felt dragon tail brushing my leggings. "Already?"

"Yes." I started to walk away. "Let Viv know I left if she asks."

"Okay." Sydney frowned as she pushed down the hood of her dragon-themed hoodie. "Catch you later!"

I didn't want to just blend in. I wanted to be invisible, and *Operation Go Unnoticed* was in effect. Viv, on the other hand, wasn't following that plan very well. After four days, she had fit right in with April and the others.

The probability of anyone noticing my absence at the party was slim, and that included Viv. Once I was farther away from the party, my feet pushed against the rough terrain, and I broke into a run. My lungs were heavy as I sucked in air, blood pumping through my veins. Something about running through the woods at night was intoxicating.

I headed toward a quarry that I had found on the second night during one of my runs. It was a good twenty minutes from the school, the distance giving me space to feel at peace. Suddenly, my foot snagged on something along the trail, launching my body toward the ground. My hands flew out just in time to soften my fall. I went to stand, cursing at myself, but froze, holding myself in the push-up position. Through the dark, a sharp stick merely inches from my eye came into focus. One more inch and I would have been impaled.

I rolled over and lay on my back, staring at the dark leaves hiding the majority of the night sky, and closed my eyes. I wasn't usually clumsy, but fatigue had been wearing on me.

After a few moments, I sat up, searching for what caused me to trip. A gnarly root poked out of the ground. I gave it a quick kick and then cursed under my breath at my throbbing toe. *Smart move.*

I stood, brushing off my dirt-caked hands, and decided to head back to the academy. It had been six days since Mom was killed and four days at the academy—my classes hadn't even started, and I was already unraveling. I started running again, slowing once I reached the tree line that opened to a field leading back to the academy.

Sweat dripped down my neck and I flapped my shirt, trying to increase airflow, and wished some of the snow outside the dome was inside. The dorms and gym were on opposing sides, both quiet, which had been good since I looked like I'd just taken up a fight with a mud creature. I glanced at my dirty running clothes and debated jumping into the lake I had just passed—I was sure the otter I had spotted swimming the other day wouldn't mind.

The hair on the back of my neck suddenly rose, alerting me that I wasn't alone. I looked up. Someone was walking across the field toward me. It was Ender Hart, and he was heading in the direction I had come from—which was nowhere near the party. As he got closer, I could make out his deep black hair and sharp jawline, and his features hinted at his Asian roots.

And he was shirtless.

I averted my gaze. After he passed in silence, I lowered my chin to my shoulder, taking in air through my nose. I couldn't place his scent. April had said he had trained extensively prior to the Academy, and apparently, he was the strongest student at Fives Academy. Not only did he rank high at a level four, but his skill set surpassed his peers. Yet he didn't have the fresh spring scent of most air mages, and I wondered what he could be hiding.

Chapter Five
Ender

———◆◦◆———

THE GROUND WAS SLICK from the controlled torrential downpour, obscuring my vision and hindering my traction. I sent a string of curses at the trainer for creating the storm around me and my opponent. Rain was more tolerable than fire—unless the rain was so fierce, it tore at your skin like sandpaper.

A rock the size of a softball hurtled toward me, and I lashed out with my hand, easily sending the piece of stone to the ground with air magic. My opponent attacked, his fist sailing for my head—wrong move. I grabbed his wrist and used his weight and momentum to send him to the ground. He sat up, grumbling under his breath, his hands splayed outward with curling fingers.

Not grumbling, conjuring.

With a sharp crack, branches from a nearby tree snapped and fell to the ground. One of the larger limbs shook and splintered, giving it the appearance of a wooden bat with nails hammered into its barrel. Fresh green stems sprouted at the bottom, coiling into legs as it stood itself upright—alive and unnatural.

I spared a glance at Leah Murphy, the elderly head trainer and head of the guards who, along with other students, had stopped to watch our session. Flame, her fiery red Agama lizard familiar, sat on her shoulder. She stood perfectly placed outside the torrential downpour and shrugged, the lizard moving with her shoulder. Only levels four and five could create a familiar, and it required creating an animal using their element, a part of their soul, and a lengthy enchantment. Once that part of their soul was gone, they couldn't create another one. The task was very dangerous and could be deadly, and it was forbidden to do before graduation. I didn't know how I felt about risking my life for one, let alone giving something a piece of my soul.

I shook my head, focusing back on my opponent and internally grinned. Creating creatures during training was unsanctioned, and Murphy wasn't going to do anything about it. That was fine. She knew I could've ended this fight as soon as it started. I was merely toying with my challenger, who had *requested* to fight me. I didn't even know his name, but he apparently knew mine.

Before the magically-made creature—which now had pointed wood chips as teeth and no eyes—could make it to me, I sent a powerful swirl of wind at my opponent, lifting him in the air. The boy's eyes widened as I pulled the wind toward me, bringing him with it and right into my fist. I let him fall to the ground, mud splattering around him and seeping into his clothes. If he wanted to fight dirty, then he could lie in it.

The rain stopped and I sighed at my soaked clothes. My white shirt was entirely see-through, my darker skin tone adding to the transparency. I pulled it over my head and balled it up, drawing unwanted gazes and flushed cheeks ... or the occasional scowl. I didn't care if people liked me or not and the few who didn't typically stayed clear of me. Well, besides this fella, now down in the dirt.

Murphy's face set, the hidden order to put my shirt back on evident in her glare. It was a look that used to frighten me, like a kid getting scolded by his grandmother who knew ten different martial art styles. As an elite level four fire mage with more than a few decades of training, she had earned her title. She had trained me since I had arrived as a freshman, and she had also trained my guardian who worked for the council.

If I had called her Murphy to her face, I would feel flames lick at my toes—enough to cause pain without causing long-lasting wounds. Even her familiar would spit little fireballs at me. They were a harmless, mere burn, but nevertheless agitating.

I shrugged back at her and grabbed my water bottle, starting to feel the exhaustion from using air magic to drag a person through the air. She shook her head disapprovingly and went on to the next training session, a much lower level. Two lower-level earth mages fought pathetically against each other.

Though her back was to me, I recognized the contender with double braids that led into messy hair balls at the base of her head—unique but more effective than a ponytail in combat. It's how she had worn her hair when I had last seen her Friday night, coming out of the woods.

"Boring." Ivy faked a yawn as she came to stand next to me. "The new girl is going to get owned by a level one."

A part of me wanted to tell her off, but she was right. The new girl received a blow to her gut.

"What'd we miss?" Gwen asked as she and Nick joined us.

"Nothing. Just the new girl getting beat," Ivy replied. "They ask all new students before their first match if they're willing to fight. New girl must've thought she could win."

"Selene," I corrected, not realizing I had spoken at first.

"Yeah, sure." Ivy waved me off and continued mocking the match.

I ignored the others as I watched the tedious fight. Though Ivy was a strong level three air mage, she annoyed me, and yet, I still managed to be in her crew. The other two weren't as terrible.

Selene tried blasting her opponent with gravel from the worn training field, but it didn't have enough force to stop the other mage. She wasn't manipulating her element well and her moves were slow and robotic ... as if they were almost calculated.

I observed closely, watching the next strike against her. She pivoted just enough—

"Ender?" Ivy's voice rose. "Are you coming?" She looked over her shoulder. The others were behind her, heading in the direction of the academy.

"I'll catch up." I looked back at the match just as Selene was slammed to the ground and the trainer ended the match. Her opponent wasn't a strong mage, nor was she skilled in fighting. It was standard to see where the new student tested in their first week, but I doubt the trainer had expected Selene to do so poorly.

"Well, that didn't last long." Ivy let out a short, derisive laugh and clapped, sending the bangs echoing across the field.

A girl that looked similar to Selene, but with contrasting hair and eyes, went to help her up, and I figured her to be the younger sister. The Thomas sisters were the talk when they had first arrived—two beautiful new girls that no student or their family had known.

The sisters started toward the dorms, the crowd dispersing as the trainers ended class.

"Hey! New girl!" Ivy said as she, Gwen, and Nick intercepted the sisters. "That was quite the show, or lack thereof. Where did you say you were from?"

I rubbed my temple, deciding if I should intervene or just walk away.

"Nowhere important." Gwen flipped her reddish-blonde hair over her shoulder. *Hair.* Something she and Ivy talked about excessively when they weren't gossiping about others.

Selene blanched so briefly that it was hard to catch. Normally, I stayed out of Ivy and Gwen's business; nonetheless, I found myself moving toward them. But before I made it to them, David stepped in.

"Now, mates, don't judge where someone comes from—especially if you haven't the faintest clue." David stood in front of the sisters. I've seen him sit with April's crew but hadn't expected him to step in for the sisters, given his supposed record. Something in me ticked. I respected him for stepping in, but an unfamiliar sensation stirred internally, hating it.

The air marginally shifted and the hair on my arm stuck up. There was static that a lower level wouldn't pick up. I glanced at David, but I didn't see any sign of magic. The water rippled inside my Fives Academy water bottle, the vibrations faintly palpable through the clear container. Vivian's hands clenched into fists at her sides, and Selene whispered something in her ear as she tugged at her arm. Right before they turned, Selene's gaze met mine and her jaw set, anger filling her eyes.

It was a look I wouldn't be able to wash away any time soon.

Chapter Six
Selene

I missed Viv even though I saw her daily. Our shared room back home was a privilege I wish I had again. Tomorrow would mark two weeks at the academy. We saw each other daily, but it wasn't the same. And now I'd upset her.

"So you're saying I can't have any friends?" Viv clutched an Algebra textbook to her chest, her knuckles turning white. She wasn't the quietest person, and since Ivy and Gwen had called us out on the training field last week, she hadn't been so subtle about her distaste for them either.

"No." All I'd mentioned was to blend in a little and avoid large gatherings. I sighed, leaning closer to her. "Mom's killer is still out there. We don't want to draw attention or for anyone to figure out we are the daughters of the *No Name Elemental* who was killed by a dark mage at her vacation home."

Gossip and drama continued outside of high school walls as well, apparently, and it had made its way here. Mom's name hadn't been leaked to the public, to my knowledge.

Viv sighed. "Has Headmaster John given you any updates?"

"No, but I'm supposed to meet him later this week." I glanced past her and down the hall, which was emptying for the next period. Everyone was moving fast for a Monday.

"It's been two weeks. Dark mages aren't known to be patient." Viv shrugged and closed her locker. "I think we're fine. Go find a guy to talk to. There's a ton here."

"We don't know if we're fine." My tone lowered, her dismissiveness agitating. She knew I wasn't interested in a relationship. Besides, her safety was my main focus, which meant there was no time for any relationships.

"I'm fine. This is blending in. I'm a teenager. Just because Mom is gone doesn't default you to being her," Viv huffed, her face reddening.

My throat went dry and not due to the cold I was getting over—seclusion had apparently weakened my immune system.

Viv turned and walked away before I could respond.

I hadn't intended our conversation to go south. My hope was for her to hide in her friend group, but the entire student body was starting to know her name—more than just being "one of the new sisters". I wanted her to have a chance at a normal life, and this was as close as it got. Something inside me found it hard to let things be that way. My *normal* for the past sixteen years of my life was different from everyone else's. I didn't socialize. Viv had the same life, just a different mindset. She still had aspirations. Mine had died when I watched Mom boil from the inside out at the hand of a water mage that had turned dark.

My head hurt, and I couldn't blame the pulsating pressure on the cold I was getting over or the daily migraines I'd been getting from caffeine withdrawal.

**

Biology lab was hardly interesting, and I was thankful training was the only thing left for the day. I needed to drop my books off at my locker first. My parachute pants—as Viv called them, despite their lack of puffiness—doubled as trousers and workout pants, so I wouldn't need to change. They were efficient, unlike her typical jeans or the school-provided trousers.

The numbers on the lockers descended the closer I got to my locker, 143. Iridescence turned the front of them from azure to indigo, most likely a byproduct of tempering steel. The lockers were secured with standard padlocks—nothing important should be kept inside. Not that there was a student who could manipulate metal, but it would be easy to break with the right tool.

Down the hall, a group of sophomores flicked their gazes behind me and magic crawled along my skin. A forceful gust of wind wrapped around me, sending my books and papers sailing across the black cobblestone floor. I ignored Ivy and her posse behind me, quelling my anger without showing a physical response. I bent down to pick up a piece of paper, but a white heeled boot stepped on it. I looked up to see who owned a boot that was overly fashionable for the middle of Alaska.

"A little clumsy, are we?" Ivy said, grinning as Gwen joined her and the two *boys* stood off to the side.

I gritted my teeth and moved to pick up my other books and papers, but before I could, another bout of wind swirled through the hall, lifting my books into the air. They perfectly stacked on top of each other right in front of me. I reached out, letting them settle in my hands, and glanced at Ender, whose hand was out in front of him.

Ivy's jaw dropped as she stared at Ender. She regained her composure and fixed her annoyingly beautiful, curly black hair that had been ruffled by the magic. Ender's gaze flicked to her, then back to me. A low grumble came from him as he scowled and brushed past me. His shoulder never made contact, but his radiating warmth still reached me.

"What was that about?" Gwen asked Ivy, and I didn't plan to stay to hear her answer.

Yes. What was that about?

I deposited my stuff in my locker and grabbed my water bottle, embossed with the academy logo, before heading to training. I'd found it on my bed as part of the welcome basket.

Training was outside again today, and time flew by. My sister sat at the corner of the field, watching. I decided to ditch the rest of my training and headed her way, going unnoticed. A perk of keeping a low profile.

Viv's class regularly ended early, and she often watched the junior and senior training sessions. I knew what she was thinking: She could take any student here, including any of the popular four. And I didn't doubt it—except one. I'd seen Ender fight, and he was beyond in tune with his element, more than anyone else his age and even most professors and guards.

"Come to scold me for being out in public?" Viv calmly asked as I sat down next to her.

"No." I plucked a blade of grass. "Just came to see if you wanted to sneak out later and eat some Oreos on the east dorm's roof."

Viv let out a low chuckle that slowly faded into silence. "I'm sorry."

"Don't be." I threw the blade of grass at her, using a touch of magic to send it flying into her face. She swirled her finger toward the blade, drawing the water in the air to create a bubble around it and sending it back at me. It struck my black T-shirt, soaking the edge of it.

We both laughed, and I realized how much I had missed us. We saw each other most nights, but it wasn't the same. Our world had been flipped upside down two weeks ago. Her mission was to live. Mine was to survive. To keep her safe and kill the mage before they set foot anywhere near her.

"I hate that you let them walk all over you," Viv said, vacantly watching the match. She meant Ivy and the others. Nick was talking to some girl, and I was surprised the four of them weren't together. I scanned the field for Ender and the other two but found him alone, leaning against a tree.

The moment I laid eyes on him, his gaze flicked to mine. This time, instead of looking away, I glared at him. I had no clue why he had helped me with my books earlier, but his stunt had only put a larger target on my back for Ivy and Gwen. At least his shirt was on—smug jerk.

"Wow," Viv said. "I haven't seen that look since Mom took away your pet bearded dragon."

"He's trouble," I said without missing a beat.

Viv went to say something, but I held up a finger. Something unidentifiable ached annoyingly in my stomach and my senses woke. Something was off.

A millisecond later, a distant scream came from the woods.

"Did you hear that?" I stood, glancing around the field. No one seemed to notice.

"Uh, no?" Viv copied my movement. We were close to the woods and everyone near us was engaged in watching the training, the hum of other students' conversations easily masking the scream.

The dull ache turned into a painful throb, and that was enough to send me into the woods. My actions were rash. I should have gotten Viv far away from whatever threat was in the woods—but my gut instinct tugged me forward. It didn't feel right, and whatever it was, I needed to get ahead of it.

"Stay close," I ordered, Viv running right behind me.

I sprinted through the woods, ignoring the brush scraping against my arms. Five minutes later, I heard a commotion as I reached a thinned-out area before the base of a mountain. Ivy stood in front of Gwen, who lay unconscious on the ground, her strawberry-blonde hair covering her own face. A thick old book lay open next to her, and before them stood three large rock creatures, their boulder heads almost reaching the top of the pines.

The creatures were conglomerated jagged rocks that ground against each other as they moved. One was about to crush Ivy with an arm that looked like an asymmetrical, monster-sized chakra keychain.

The flutter of magic thrummed along my spine as heat pricked at my hand. I called on my magic, and it flowed from my hand with ease. It merged with a nearby tree like an invisible tentacle and I closed my hand, my magic wrapping around its trunk and embedding itself—compliments of my earth magic. With a little more push of magic, the roots ripped from the ground and the tree crashed into the rock creature. The creature fell, causing the ground to shake. That probably got the academy guards' attention.

Ivy turned to me, eyes wide with shock and her umber skin a ghostly pale. Blood soaked through a hole in her leather pants, and she shifted her weight to her uninjured leg. Behind her, the other two rock creatures were advancing, and I kicked into action.

"Viv. Grab Gwen and get them out of here." I picked up the book and tossed it at Ivy. "Go warn the headmaster."

"What?" Viv clamored. "I'm not leaving. They can take themselves."

"Vivian!"

She knew Ivy couldn't carry Gwen with a bum leg.

"Fine." Viv rolled her eyes and went over to Gwen, picking her up and throwing her over her shoulder in a fireman's carry with a humph. She glanced at Ivy. "Come on."

They disappeared into the woods and I turned to face the two oncoming threats as the third stirred on the ground.

Now *this* was my kind of party.

Chapter Seven
Ender

"Take her!" Vivian shouted at me. Gwen was slung over her shoulders like a heavy rag doll.

"Where's Selene?" I slowed but didn't completely stop as I scanned the three of them for injuries. Ivy clutched a book in her hands, her face alarmingly pale as she hobbled next to Vivian. Gwen's sides slowly rose and fell, indicating she was alive. Other than that, they seemed fine. My gaze briefly fell back to the rough, brown leather-bound book with gold calligraphy. Its title easily identified it as a forbidden book of creature summoning spells, and it was supposed to be locked in the library basement.

"I need to go help her." Vivian took a step toward me, clearly indicating for me to take Gwen from her. Instead, I started in the direction they had come from.

"Hey, wait!" Vivian called after me. "Prick!"

I couldn't help a small smile as I ran. Besides a match or hidden scowls, no one vilified me to my face or held my glare. The Thomas sisters weren't afraid to.

The ground shook again and I pressed harder, uneasiness settling in my gut. I'd never seen Ivy so quiet or pale; she was always up for a challenge. Up ahead through the trees, I could make out Selene. When

I reached her, her arms were stretched in front of her, aimed at a giant pile of rocks underneath a tree. The pile started to shake, and off to the side, another heap of boulders shuddered underneath a nearby fallen tree, slowly getting taller as it formed into a sentient being and stood.

Rock creatures. Someone powerful had to have summoned them because not only were there two, but there was a third behind them. And neither Ivy nor Gwen was an earth mage nor powerful enough to summon creatures like this.

"What are you doing here?" Selene gritted through her teeth, her chest barely rising faster than a normal rate.

"I should be asking you what *you* are doing?" I examined her and then the rock beasts—the trees hadn't been knocked down by them. Ivy was strong, but not strong enough to uproot a tree of that size with her air magic, let alone do it twice. There was no sign of Gwen's water magic, and Vivian was only a level two water mage.

The rock creature behind the others made its way toward us, its empty orbital sockets somehow managing to still devour us like prey. Selene sent boulders flying into its head, slowly causing it to step backward. Because these were made with earth elements, it would be easier to destroy them by controlling them with earth magic. Unfortunately, if you didn't create them, your magic wouldn't work to manipulate them—unless the creature was weak.

I twisted my hands, circling them in small motions as the cold touch of my magic singed the insides of my fingertips. A small tornado formed and grew as my motions became wider until it was the size of the creature. It acted as a small distraction but did not stop it.

The creature was too heavy for the tornado, so I changed tactics and sent whips of air against its stony body, slowly crumbling its exterior. The air slashed through its arm like a sword, cutting it off and making it crumble to the ground. Selene uprooted another tree—much smaller than the first two—and sent it crashing into the creature. It fell to one knee and braced itself with its only remaining arm. The rocks and pebbles from its chopped arm moved, piling on each other and sticking together like magnets. After the creature's arm reformed, it reattached itself so it was whole again.

We continued our attacks. Once we would take one down, we focused on the next one closest to us. They were slow, and we used that to our advantage. But despite our best efforts, they continued to get back up again. My magic left my blood flowing like a river of ice as I sent strike after strike. At one point, I focused on pressurizing the air around the approaching rock creature with enough force that should've crushed the majority of it but only impacted a single boulder on the edge of its body.

"We need a different strategy," I shouted to Selene and glanced at her. Her breathing was now quick. She was getting tired, and so was I. Magic used endurance and was similar to running or lifting weights.

Selene held my gaze and nodded before looking back at the creatures. Her brows set, determination spreading across her face, and somehow, I knew she understood the creatures would wreak havoc on the academy if they made it past us.

One of the creatures was still down after our recent attack, and the other two were slowly advancing. Selene knelt, placing a palm to the ground and closing her eyes. Cracks spread around her hand like a spider's web, and a fissure broke through the earth, trailing toward the creatures. It ran underneath their stone-stubbed feet, and a rift formed behind them, the dirt falling in on itself.

"Now!" she shouted and glanced at me. I nodded, realizing her intentions.

I breathed deeply, focusing all my magic. With a giant push of my hands, I sent a forceful gush of wind toward the two creatures. The wind sent them toppling backward into the crater. The small internal frosty hum of my magic faded, the entirety of it depleted.

The magic-charged air stilled, creating a blanket sensation. The air along my arms should've risen at the abrupt change, but it didn't. The thin blades of grass and pebbles at my feet began to shake, and a loud pop echoed through the air like thunder. The edge of the mountain behind the creatures cracked like something out of a movie.

Selene had her hands out, palms facing the mountain. Sweat laced her forehead and her cheeks were flushed. Her mouth moved, whispering words I couldn't hear. In a swift motion, she brought both hands down. Boulders came tumbling down like a landslide and covered the rift, piling a good twenty feet above ground.

I looked back at Selene. She clutched the ground, fisting the dirt as she held herself up. It took a moment to come out of my stupor and race over to her. I reached out as she tilted her head up, her expression unreadable. She hesitated before taking my arm. Her hand brushed against my skin, sending a small shock through my arm.

That was new ... and different.

I pulled her up and we froze with my arms underneath hers, her face inches from mine. The heaviness of the charged air still didn't make my skin crawl. It was like the inferno of her magic and the iciness of mine happily intertwined as it dissipated. The only sound in the quiet forest was our breathing, and the beating of my heart drummed in my ears. I swore I could feel her heartbeat like my own. Her rich brown eyes looked at me as her mouth parted, accentuating her cupid's bow. She was breathtakingly beautiful.

"Sal!" Headmaster John shouted as he emerged from the forest, Aura right behind him. Murphy trailed behind him with more guards. Selene tugged out of my grasp, her cheeks reddening even more.

Different felt good.

Chapter Eight
Selene

I SHOOK MY HEAD, clearing the mixed thoughts and emotions jumbling my brain. Using that much magic must've exhausted me to the point its fumes were altering my brain function because nothing else could explain what I had just felt. The air was charged, and when my arm touched Ender's, a little electric zap went off.

But I had felt it in my chest, not just where our skin had met.

Aura prowled over with dark eyes and hackles raised, hissing at the rocks behind me. This was the first time I'd seen her so hostile.

"Are you both okay?" John asked as he reached us.

"Yes." I answered too quickly.

Ender watched me, and I didn't like it. He had seen more than I wanted him to, but it was the only way to save the academy and stop the rock creatures—at least two of the three. The third still lay in a heap off to the side, no doubt about to pull itself back together. But had my actions jeopardized Viv's safety at the academy? I should have just let the guards take care of it. *Stupid.*

"Good." John's gaze narrowed behind me, taking in the scene. "Take your sister and go to the gymnasium with the other students in lockdown. You too, Ender."

"My sis—Viv!" I yelled as I spotted her among a few guards. She shrugged and made her way over. "What are you doing here?"

"Wanted to make sure you were okay." She looked between me and John, who shook his head, then opened his mouth to say something but stopped when the unburied rock creature stirred.

"Go. Now," he ordered the three of us. Even Aura glared at us as if she was giving us the command.

I composed myself, hiding my exhaustion, and nodded. I tugged Viv back toward the academy, Ender following suit. They had enough hands and would be fine against just the one. I wasn't about to show anyone else what I could do—and I had exhausted almost all my magic. Hopefully, they thought most of the damage and magic in the air was from the creatures and not from two students.

I spared a glance at the head trainer as we passed. She had been with the group in the jungle the day the headmaster had found us, and with this incident, there was no doubt she would have her suspicions of us, if she didn't already know. The little lizard sat on her shoulder, its head twitching to the side as it watched us.

We made it to the end of the tree line leading to the academy. The massive structure that housed the gym came into view, but I strode right past it, toward the main building.

"Where are we going?" Ender asked from behind me.

"*We're*"—I pointed between Viv and me—"going to the cafeteria. I'm hungry."

Ender didn't break off toward the gym. Instead, he kept his stride a few paces behind us.

"What did he see?" Viv whispered, leaning in close.

"Enough," I said, keeping my voice low. "I'm more concerned with what the headmaster will think." *I can handle Ender.*

"So much for staying under the radar," Viv mocked.

"So much is right." I sighed and pushed open the cafeteria door.

The oak wood tables were empty, as expected during a lockdown. I walked across the walnut floor and into the kitchen, which was off-limits to students. Where everything in the cafeteria was wood, everything in the kitchen was stone or marble.

My muscles were fatigued, my body drained, and I was starving. This had happened often after training sessions with Mom, especially when I fought the creatures she conjured. Our little secluded paradise gave us the privacy and room we needed for such sessions, and I would be ravenous and exhausted afterward.

The food trays had been picked up from lunch, and dinner hadn't been set out yet. A large stainless-steel fridge sat just beyond a stone island, and I made my way to it. Viv stood right behind me as I opened it.

"Lame." Viv swatted at the air and walked away.

There was salad, subs, sandwiches, and some soup from lunch. I grabbed a random sub and made my way back over to the island, ignoring Ender, who stood by the door and watched me. I hoisted myself up and began stuffing my face.

"Not awkward at all." Viv rocked on her feet. "You know what ... I bet they're hiding the dessert in the back." She went through a set of swinging double doors before I could finish chewing and protested. I would have to yell at her later for leaving me alone with the arrogant air mage.

Ender came over and leaned back against the island next to me. I pretended he wasn't there as I pushed the lettuce falling out of the sub back in and uncrossed my dangling legs. Even though his shoulders were relaxed and his arms were back against the counter, I was always prepared for an attack. My position made it awkward to fight if needed, but I could easily jump down.

"Level two, huh?" He sounded ... *amused*? I didn't look at him while I ate.

John had tested us the first day we arrived using the standard test employed throughout all academies. Mom had warned us that someday we might be put in a position where we would need to be tested. She had taught us how to trick the test into thinking we were a lower level by tucking away our magic and only allowing a small amount to seep from the imaginary little box in our chest while our blood was drawn.

Deceiving the test was harder than it sounded; it used our blood and scanned for both the element and potency by using a device that had been made centuries ago. The devices weren't common because the mages who had created them no longer existed, and the spell had disappeared along with them. Somewhere in the world, there most likely was a group of mages creating a new and *improved* device.

"Selene ..." Ender faced me, his voice dropping as he kept an elbow on the counter.

"Sal," I said.

"What?"

"I go by Sal." No one had called me Selene until here, and I had to correct every single student and professor. Then again, I had only ever really talked to Mom and Viv growing up—or the birds and iguanas. But no one needed to know that.

"Moon goddess," he said, and I raised an eyebrow. Yes, Selene was the name of the moon goddess, but how would he know?

"I read." He shrugged, answering my unspoken question.

"Or you're just a creep," I said.

"It's a beautiful name. It suits you. I wonder if the goddess was also a spitfire."

I almost dropped my sandwich. He was grinning, and annoyance flared inside my chest.

"Why did you help me?" I asked, and he took a moment before responding.

"They would have destroyed the Academy," he said matter-of-factly.

"No—with my books in the hallway."

Ender looked at me, his lips pressed in a flat line. I held my breath, waiting for the truth that it was for selfish reasons: a ploy to aide his stature or something along those lines.

"You worked up an appetite," he said instead, nodding toward my almost-gone sandwich.

"You're a smug jerk." I took another bite of my sandwich. His apparent confidence in himself, frequently being shirtless, always finding a way to annoy me ...

"They have cake!" Viv burst through the door with a decent-sized piece of chocolate cake on a plate. "It must've been some teacher's birthday."

Viv stopped and looked between us, the door swinging closed behind her. I bet she felt the tension in the air because I sure did.

"Bad timing." She glanced at me. "Should I go?"

"Yes," I said. "*You* and *I* should go."

I hopped off the counter, sandwich in hand. There was no way I was wasting food, so the rest was coming with me. I contemplated taking another, but Sydney always stored snacks in our room. That would satisfy me enough so I could retreat there until I had to come out.

On second thought, I wanted another sandwich. I walked over to the fridge and grabbed another sub, then tucked the wrapped sandwich between my arm and side so I could easily eat. Without looking at Ender, I left the kitchen with Viv.

I had been worried about the headmaster, not Ender. I would have to tread carefully with him.

Chapter Nine

Ender

I SPUN THE CARDBOARD water bottle on the table, tuning out Ivy and Gwen's mundane conversation. Gwen had recovered from yesterday's rock creature attack, having spent time in the infirmary with Nurse Adair. The two of them acted like nothing happened. Ivy's leg was covered by her pants, but she still favored it when she walked. I had questions but didn't ask. I wasn't going to get in the middle of whatever illegal magic the two of them had tangled themselves up in.

For the fourth time, I glanced over at the table Selene and her friends usually sat at for lunch. She wasn't there.

"Hey, man. You okay?" Nick asked.

"Yeah." I stopped twirling the bottle. "Just distracted."

Nick's gaze followed mine to Sydney and Denise. If it had been dinner, I would have assumed she was with Vivian, but she had a different lunch period.

"Ah." Nick smirked and leaned back in his chair, running a hand through the curly blond hair he took an inordinate amount of pride in. "She's not even over there. Or is that the problem?"

"It's not like that," I said, my voice low.

"Oh, come on, man." He patted my back with a thud. "I'm just messing around."

"Hmm," I grunted.

Nick was the closest I had to a best friend. He was flawed, but so was I. His biggest problem was following Gwen around like a mindless lovesick puppy. I vowed to never lower myself to such behavior.

"I'll see you later." I stood, grabbing my bottle, and headed toward the door leading to the end of the courtyard.

"Where are you going?" Nick called from his seat.

"Fresh air," I tossed over my shoulder. A walk would do me some good.

"Where is he off to?" Gwen asked.

As I got farther away, I barely heard Nick say, "Chasing tail."

I shook my head and walked outside, the urge to feel fresh wind against my skin beckoning me. I stopped short of the field, intending to cross it and go into the woods for a short walk, but Selene sat under a tree with her nose in a book. Her brown locks fell just below her shoulders—not in her normal braids. The wind caught a few of the strands, blowing them across her face.

I rubbed my eyes with one hand, feeling pressure build behind them, and sighed, then started toward her. Why? I didn't know.

Chasing tail, maybe?

I passed David, who looked up from his own book as I walked by. Normally he sat with Selene, Sydney, and Denise. He had probably chosen a shaded picnic table outside rather than the girls flaunting over him in the cafeteria. He would learn just like I had—don't be friendly and the ones with any self-preserving instinct will stay away.

My shadow fell across Selene, blocking the sun, and she looked up. Her eyes narrowed when she recognized it was me, as if I was the most insufferable thing at this academy—more so than the notorious Professor Eaten, who's rumored to eat students.

"What do you want?" She didn't take her eyes off me.

"Learning anything interesting?" I asked, avoiding the question I didn't have an answer to.

"Not anything I don't already know." She sighed and her cheeks reddened a touch, as if she hadn't meant to say more than one word.

I glanced at the cover—*Water Magic and Its Beyond*. "You know everything about water mages despite being an earth mage? Is that because of your sister?"

"My mother taught me everything my sister and I needed to know." She flinched, and I couldn't help but notice her use of the past tense. I could relate—my parents were gone. Priscilla Hart raised me and was the only blood relative I had. She was a distant cousin, but she took me in like I had been her own, and so had Mr. Scott, her elderly assistant—we had called him the house manager.

"Sounds like she was very knowledgeable." I nodded.

"She was." Selene went back to her book.

I ignored her blatant hints to leave her alone and sat next to her, intrigued by Selene Thomas, even if she wasn't going to tell me anything. Talking wasn't the only way to learn things about someone—actions alone spoke a great deal.

Selene closed her book and huffed. "Seriously. What do you want?"

"I'm just enjoying the sun." I grinned. Something about the blush of irritation on her cheeks warmed me. Her honest refutation, instead of groveling like the other academy girls, was refreshing. I didn't deny my good looks, and I trained hard. Some of the lusting led to resentment by other students.

Selene went to stand.

"Wait." I put up a hand, stopping her. "How did you know the academy was in danger?"

She eyed me for a moment before slowly settling back down. Her gaze was locked on the grass in front of her as she cracked each knuckle of her right hand with her thumb.

"Something felt off. I thought I heard a scream in the woods," she said after some hesitation.

Huh. She was going to talk—at least a little.

"What do you mean, *felt off*?" After she had stood up that day, I had suddenly felt a bit ill, but I hadn't known why.

"I'm not sure." She took a deep breath. "Did you tell anyone"—the cracking sound of her knuckles drew my attention to her hand and then back to her—"what happened ... what I did?"

"No." I met her gaze as she watched me with regard. "And I won't."

The headmaster had talked to me briefly, but I hadn't told him exactly what she did. Ivy never asked, and Gwen had no recollection of that afternoon. I had a feeling Selene didn't want anyone to know. She had torn apart the sides of a mountain. Her power was stronger than mine as a level four, and that wasn't common.

She had to be a level five earth mage.

Chapter Ten
Selene

I slammed the book shut, the sound echoing through the massive library. A few students glanced my way. It was Thursday afternoon and most students were attempting to finish their assignments before the weekend. None of them seemed concerned about the event that took place Monday; that is, if they were even aware of the danger they could've been in if the rock creatures made it to campus.

The library was the most beautiful, enchanted library I'd ever been in—the only library I'd ever been in—and a fresh sage aroma should have helped quell my anxiety, but it crept along my skin, staying attached like little weights. I rocked back in the wooden chair and shoved aside the book I'd been skimming, revealing dark knots in the wooden table.

There hadn't been a single book that contained any useful information about who may have killed Mom. The black circle on the dark mage's palm must indicate they were from a clan, as John had suggested, but I couldn't find any locations of previous clans or names. The books barely even touched on blood or dark magic. It mentioned that dark mages, if powerful enough, had some control of all the other elements—which I knew—and basically stated how terrified you should be if you ever encountered a *turned mage who dipped into dark magic and killed an innocent, consuming their soul.*

I let my head fall back, sighing at the massive glass-domed ceiling, then glanced at the upper two levels of the library. Three stories with stone bookcases all filled, and I'd come up empty so far.

My mother had told me stories of the dangerous spells hidden in the books in the academy's forbidden basement, and I believed I had encountered it Monday. There was something else I wanted to look into before planning to sneak into Fives Academy's basement. I stood, slinging my bag over my shoulder, and grabbed my books. I placed them in the return cart and headed over to the librarian's desk where a tall, slender man with grey-speckled black hair stood.

"Miss Thomas." The elderly librarian nodded. "Checking out another book?"

"Not at the moment." I had taken the first book without checking it out and it had practically seared my hands the moment I stepped out of the library. The academy took great care keeping its books safe and accounted for. "I was hoping you could tell me where the yearbooks are kept?" I specified to the librarian one of the years my mother had attended.

"Ah." The librarian adjusted his wood-framed glasses. "Your mother's senior year."

I tensed but told my body to relax and carefully chose my next words. "You *know* my mother?"

"Yes." His head slightly tilted before giving me a warm smile, and I couldn't tell if my lack of past tense had thrown him off. "I've been here awhile. You look just like her."

"I get that a lot," I lied, not wanting to give anything away about my previously secluded life and unsure if he knew what had happened to my mother. "Did you know her well?"

"Not particularly well," The librarian said. "She did visit the library daily."

"That sounds like her." Mom loved her books. "Her senior yearbook is available?"

"Yes." He waved above me. "The yearbooks are on the third floor opposite the greenhouse—in the back corner."

I nodded in thanks. I'd have to watch what I said around him.

I headed toward the wooden stairs, careful not to trip over the large vines weaving through them like the steps were in a jungle. The stone shelves were sprawling with vines and blooming purple and yellow flowers. Glass windows on the far side rose all three floors, like a looking glass into a magical library sanctuary.

I reached the top of the stairs and headed in the direction the librarian had indicated. The yearbooks were in a back corner, and I quickly found the one I wanted. Snatching it, I headed to the nearby table and began flipping through the pages. Midway through, my hand froze. A young version of my mom stood at a lab table, working on some kind of creation next to a young, handsome student with broad cheekbones and a narrow nose—her lab partner. I studied him a little longer, his features becoming decipherable. *Headmaster John Sanders?*

John hadn't acted like he knew Mom, and in the photo, they were both smiling together. Which reminded me ... I pulled out my phone—which John had annoyingly given to Viv and me after the rock creature incident in case we needed to contact him—and glanced at the time.

Shoot.

I had a meeting with him and was going to be late if I didn't leave right away.

Good.

I could question him about being lab partners with Mom.

I grabbed the yearbook and headed down the stairs. The librarian didn't say anything when I asked to check it out. Once it was, I shoved it in my backpack and left for John's office. I knocked on the door before trying the handle, surprised to find it unlocked and the room empty of the headmaster. Aura briefly raised her furry little head from her curled ball on the desk, not caring about my intrusion.

After a short walk around his office, I went over to the chairs to sit but paused and stared at his desk. Now was my chance to find out if he was hiding anything. I rummaged through the papers on his stone desk and the little fox cracked an eye open but closed it midway through my digging. Nothing stuck out to me.

I began searching through the ebony wood drawers of his desk until I came to a bottom drawer that wouldn't budge. It had a tungsten lock.

Smart choice, Headmaster.

If I was hiding a key, where would I keep it? I searched the open drawers again, checking for the obvious spots. Aura raised her head again, giving me a curious glance before stretching and coming to sit at the end of the desk. Sun glinted off her collar as she yawned.

"Don't worry," I reassured the little fox. "I'm not here to cause any harm to your master." Aura tilted her head, the dangling oval charm catching my eye. "What do you have there?"

I held out my hand, and she sniffed it. Once I was sure she wouldn't bite my finger, I ran my fingers through the white fur on the top of her head, slowly making my way to her chin, where the charm was. Upon further inspection, I realized there was a release button on the charm and a faint tingle of magic radiating from it, only palpable when touched.

"I'm going to take your collar off, okay, girl?" I softened my voice as if I was talking to a kid. She only blinked at me, and I took that as my cue, slowly unclasping the collar. Once I almost had it off, she let out a little hiss, showing her teeth. I pulled my hands away, collar clutched in them.

Aura licked her paw and then went back to her corner, circling three times before lying down.

Okay, then.

I pressed the button and a small key folded out. Magic and mechanics working together at their finest. Holding my breath, I tried it on the drawer, a small thrill of triumph running through me when it clicked open. I went back over to Aura, testing her temperament by getting in her space before reaching around her neck with the collar. She didn't move, only gave me narrowed side-eyes. I clasped it back on and went over to the drawer, opening it farther. I was running out of time.

An old phone rested on top of some papers in the corner. I picked it up and pressed a button. The screen lit, and it was still open to a message to a seven-digit number.

They're coming.

The door to the office started to open and I dropped the phone in the drawer, closing it with my shin. I stood up straight as John walked in. He eyed me wearily, taking in my position behind his desk and then glancing at a sleeping Aura.

"Anything I can help you with?" He closed the door, clutching a cardboard box to his chest.

"You're late," I said, deflecting the attention off me and striding to the other side of the desk where I was supposed to be.

"Yes. I apologize." He gestured with the box in his hand. "I had something to pick up. I see your sister has not arrived yet."

"My sister?" I asked. "She's joining us?"

"Yes. Viv—" The door to his office opened, cutting him off as she strode through.

"I was summoned by a guard?" Viv glanced from me to John. "I would like to make it known that a simple text goes a long way."

"Yes but delivering a message through a guard ensures that you receive that message in a timely manner. It cannot be left unread in your inbox or ignored." John strode over to his chair and set the box on his desk before sitting down.

She sat in the chair and I followed suit, giving her a shrug. She didn't attend our meetings for one simple reason: She didn't want to. The benefit was that it didn't allow her a chance to accidentally say something she shouldn't. The thought made me cringe. Had they found something?

"Any news on our mom?" I asked and noticed his gaze dart to the box in front of him.

"Unfortunately, no. There have not been any new findings." He took a moment, studying me and Viv. "Your mom is here."

John opened the box and gently pulled out a sleek, handmade-looking octagon urn, setting it on the desk. Aura jolted from her sleep, trotting over. She let out a mournful howl and lay down on her belly, staring at the urn. Foxes were intuitive, I suppose.

"I am so sorry," John began. "If I can help either of you in any way—"

"I just want to find those responsible." My eyes fixed on Mom, and I grabbed Viv's hand. She only nodded. If they were found and taken care of, she would be safe.

"I do too." He rested his hands on his desk, clasping them together.

"Black walnut?" I asked about the urn, staring at the smooth color variants in the dark surface.

"It is." John nodded. I waited for him to explain its significance, but he remained silent. Not that I needed an explanation, and Viv most likely knew. Black walnut trees signified spiritual wisdom and guidance, as well as resembling the strong link between people and nature. Picking out her urn hadn't crossed my mind. John—or whoever had decided—had chosen well.

My heart ached as tears threatened to fall. Without her ashes, it was easier to pretend she could still be alive somewhere. I knew she was gone—I had seen it with my own eyes. There was no surviving a horrific death like that.

A tear rolled down my cheek. Reality sucked.

I swallowed and wiped the tear away. Wallowing wasn't going to help avenge her or keep Viv safe.

"I'm going to use the restroom." Viv stood, letting go of my hand.

"I'll join you," I said and stood, not wanting her to be alone.

"Sal. Please." Tears traveled down her cheeks. "I just need a moment. I'll meet you in the hall?"

"Okay." I nodded and hugged her.

She pulled away and walked out of the office. I faced John, who remained sitting. There was one thing he could clear up.

"You didn't tell me you were in my mom's class *and* lab partners," I said, letting a bit of harsh accusation seep into my tone.

John was quiet for a moment before a grim smile tugged at the corner of his lips. "Yes. We had been lab partners."

"You led me to believe you didn't know her," I said.

"I don't recall saying I didn't know her." He tapped a finger on his desk. "We were classmates. She was a very caring, gentle soul, and very educated. She was kind to all other students, including me. I want to find who did this to her, Selene, and I won't stop until I do. I promise."

My jaw clenched but I found myself nodding, wanting to believe him. But he was hiding something—and he was darn good at it.

Chapter Eleven

Selene

"Welcome back." Sydney lounged on her bed, drawing on her tablet. "Are you coming to dinner with us tonight?"

"Not tonight." I went farther into our room, Viv walking in behind me. Sydney had been the one to convince me to go to dinner the last few times. She was growing on me, but I didn't have an appetite and Viv and I needed time together. I clutched the box in my arms.

Sydney looked up, her expression falling when she saw us.

"No problem. Maybe tomorrow." She set her tablet down and climbed off her bed. "I think I'm going to go for a walk before dinner. Let me know if you need anything."

I nodded, and Viv kept her head down, her hair falling into her face. Sydney wasn't going to go for a walk—it was raining—but the privacy was appreciated.

Once the door closed, I set the box, which was still nested inside my jacket, on my bed. I had put the urn back inside its box, not wanting to draw attention on my way back to my dorm. A student walking around with an urn would raise enough questions.

My shirt was drenched but the box remained dry.

I turned to face Viv but before I could say anything, she ran into my arms.

"I'm so sorry," she sobbed.

"You have nothing to be sorry about." I wrapped my arms tight around her.

"What I've said before … I'm," Viv's chest heaved as she tried catching a breath, "I'm not okay, Sal. I miss her."

"I do too." I squeezed her tighter as her tears dampened my shoulder.

"It's my fault." Viv's voice cracked. "Why don't you hate me?"

I pulled back to look at her, pushing her wet hair out of her face. "It's not your fault."

"It has to be." She sniffed, mustering up enough composure so she could speak clearly. "All because I had wanted to go into town."

I didn't let myself react, but I remembered the night she was referencing very clearly. Mom had gone into town earlier that week to get some supplies. A few days later, she had come down with a cold. The third night of what we believed was the flu, she was starting to feel slightly better but was exhausted. She had fallen asleep in her bed early that night, unrousable.

After my shower, I had gone to see if Viv wanted to go lay out on the cool sand and watch the stars at our secluded Caribbean island home. When I couldn't find her, I began to panic and checked out front. The side-by-side was gone and nailed to the tree where it was normally parked hung a note with Viv's handwriting.

Went into town. Be back in two hours. I would have invited you, but you'd say no. Maybe next time.

-V

My panic had turned into agitation. She had known we weren't allowed to leave unless it was authorized by and with Mom, and that rule was to keep our family safe. Viv had even turned off the perimeter alarms. I had hopped on my bike and went after her, knowing it was going to take me at least thirty minutes of hard pedaling to get to town.

I had found the side-by-side hidden off the path. Leaving the bike there, I had begun searching through the small town—it shouldn't have been hard to find her. It hadn't been until I heard a couple grunts outside a row of houses that I found her. When I had rounded the corner, she was holding a cat as three boys sat on the dirt, a mix of shock and anger in their eyes.

"V," I said, not wanting to use her name, "what happened?"

"They were picking on this poor little thing." She strode toward me, stroking the diluted tortoise shell cat who happily purred in her arms. "I didn't use any magic," she added quietly.

I had glanced behind her at the boys on the ground, checking to see if they picked up on her whisper. Two of them were rubbing their shoulders while the other was slowly making his way to his feet. The one attempting to stand appeared to be slightly older than me.

"Come on. Let's go." I put a hand on her back, leading her toward the way I had come and eyed the content feline in her arms. "We can drop the cat off at a building a few blocks up."

Vivian snapped her head in my direction. "She likes me. She can ride in my lap."

"We are not taking her home." I scowled. "Mom's not going to believe that a cat wandered that far out into the forest. She'll know it came from town."

"You're ..." Viv stumbled with her words as she glanced at me. "You mean you're not going to tell Mom?"

Not if Mom doesn't find out on her own.

Instead of answering her question, I nodded in the direction in front of us. "I saw cat food and little huts made for the street cats underneath a canopy. She'll be fine there."

We dropped off the cat—Vivian no longer arguing once she realized she couldn't take it home—and continued making our way to the side-by-side and my bike. But before we made it, a shadow fell in front of us and I recognized him as one of the three boys Vivian had downed. He had been the one getting to his feet.

Based on his frantic breathing, he must have run to be able to cut us off. He wouldn't have been a concern if he hadn't been pointing a small firearm at us.

"Crap," Vivian muttered.

Crap was right. The hands of the teenager were shaking, but his narrowed eyes and set jaw didn't hold back his determination and the anger fueling him.

Was he drunk?

I didn't have time to ponder that question because his finger squeezed the trigger. Viv was already starting to dive, but I dove at her anyway, covering her as we fell to the dirt. The closest cover was a tree to our left and a building to our right, but neither were close enough. The boy fired two more shots, missing each time.

Yep. Either he's drunk or has awful aim.

While Viv and I stood, I tried to think of a way to subdue him while avoiding getting shot—and without magic. We couldn't let them know what we were.

Before any ideas came to mind, another shot came from behind me and a touch of static filled the air as a bullet whizzed by my shoulder. I swirled around to see one of the other boys flying into a nearby closed mini store, a blue barrel full of liquid rolling after him. Viv had her arms stretched out, having used her water magic to strike the boy with the water barrel. Being a level four water mage, she could be dangerous. If she hadn't used her magic, I probably would have been down with a bullet in my chest.

The assailant's eyes had widened, and he briefly lowered his gun. When he went to raise it again, I projected my magic, feeling the cool, smooth surface of a nearby rock, and flung it at his head. He fell to the ground. I hoped the rock had hit him hard enough that he would forget the last hour.

"Let's go," I said to Viv, and we started running, unsure where the third boy had gone.

The memory dug its sharp nails into my mind. It was my duty as Vivian's sister to protect her—instead, I chose to be her friend that night. If I had told Mom what had happened, she would have taken precautionary measures, and honestly, we might have relocated. Mom would have been alive if I had been more mature instead of worrying about the consequences for Viv and that she'd hate me. My shortsightedness had opposing deadly consequences.

"No. Viv." I put my forehead to hers. "Do not put the blame on yourself. There are a hundred different ways the dark mages could have found us. No one would have believed three drunken teenagers. Plus, do you really think they went around saying they were shooting at a couple of girls who could move objects with their minds?"

Actually, that's probably exactly what happened—or a version of it. But sometimes, small lies help protect a person from themselves. Mom had always been careful on her runs into town, but I wasn't going to let Viv think it was her fault—I could have prevented both that night and Mom's death.

Viv pulled back, looking at the urn on my desk. She set her shoulders back, a sign that she was building her walls back up. I couldn't tell if she believed what I had said, but I had my doubts.

"I don't think they're gone," Viv said after a moment. "The dark mages who were after Mom, they'll find us."

I looked across the room, staring at the abstract art hanging on Sydney's wall, the reds and blues mixing together like hot flames.

And I would do my best to keep them away from Viv and prevent them from hurting her.

Chapter Twelve
Selene

My phone rang and I glanced down to see a picture sent as a group message to Sydney and me from Viv.

"It looks like they're up to no good." Sydney laughed. "Especially at nine o'clock on a Friday night."

Our phones chimed in unison as another message came through, asking for us to come join them in the woods behind the gym. I sighed at the mental picture of Viv and April somewhere outside in the dark. A relaxing night in and an evening run sounded like the small piece of therapy I needed after getting Mom back yesterday.

"Should we go?" Sydney, who was sitting on her bed, looked at me.

"No." I hopped off my bed and started to put my sneakers on.

"No?" Sydney raised a brow.

"No. We shouldn't," I answered, glancing around our room. Compared to the rest of the Academy, the dorm rooms were blander with less greenery, and unlike the library, the lights were from regular chandelier light bulbs and not hollowed-out quartz stone. They were most likely powered by the solar panels on the garage and staff dorms. The enchanted phantom fire used as candles or inside quartz was a safe option, as it contained no heat and couldn't cause any harm. It was disappointing they hadn't incorporated it into the dorm rooms.

"But we're going?" Sydney eyed me as I stood, sneakers on.

"But we're going." I put my hands on my hips. "I can't let Viv get into trouble with the guards, and if they go out farther, they might be out of range for our messages to get through."

The real reason was that I didn't want Viv wandering the grounds at night with just April. The academy wards were strong, but so were dark mages.

"Cool. I was getting bored of this piece." Sydney tossed her tablet aside and hopped off her bed, revealing her drawing of a beautiful tree with red flames licking at its base. She seemed pleased to get out of the room, and I wondered if that's why she'd already snuck out twice this week in the middle of the night.

I didn't bother with my jacket and headed out the door. My T-shirt and pants would suffice, though night did cool down ever so slightly. We made our way past the gym, where dark woods greeted us. My heartbeat quickened. I didn't see them, but this was where they said they would be.

"I bet they're goofing off with magic in the woods." Sydney snorted as she snapped her fingers. A small trill of fire shot from her index finger and thumb like a candle, emitting a small glow around us.

Yesterday, Viv had broken down in my arms. Today, I wasn't surprised she wanted to be adventurous. Adrenaline was a distraction.

"Alright. Let's go." I started toward the woods.

After a couple minutes of walking, multiple flares of light shined through the woods. I recognized the spot as we came up on it—it was where the Halloween party had been. Wooden chairs and logs were scattered throughout, surrounded by torches. It was too quiet. Goosebumps rose on my arms and I knew we weren't alone. My fists clenched—

"Surprise!" Vivian and April shouted in unison as they jumped out from behind a tree.

I lowered my arms, hiding the fact that I was on the verge of blasting them with magic. I closed my eyes to help quell my nerves, and opened them again. Other students started revealing themselves from the shadows, and somewhere, someone started playing music through a speaker.

"Happy Birthday, Sal!" Viv came up to me and gave me a hug, her familiar fresh rain scent feeling like home. "You didn't think I would forget your seventeenth birthday, did you?"

I angled my body toward Viv in hopes of avoiding a hug from April. Guilt etched my gut but didn't linger—I wasn't as fit for this life as Viv.

"Did you know about this?" I asked Sydney, who glanced at the students around us.

"Actually, no." She frowned and turned to April.

I relaxed once they started talking and the attention slowly drifted from me.

"Who are all of these people?" Honestly, I had thought Viv had forgotten about my birthday. But I didn't mind if she had, and from the looks of it, I would have preferred it.

"Well, it started with only a couple of people ... April, Denise, Joseph, and me." Viv blushed. "Then it just kinda got big."

"Just *kinda* got big?" I saw Ivy and Gwen in the distance near a newly lit fire pit, the light flickering across their faces.

"I didn't invite them. Ivy, Gwen, and Nick came on their own accord." Viv followed the direction of my glare. "But I did invite someone you talk to."

Viv nodded off behind me and I turned to see Ender. Though he was talking with Nick, his gaze was on me. He casually leaned against a tree with his arms crossed, seemingly carefree, but the tapping of his finger caught my attention. That wasn't in line with untroubled.

"Thank you, Viv." I turned back toward her. "But you know I'd much rather spend the night in ... or alone."

"I know." Viv frowned. "I was hoping it would help distract you and help your life be a little more teenager-like. You know, take the *big sis* stress load off for once."

Ha. Sisters think alike.

"Not all teenagers like parties, and I just prefer getting the stress off differently." I crossed my arms. "Like we used to do on our weekends—have a movie night or sit out on the beach with the stars. Go for a nice run."

"Can I make it up to you tomorrow night with a movie?" Viv sagged her shoulders.

"Sure, but just you and me." Even though I was slightly frustrated, I wasn't angry. She'd tried, even if it failed. Tomorrow we would discuss boundaries with her so-called presents.

"Yes." She nodded and her smile came back. Her gaze flicked behind me and her grin grew even more. "Time for you to broaden your horizons. Looks like you have your first guest to talk to." She nodded behind me again, but I didn't need to look to know who was approaching.

Viv got April and Sydney's attention and waved to them to follow her. They both had huge smirks when they realized why they were being ushered away. It hadn't gone unnoticed the day Ender intruded on my lunch break and sat with me outside.

"I hear a *happy birthday* is in order." Ender's deep voice sent shivers down my spine and a light scent of cedar and bergamot wrapped around me.

"Happy birthdays are never in order." I turned to face him, and my breath hitched at his nearness. "Unbeknownst to me, I apparently have a birthday party tonight."

"You don't approve?" Ender gave me a one-sided grin, and I had to tell my insides to cool the random spark of heat.

"Vivian outdid herself." I should've seen this coming. She'd always made our birthdays as extravagant as she could. I always thought I had everything I needed—her and Mom. She, however, had still been lonely. "She tries."

"She cares." He shrugged. "You look out for each other."

I didn't have anything to add, so I nodded awkwardly. His hands were in the pockets of his shorts—more along the line of carefree—and his finger was no longer tapping.

Ivy and Gwen started toward us and I held in a big sigh, not wanting to show Ender how much their ruses irritated me. But they didn't stop as they neared us. Instead, Ivy gave me a curt nod and continued past us.

"That's new," I commented. Ivy wasn't one to have manners, especially if I was with Ender.

"She'd probably be dead if it wasn't for you," Ender said. "They both would be."

"Sure." I wouldn't have suspected that saving her life would've changed her attitude toward me. She now knew I was much more powerful than I had let on, and mages tend to either fear or crave power—or both. Her nod was more along the line of respect, which was doubtful.

"She may be evil, but she has her limits."

I couldn't help the awful snort-laugh that came from me. Ender raised a thick brow.

"You admitted she's evil," I said, trying not to laugh. "Why do you hang out with her?"

"Why save her if she only makes your life more difficult?" Ender glanced at the other students gathered around. "There's good in almost everyone—it's just buried. Life has a way of shaping everyone differently."

I mulled his words over. They held some truth, but I wasn't so sure *almost* cut it. More like half. It was a single dark mage that had killed

Mom, but there were two other dark mages present during the attack. All three were well beyond the almost category.

Ender began tapping his finger inside his pocket as he stared off at the party. A small rush of anxiety suddenly trickled along my shoulders, causing me to rub my palms together even though my hands weren't cold.

"Want to go for a walk?" I asked, my feet practically begging me to leave.

Ender looked over at me, his forehead creased. "Won't you be missed at your own party?"

I looked around and found my sister and Sydney. They were with April and a couple of others, all of them laughing.

"No, I don't think so." I smiled. It was nice to see my sister having fun. Not to mention I was more comfortable with her being out here, especially with all these students around.

I went to turn and walk but stopped before I ran into a tall figure directly behind me—and almost into Ender's arm, which he had held up to prevent the collision.

"David." I greeted him as Ender lowered his arm. I hadn't heard him come up behind me.

"Sorry. I didn't mean to alarm you." He gave me a sympathetic smile.

"You didn't." *He had*. I needed to be more alert and hadn't realized he had approached—I couldn't afford to not be aware of my surroundings.

"I just wanted to say happy birthday and I'm sorry I'm late," he said as he glanced between Ender and me. "It seems like you're on your way out, though. I don't mean to hold you up if that's the case."

"No, that's okay." I didn't much care to talk with him—let alone with most anyone—but he had so far been kind to my sister and me. "Parties aren't for me."

"Even though this one is for you?" He laughed.

"Even more why it isn't for me," I said, causing him to laugh even more, and I could *physically* feel Ender tense next to me.

"Alright, alright." His laughter faded. "Have you seen April? She's upset I missed the first part of the surprise."

"Yeah." I pointed over my shoulder. "She's over there."

"Ah." David nodded. "Thank you."

David left, and Ender and I started walking toward a path in the woods.

"You don't like him very much," I said once we were out of hearing range.

"He's alright," Ender replied, his gaze straight forward as we walked. I wanted to ask why he had tensed during the interaction with David then, but I didn't want to pry.

I sent a message to Viv, letting her know I was headed out, but it didn't go through. The music and glow from the torches faded the farther we got away from the party. A small part of my rational reasoning screamed at me that it was a stupid idea to walk alone with a boy at night in the middle of the woods—I should've at least turned around and told Viv or Sydney.

I went anyway.

Chapter Thirteen

Selene

MONDAY HAD APPROACHED QUICKLY, especially after the party and last night's movie night with Viv. I crossed the threshold into the library, heading toward my usual table in the back. Mara, the librarian's assistant, sat behind the checkout counter. I saw a flyer for a paid student greenhouse aide position and wondered if the library assistant was also paid or if she volunteered during her free blocks and spare time. Down the road—if we were still here—it would be pleasant to have a position at the library.

I stopped when I saw Ivy blocking my path, her gaze pinning me. I tilted my head to the side, waiting for her to say something as she clutched her books to her chest. She took a deep breath and let out a silent sigh. Her shoulders rolled back so she stood taller, and she took the few steps left between us.

"I need to talk to you," she whispered, her glare losing a touch of its harshness. "It's about that night and the book."

It had been a week since *that night*. I glanced around. No one was in sight, so I impatiently nodded for her to go on.

"Um ..." She squirmed. "First, thank you, and I guess I'm sorry. Second, the book ... the spell wasn't supposed to go like that. It was supposed to help enhance our powers, not summon those creatures. It had an odd presence."

"What do you mean by an odd presence?" My brows narrowed.

"It just didn't feel right." Ivy glanced around, her eyes darting everywhere. "The spell had been changed, and I don't know how, but when I was performing it, I *thought* of you. It manifested differently."

"You *thought of me*?" If my eyebrows could raise any farther, they'd be touching the vaulted ceiling.

"I don't know..." She sighed. "Like... like your name just popped into my head and that those things were meant to find you. It was like waving your shirt in front of a bloodhound."

"So a power amplifying spell was turned into a summoning creation spell?" I asked, unconvinced.

"It was only supposed to be temporary." She waved a hand in the air. "I didn't know it was going to do... *that*."

"Did you inform Headmaster John that it was you?" I asked.

She shook her head. Of course she didn't.

"I didn't tell him how they were summoned. I returned the book that night." Her paranoia got the best of her as she glanced behind me. "But he did give Gwen and me detention every day for two weeks, including the weekends. He said it was for skipping class."

The headmaster was smart. Surely, he had suspected more and that long of a detention hadn't been just for skipping class.

"How did you return the book?" The doors were usually spelled and locked.

"I hid in here until closing. The doors were unlocked. No spells. Nothing. I was going to see what I could do—I hadn't expected them to be unlocked."

I felt a presence and glanced up. Ender stood on the next level, leaning over the railing. Ivy followed my gaze, her jaw clicking shut when she saw him.

She dipped her head. "No one knows about the book, and I didn't tell anyone about you."

She made haste and left the library. Did she just blackmail me? She knew I wasn't a level two. She also must have assumed there was a reason I had played my magic so low.

I glanced up at Ender, who had begun walking toward the stairs. I continued to my table, setting my books down, then turned to face my visitor.

"What was that about?" Ender asked.

"Oddly enough, she thanked me," I answered. His lips pursed—he knew it was more than that. "And she apologized," I added, though does adding *I guess* to an apology make it an apology?

"Did she give you specifics …" He cocked his head ever so slightly. "For her apology, that is?"

"No." My cheeks flushed as he took a step closer, invading my personal space. "I would assume for all of her *hilarious* insecure and narcissistic bullying?"

"Because that is very *hilarious*." His annoying playful half-grin showed for a split second, then vanished as he silently watched me.

My heart ramped itself up to an uneven pace and I internally struggled to subdue whatever emotions were betraying my body. Yes, Ender was invading my space, but I could handle him. Whatever Ivy had done was risky, and the information she had just informed me of would be harmful to anyone who knew. Ender had made a great ally in taking down those rock creatures, but he didn't need to know about the—

"Was it about the book?" His face was set, practically demanding an answer.

"A book?" I played dumb, my voice awkwardly pitching up a couple octaves.

Ender slowly shook his head and glanced off to the side before looking back at me.

"I saw it in her hands that night. It's dangerous." He searched my face. "Selene ..." His voice was low and hoarse. "If—"

"Ender!" a small, raspy voice came from behind me.

I turned to see a tall, slim older lady pushing a custodial cart. She smelled faintly of spring flowers and a touch of dirt. Her sleek grey hair was pulled back into a tight bun. I had seen her around a few times. She was the head groundskeeper—inside and out. It was logical to have someone in touch with nature as a groundskeeper, considering all the ornate greenery and flora lining the interior and exterior of this entire place.

"I have something for you." She rummaged through a purse-looking bag hanging off the side of the cart and pulled out an elegant cupcake garnished with flowers that was safely kept inside a clear container. "Happy birthday!"

"That's lovely." Ender gave her a warm smile as she handed him the cupcake. "Thank you, Miss Lee."

The older lady's smile brightened as he took the container and then her gaze drifted to me. "And who is this?"

"This is Sal." Ender waved at me, and I swiveled, surprised he'd used my nickname. "She and her sister started about a month ago."

"It's very nice to meet you, Sal." Miss Lee held out a hand, and I took it. She looked back at Ender. "I'm sorry I missed your birthday on Friday."

"Your birthday was Friday?" I asked, surprised he hadn't said anything. They both glanced at me. "I'm sorry. I just hadn't realized we shared the same birthday."

"Oh. Ender here is humble. I doubt he's told anyone the date of his birthday since he's arrived." Miss Lee rubbed her hands together. "Well, this academy isn't going to clean itself with all you kids running around."

"Thank you for the cupcake, Miss Lee," Ender said. She nodded, smiling brightly, and left.

"That was odd." I watched as Miss Lee left the library. "I haven't seen anyone bring you a cupcake or flowers." With the amount of girls fawning over Ender, one would think they'd be lavishing him with gifts.

"She always does." He laughed.

"And she's the only person who knew it was your birthday?" No one had said it once to him that night, and if students showed up to mine—even if it wasn't for me and was for the party itself—I imagine a party for him would have been massive.

"I don't care for the attention, so I don't mention it. Birthdays had come up in a conversation a while ago with Miss Lee. She spent a lot of time helping me. I would be out late in the garden and she'd have to kick me out." He waved a hand in the air, mimicking getting booted. "She eventually realized I wasn't in there to just fool around but was trying to remember what forsaken plant was what. She helped me pass my botany science class in ninth grade. I had been failing."

"That makes sense." I headed over to the chair and sat down. That explained her subtle earthy scent.

"It makes sense?" He grinned as he strode over to the table. "That I was failing Botany class?"

"Oh." I was the definition of being socially inept. "Umm, no. Just the relationship between you two. Everyone else here seems to either hate you or wants to bow down and kiss your feet. Granted, she's probably triple your age."

Ender raised an eyebrow, and I internally cringed.

"I meant in a mentorship relationship," I said.

He laughed as he pulled out the chair opposite me and sat. I eyed him. Was he really going to sit with me while I studied—well, did research?

He gave me a small grin before grabbing a random book that had already been on the table and opened it.

Neither of us spoke until it was time for me to head to my Elemental History class.

Chapter Fourteen

Selene

Two days later, I was wishing Thursday was Friday. I had already attended my Elemental Laws in the Human World once this week and couldn't bear it again today. So I went for a run. All the classes I had been enrolled in felt moot. Vivian and I had been taught year-round; we were way ahead of the academy's curriculum. My mom's wealth of knowledge was far greater than I had realized.

The fresh air did nothing to suppress the anxiety rising inside my chest as I ran. Based on the knowledge Ivy had given me in the library two days ago, someone was trying to kill me. It meant someone had found me. *But who?* Viv hadn't been attacked—yet. The culprit had to be inside the academy if they tampered with the creature spell book. Was it a dark mage?

But the *someone trying to attack me* wasn't the main perpetrator of my stabbing, piercing anxiety—Viv could be in danger, and I had no idea from who.

My stomach twisted at the possibility of the academy no longer being a safe haven and at the old memories of Mom. I pumped my arms faster, pushed my legs harder. The brush blurred by as I dodged hanging twigs and jumped over knobbed roots. The quarry wasn't too far from my location, and I hoped to clear my head there.

Something hit my ankle and I fell, my hair snagging on a branch. That hurt. I flung my hands out just in time to save my face from hitting the ground, my palms and knees burning. This all felt too familiar, like déjà vu—except this time, my face wasn't almost skewered. I rolled over to see what I had tripped over, but there was pressure around my ankle. Then suddenly, I found myself being dragged through a prickly brush.

An emerald green vine was snuggly wrapped around my ankle, and it was pulling me. I lashed out with my magic, sending a sharp fragment of rock slicing through it. The vine turned black from the inside out, decaying until it had crumpled into dust, which meant it had been created.

I attempted to stand so I could see who was attacking, but another vine wrapped around my throat, squeezing instantly. I pulled at the vine and tried to control it with my own magic, but I couldn't—its mage must be using enchantments. My hands and magic searched the ground around me, trying to feel for the rock again, but more vines bound my wrists, constricting them against my body.

My heart pounded against my chest, its uproar banging all the way to my eardrums, and black and white spots obscured my vision. Without movement of my wrists and arms, my ability to use magic was hindered. There was no one in sight, and my earth magic wasn't going to get me out of this. Whoever's magic it was, it was strong, and I had to do something.

I resorted to a trick Mom had taught me and ignited flames across my skin, commanding them to burn anything that wasn't my skin and clothes. It was a spell that would drain me fast but would incinerate the vines.

The vines started to wither away. I thrust my arms out, breaking the rest of the vines and sending a burst of air outward into the woods. Small smoke trails of burnt foliage and flattened plants circled me. I took the moment to recover and try to find my attacker, but they were nowhere to be found.

I glanced down at my shirt, where the heat from the flames had incidentally melted a small area, and I rubbed my wrists where bruises were already forming. The attack didn't feel like the one back home.

The danger was evident, even if it hadn't been a dark mage.

The hatch to the east dorm's roof opened, and I didn't bother checking to see who it was. I had sent an SOS for Viv to meet me after the attack.

"Sal. What happened?" Viv called from behind me.

"I was attacked in the woods." I had texted Viv and changed my clothes while Sydney was at class. My pullover's sleeves covered my wrists, and my hair covered just enough of the red marks around my neck. "Their magic is strong."

"Did you see them?" she asked as she came and sat on the ledge next to me. The sun would fade fast thanks to the shorter daylight this time of year.

"No. I was blindsided." I casually swung my dangling feet off the roof as if someone hadn't just tried to kill me. "There's more."

I filled her in on the details and then my conversation with Ivy.

"What are we going to do?" Viv asked.

"I don't think you're a target—for now," I said. "But we have to be careful. The magic doesn't feel dark, just powerful, so it's not the dark mage. I think we're still safest here." I thought for a moment about why it had so happened to be Fives Academy guards and John who had found us. "Have you seen the headmaster use magic?"

"No." Viv tapped her dangling feet together. If either of us fell, we wouldn't be harmed. I could use air to help carry me to the ground, and she could create and control a solid enough water bubble to lower her slowly, although her magic would be drained. "Why?"

"He's the reason we're here. And that message on his phone." I had told her about the locked-away phone, which she didn't think was odd—or didn't want to believe it. "It doesn't add up."

"Something doesn't add up, but I don't think it's him," Viv said. "If he knows you're an ether mage, why not kill you before you arrived?"

I sighed. I had no clue. But someone at the academy must've found out I was an ether mage and that was a problem.

Chapter Fifteen

Ender

A BASEBALL-SIZED MARBLE HOVERED above my palm, using more air magic than a tennis ball would need, due to its weight. I shut off my magic and it dropped into my hand before I tossed it in the air again, circulating my magic around it and causing the marble to swirl.

"I'm meeting up with Gwen and Ivy and then we're heading to the fountain." Nick hopped off his bed, openly staring at me. "Bro, you've been doing that for over an hour. You coming?"

"I'm good." The academy was throwing its twice a year informal social, Night Out. It was Friday, and they'd play a movie and have elemental games on the front lawn by the dragon fountain. It was one of the few times the dorms and entire back end of the academy were quiet. I was content with not going.

"Suit yourself, man." Nick waved me off. "A certain someone might be there."

With that, he left, and I let the large marble fall back into my hand. I hadn't talked to Selene or seen her the last half of this week, and something heavy weighed in my gut. I sat up and tossed the marble to the foot of my bed, its weight sinking into the stripes of my grey comforter. I checked my phone and didn't see a response from Selene, although she hadn't been thrilled when she found out I had convinced Vivian to give me her number.

I stood and tossed my sneakers on, intending to find Selene, who I presumed would be anywhere but at the front of the academy tonight. My first thought was the library, but something about it felt off. I went with the small feeling in my gut and headed to the gym.

The heavy wooden gym door made an echoing noise when I opened it. The massive space closely resembled a normal school gym—besides the stone walls to keep magic training sessions contained.

Selene was in the far corner, her uncovered fists striking a sandbag that hung there. Her hits were rushed, uncalculated. She glanced at me as I approached, lowering her raw knuckles. The heaviness in my chest dissipated but didn't entirely disappear at the sight of her.

"Following me, are we?" She grabbed her water and took a drink, her chest heaving up and down.

"I'm starting to think you just end up at places where you think *I'll* be at." I gave her a lopsided smile.

She lowered her water and narrowed her eyes, her chin tilting the slightest in defiance—a look that was growing on me. Her gaze lingered on my joggers and shirt, no doubt validating that I had truly intended to come to the gym. She set her water on the floor and put her hands on her hips.

"Want a live punching bag?" I nodded at the sandbag she'd been taking her frustration out on.

"I don't think that's a good idea."

"Why not?" I waved my hands in front of me and walked closer. "I'm dressed for the part. Almost."

I tugged my shirt over my head and tossed it to the side. I never liked training with a shirt on and part of me was pleased to see her blush as she averted her gaze. She muttered something under her breath and it sounded something like, *Cocky, are we?*

I couldn't hide my amusement.

"Fine." Selene waved for me to come closer. For the first time, I could see the shadows of dark circles underneath her brown eyes, and her hair was only half up, covering parts of the collar of her jacket, which had been zipped all the way up like a turtleneck. She seemed like she was hiding, constricting herself—being something she wasn't.

"One second," I said and turned toward the door.

"Tapping out already?" she called after me as I took a few steps.

"I understand what it's like when you can't use your magic, and I have a feeling you haven't truly used it in the last two weeks. It's a painful itch you can't scratch," I tossed over my shoulder as I locked the door with my air magic and turned back toward her. The back door was already locked. "So, use it."

The corner of her mouth turned up in a small smile for a fraction of a second—one that I couldn't quite get a read on.

"Why do I feel like this is a trick?" she cocked her head to the side, studying me. She was a level five earth mage and most likely hadn't been able to use her full power since the rock creatures.

"It's not." I opened my arms, metaphorically showing I had nothing to hide. "I'm not sure what your story is, Selene, and it's not mine to ask, but I understand pain." *And loss.* That pain had resurfaced recently, though I didn't have a reason for it to.

"While that sounds like fun—and obliterating—let's have a match with no magic use." She crossed her arms as if she was challenging me, and I grinned.

I nodded and she charged, not giving me any time to think. Her knee lifted in the air, preparing for a kick. I pivoted so the blow would land on my stomach, but her kick never came. A knifed hand came at my neck and I adjusted automatically, barely blocking her attack. Her first move had been a decoy and her true attack stayed hidden until the last second, something that takes practice.

"You are clearly well trained." I shifted on my feet, preparing to defend myself.

"So are you." She nodded at my stance. I had shifted my weight to the balls of my feet, just like Priscilla had taught me.

I shrugged. "I've had training since I was—"

Selene attacked again, this time partially succeeding at getting a knee to my stomach. I smiled. *This will be fun.*

A good thirty minutes passed with us sparring back and forth, no successful takedowns and only soft blows on both sides—if they weren't deflected. Despite the anger she was clearly carrying and her firm strikes, she hadn't landed anything bruise-worthy. The first day I saw her train, I had sworn I saw her pulling her punches and leaning into her blows. Now, I was positive that was exactly what she had been doing.

"Why are you really here?" She breathed, and I evaded her kick to my midsection.

"You're refreshing." I went to grab her ankle before her foot descended, but she dodged it. She was fast and efficient, and I had to admit I was tiring. But the hint of sweat across her brow told me she was too.

"Refreshing?" She quirked an eyebrow.

"Yes," I said between spars. "You don't fangirl over me, and you're not afraid to put me in my place." It wasn't solely that pull, or whatever it was, that led me to her. She was different. Beautiful. Exciting ...

My back slammed against the ground as Selene straddled me, having taken me down in the fraction of a second that I had let my mind drift, her forearm braced against my neck.

"That's why it seems you can't leave me alone?" She grinned—playfully.

I looked up at her. The overhead mage lights illuminated behind her, causing a slight shadow across her face. Her grin faded as we stared at each other, our match briefly on hold. It was like I could hear her heartbeat with the same rhythm as my own, and each area of her body that touched mine was fire.

"There's something else." I studied her, her pupils widening. "You feel it too."

I took her moment of hesitation and grabbed her hips, flipping her over and gaining the upper hand. We switched positions and I bound her hands over her head.

"It—" The joke that had been on my tongue slipped. A ring of blue and purple around her neck caught my attention. With this angle and her neck more exposed, I could make out the fresh bruising.

I glanced at her wrists and gently pushed the rest of the fabric up her arm with my thumb. Matching bruises wrapped around each of them.

"Selene ..." I got off of her but stayed on my knees next to her. "Who ...?"

I couldn't get much more out because I bit down on the inside of my cheek, blood pooling in my mouth. I hadn't meant to draw blood.

"I'm fine." She sat up and brushed off her pants as if we had been rolling around in dirt.

"Who did this to you?" I tried to keep my voice soft, but I couldn't help the edge of anger that laced it. I hadn't known ...

"I'm okay." She stood and offered me a hand. "Really."

I took it, surprised at the gesture despite us both knowing I didn't need it. Hot rage flitted through my veins and I searched her face for any give, hoping she'd tell me who had attacked her. They had a death wish.

She glanced at the floor, then back up at me, sucking in her bottom lip.

"Vines," she said, and I patiently waited for her to elaborate. Her magic and fighting skills were powerful—I couldn't imagine another student being able to do this to her.

After a moment, she continued. "I was running in the woods when I was attacked. I didn't see who it was." She sighed. "You wouldn't happen to know how to find all earth elementals that have attended or worked, or still do, at Fives Academy, and their levels? Basically, anyone that would have access past the wards?"

I thought for a moment and glanced over my shoulder out of instinct. "There's an archive of students and the academy staff that's updated at the end of each school year." That was one of the meaningful things to come out of Ivy's yammering.

"Where's the archive? Headmaster John's office?" Selene took a step forward, a glimpse of hope in her eyes.

"The library."

"Okay," she said and grabbed her water, brushing past me.

"Selene." I grabbed her arm gently, and she whipped her head around. I half expected her to punch me in the throat for touching her. Instead, she stared at me, despair in her eyes as if she could not only hear, but also feel the doubt in my voice. "It's in the basement."

"The locked and warded basement that is completely off-limits and dangerous. That basement?" She nodded at her own question in understanding as she spoke. "Noted." She headed for the exit, not bothered at all by the impossible mission she was embarking on.

This girl was going to be the end of me.

Chapter Sixteen

Ender

Even the librarian of the academy, Mark Hastings, wouldn't be in the human literature section—no one ever was. We were at a magical school to learn magic, and if students didn't borrow books from this area, it wouldn't need attending to. Mr. Hastings hadn't seen Selene and me enter and sneak to the third floor, where we planned to wait for the lights to turn off, the sign Mr. Hastings had closed up for the night.

Because it was Friday, along with the Night Out event, students were scarce. If anyone entered, we were unable to see them from our spot behind the wall of mundane life books—a very quiet section of the library that smelled slightly stagnant from the lack of foot traffic.

"You said you knew pain?" Selene quietly asked. She sat against the stone wall across from me, our knees bent and feet lining up next to each other.

"From loss." I moved my arms from my side and rested them on my knees. "More so the loss of past and future memories. My parents died when I was little. They got caught in a robbery."

"I'm sorry. That's terrible." Grief filled her voice and it radiated off her, mixing with mine.

"It's not so bad," I added. Being so young, I didn't remember the event—or I had blocked it out. "My cousin raised and trained me. She treated me like her own."

"I never met my dad but lost my mom recently. She had trained me." Selene's gaze dropped to her hands, her fists clenched. "Losing someone no matter at what time of your life is hard."

"That's why you and your sister are here." It started to make sense. She'd mentioned her mom had taught her a lot. Why start this late in high school at Fives—unless her sole guardian was gone.

"She—" The lights turned off, causing Selene to go quiet and pressing her lips together as if she realized she shouldn't say her next words.

The moonlight from above shone through the giant glass dome and onto the shelves and vines, giving the vibrant greenery a mute, dark color. I glanced at my phone and showed her my screen. It was just after ten. I gently nudged her leg with my foot, hoping to ease the tension from the quiet of the library and sudden drop of conversation. She dipped her chin, narrowing her gaze at me, but the tight skin around her lips told me she was suppressing a smile.

We waited the next half an hour in silence until we descended the stairs toward the checkout desk. Behind it was a locked solid oak door, but Selene had said she had a plan. She asked me to keep an eye out, and when I turned back around, she was kneeling in front of the now opened door.

"They don't teach that at Fives," I murmured.

"No," Selene whispered. "They don't."

I watched her as she stood and stepped inside, holding the door open for me to follow. We stepped into an ornate room with red carpeting and matching red velvet furniture, the door closing behind us. The wood walls were carved with elemental symbols—some I recognized from my enchantment class were allegedly to ward off evil spirits. An empty gold vase sat upon a small wooden table—a fancy, pointless display, in my opinion.

Another double door, similar to the one we had just entered, was on the other side. Two large symbols in the shape of a diamond with a line striking through it took up the entire middle of each door. It bore a slight resemblance to the symbols at the front gate.

Without hesitation, Selene grabbed the golden knob and turned it. The door pulled open and she looked it up and down.

"It's not warded."

I walked over to her and studied the door. "Apparently not."

She glanced at me, her forehead creased. "The ward wasn't up when Ivy came either. It's supposed to have an enchantment specific to each element for deactivation."

"Something's not right." From my understanding, the door was always locked and warded to keep out anyone who didn't have the enchantment. Having an enchanted door leading to the library basement was expected, but the detail of it having an enchantment specific to each element so a singular mage couldn't access it on their own was not. Miss Lee had discussed the enchanted door during one of my tutoring sessions, and somehow Selene had known about it. Though it was designed to give access to multiple mages, I imagined only a select few had access. "You had a plan to open it?"

"No." Selene entered and started down the hallway.

"Woman of few words," I mumbled, jogging after her as the door closed behind me with an echoing thud.

A spiral staircase marked the end of the hallway, the center of the stairs a dark abyss. My nonexistent acrophobia was unfazed by the lack of guard rails, however, I wasn't a fan that the bottom wasn't visible. We had to get in, find the Academy Directory book, take pictures of the pages, and get out.

Spelled torches lit our way as we descended the steps. The smooth stone was one I had heard about—melted together like cement so not even the strongest of earth elementals could manipulate it. We reached the final step and walked down a short tunnel that led to a massive opening. I laughed.Rows upon rows of bookshelves spread across the entirety of my sight. This wasn't going to be easy.

"Where's all the dust and cobwebs? It's not matching its vibe without them." I ran a finger along a surprisingly clean shelf.

"Air preservation spell. They're alphabetically ordered," Selene said, pointing to the gold letters marking each shelf and getting straight to business. "I'll start with A and you start with D. If it's not under academy or directory, we'll check F for Fives, then S for staff."

"Yes, Captain." I saluted and she looked back at me, pinning me with her *I'm going to kill you* look. I couldn't help but smile as I turned toward aisle D.

It surprisingly didn't take long for me to find the book: *Directory of Staff and Students*.

"Got it!" I hollered as I plucked it off the shelf.

"Shhh!" Her hush came from a few aisles down before she met me.

"What?" I waved around us. "No one's here, and it's not like anyone can hear us."

Selene shook her head and grabbed the book, looking it over.

"Can you hold it open?" she asked as she pulled out her phone.

"Selene Thomas. Was that a question instead of an order?" I opened the book, grinning.

"Maybe it shouldn't have been." She tilted her head down at the book, as if she was trying to cover the small twitch of her lips—the start of a smile.

My gut sparked, like a match had been lit.

Selene had started taking photos in a section of the book but was stopped by a low, distant growl that echoed from the opposite end of the basement. I strained to see, but all I saw was the row of bookshelves leading into a black void.

"Selene," I said as she rushed to take more photos, "we have to go."

I closed the book and grabbed her arm, ushering her toward the stairs. I had no clue what made that sound and didn't intend for us to stay to find out. I went to toss the book on a nearby shelf, but Selene snatched it out of my hands.

"I don't have enough information." She tucked the book under her arm, taking it with her as we jogged. "The ward is down. I should be able to bring it upstairs."

Another deep growl—much closer this time.

"Run," I said, my voice deep. We took off in a sprint.

We reached the stairs at the end of the hallway, and I glanced up at the steps leading into the darkness. We had a long way to go.

Another demonic growl, and I turned just in time to catch a glimpse of a large shadow before the torch behind us extinguished.

Selene muttered angry verbiage next to me and took a fighting stance—she must've seen it too.

Whatever was down here had to be powerful and dangerous. Selene was powerful, and I was strong. We took on three rock creatures, but this? We could stay, find out what it was, and fight. But I wasn't going to chance Selene's life on it.

I scooped her up with one arm, holding her to my chest, and used my other hand to summon my magic. It swirled the air around our bodies, lifting us off the ground. My palm stung as I held it out, trying to focus on control instead of Selene's warmth pressed against me. Two hands would've made this easier, and flying in itself was already energy depleting.

Somehow, I was able to keep a steady pace. This was the first I've flown carrying someone else—and it felt right. My arm squeezed tighter around Selene's waist, her arms wrapped around my neck. She held tightly onto the book, its corner jabbing me in the back.

The ceiling came into view, marking the top of the stairs. Almost there ...

Something sharp struck my leg, embedding itself, and I gritted my teeth against the pain. I held on tight to Selene and glanced down. A long purple—almost black—tentacle covered in suction-like cups but with sharp, tiny teeth burrowed through my pants, piercing my calf. My blood burned like scalding water and then tingled before rapidly fading. The tentacle released and disappeared below.

My magic vanished when the tingling ceased, causing us to fall into the abyss. Air threatened my lungs and my heart raced as we fell. My magic was out of reach and there wasn't anything usable for Selene's earth magic in this cursed stairwell. I reached for her, grabbing her and pulling her tight to my chest, and flipped over so I would hit first.

Wind abruptly blew against my back and our bodies stopped just above the stone floor, saving us from a splattering fall. I glanced up at Selene. She had her arms out just enough at my sides, the faint current of air flowing from her palms. Her gaze met mine, a hint of uncertainty wrinkling at the corners of her eyes.

The air cut off and we fell the remainder of the way, Selene falling on top of me. Her lips parted just a touch, and all I had to do was arch my neck and they'd be touching mine. As if she read my thoughts, her gaze lowered to my mouth. My body was transfixed, like I was being held down, yet I felt the lightest I'd ever been.

A growl came from the hallway and I snapped my head back. Upside-down, red glowing eyes were locked onto us—its prey. The shadow outlining it told us it wasn't human. Selene jumped up with her hands out in front of her, readying to fight.

"You're an ether." I got to my feet, shaking off the haze and standing next to her. "Ethers don't exist."

"You got bit by a *Demonher Rattus*." Selene drew in a breath. "Your magic will return soon."

"A what?"

"A ginormous magic and blood-sucking demon rat." Selene cracked her neck as she stared at the glowing eyes—which were fiercer right side up. Her gaze dropped to the directory book just beyond the rat's reach. It must've dropped from her hands and slid when we fell. "Where there's one, there's more."

Two small, red glowing circles lit the dark space as if on cue, and then suddenly a large rat the size of a panther leapt out of the shadows. Before it could reach us, Selene whipped it into the wall with her air magic. Its oozy leathery skin left a trail on the wall as it fell to the floor. It slowly stood, shaking off the fall, and its tail, with scales like an alligator, straightened.

Another demon rat reared its ugly head just beyond the first, its jagged snarling teeth dripping with drool. They simultaneously attacked—the first one lunging toward me and the second hurling its weird tentacle tongue toward Selene. I ran, grabbing the slimy tongue with both hands before it reached her.

This position left me wide open to an attack, and the other rat changed its course and rushed me. It chomped at my neck, but Selene blasted it a second time with air magic before it could take a bite. The slimy warm tongue pulsed in my hand, then started to recoil, managing to slip from my grip.

The first rat began to move. Its head sat at an odd angle, thanks to the way it had slammed against the wall, but it contorted itself back into place and rose. These creatures should have died—they were *living* and made of skin and dark, thick blood, unlike the rock creatures.

"Curse dark magic," Selene muttered under her breath. *Dark magic?* There shouldn't be dark magic inside the academy.

My magic slowly began to stir but wasn't ready to play yet. A third demon rat emerged behind the first two. I spared a glance at Selene. She braced herself, and I had no idea what she was capable of, but her beauty and resilience did something weird to my heart. I doubt most people would be standing up to three man-eating immortal rats.

I searched the ground near us, but there wasn't anything that I could use as a weapon. My fists clenched, ready to fight these vermin. A flash of light blinded me for a split-second, and sweat broke out on my neck from a sudden heat.

Selene had turned her hands into a blowtorch. The flames were almost blue—enough to incinerate anything in their path. But the blue and orange flames were not enough. The hideous rat slowly crawled through the flames toward us.

"Go!" Selene yelled at me.

"You're crazy if you think I'm missing this rat-roast!"

I saw the slight shake of her head before she faltered. Blue flames were challenging to create and hold on to.

Something shifted inside me ... *my magic?* ... and I moved on instinct, pushing my hands with my palms out next to hers, almost as if my thought-to-be-depleted air magic aided her fire. The blue flames grew, taking over the orange fire, and I thought my hands were going to melt off. A desert did not compare to this heat, and it smelled like an animal had died in the walls years ago.

After a long second, the flames died, leaving three piles of ash behind. Two more growls came from the shadows.

"This roast is getting too hot." My magic was slowly coming back, but I felt like I had just fought against three level four fire mages. "Let's get out of here."

I started toward the bottom step, gesturing for Selene to go first. She shook her head and grabbed my hand, tugging me toward her. I let her pull me close. Wind swirled around our feet and up to our chests.

She was flying us out of here.

Our ascent was quick and the landing at the top was rough. My knees bent, bracing as we landed. Selene faltered and I reached out, wrapping an arm around her. Her eyes narrowed, but she took the help as I steadied her and supported her through the door, the directory still on the basement floor.

Chapter Seventeen

Selene

Heavy breathing rasped nearby, and it took me a moment to stir from my slumber, interrupting a dream of the encounter Ender and I had with the *Demonher* rat the other night. That much firepower had drained my magic, but when Ender joined—despite his magic being depleted—mine grew, as if it was expanding to him for strength. Between the energy and the sickly ginormous rats, it was something I wouldn't forget any time soon. Mom had taught Viv and me about them, even though the chances of encountering one was rare. There were three ways to kill it—incinerate it, decapitation, or cut out their tongues. The later took much longer as they slowly bled out, and the cut had to be precise—if their tongue wasn't extended and severed close to the base, it wouldn't work.

I sat up, pushing the grey cotton sheet off my sweaty body. One glance at the clock told me it was nearly two in the morning. Sydney sat upright in her bed, her shadowy figure revealing she was breathing heavily, her chest heaving. The lamp's switch clicked as I turned it on, careful not to use my fire magic as a source of light. Her pale cheeks were wet with tears and she stared in front of her, clutching her red comforter. She didn't even register that I had turned on the light.

"Sydney?" I kept my voice soft and hopped off my bed, making my way over to her. "Hey. Sydney. It's alright."

When she didn't bother to look my way or seem to calm down, I climbed onto her bed next to her. I opened my mouth but before I could say anything, Sydney leaned into me. She sobbed into my shoulder and I wrapped an arm around her, too shocked to say anything.

We sat like that until she calmed down and was able to breathe. I had a feeling this was the reason she typically snuck out at night—she'd leave before she had a panic attack.

She had woken in the middle of the night last week, her face pale, her chest heaving, and tears streaming down her cheeks. Normally, I let her leave without a word, thinking that was what she wanted. This time, I had caught her before she left and just sat with her until she could breathe again. Sydney had thanked me, but she hadn't let me in.

An hour passed after Sydney had fallen back to sleep. I, on the other hand, was not going to be able to sleep. The room was dark and the dorms were quiet at the early hour of four in the morning on a Monday—and the darkness would stay until midmorning. *Thanks, Alaska.* I missed the sunny days back home in the Caribbean. And I missed coffee. But I had given it up after Mom passed, despite the raging caffeine withdrawal headaches. It reminded me too much of her.

Mom's senior yearbook sat at the foot of my bed, and I stared at the unexciting black and gold synthetic leather cover. Leaving the Fives Academy directory on the basement floor had stung. I was hoping to be able to use it to cross-reference earth mages currently at the academy—or even from my mother's class—and figure out who was attacking me. The photos didn't appear to be helpful. At least I had the yearbook. Someone at the academy had attacked me and it might lead me to them. They could've known Mom.

The bed groaned as I sat up and grabbed the book. I didn't want to wake Sydney, so I snuck out of our room and made my way to the rooftop. A soft breeze swirled around my messy bed hair. The leaves rustling and the occasional chirp from an early bird were the only sounds on campus. Light reflecting off the half-moon cast over the grounds, giving just enough glow to be able to see.

Movement in the field coming from the direction of the main building caught my attention and I knelt, taking cover behind the parapet. I didn't want a teacher, or the night guard, to spot me. As the figure came closer to the dorms, I relaxed, realizing it was just David. He was dressed for the day and appeared to be holding a book, like he had tried to go to the library. A small twinge of disappointment struck my gut. *Had I seriously been hoping it was Ender?*

I shook the thought away and turned my back against the parapet, focusing on the yearbook. My finger grazed the straw wrapper I had used as a bookmark and opened the book to that page and then flipped it to the next one.

My finger halted at the edge of the paper.

Was I seeing doubles?

I slid the yearbook across the desk in front of the librarian, the binding not sliding across the wood as easily as I'd hoped. When it was evident John wouldn't be in his office before classes started, I went to the next person who I thought would give me answers. I pointed to a single picture among the rows of squared portraits.

"Ah, yes." The librarian adjusted his glasses as he looked at the picture I pointed to. *Mark Hastings, Librarian* was captured underneath. "After many years, the photos are homogenous. I would like to believe this particular year is the same."

I blinked at Mr. Hastings, my finger still pointing to his younger profile. If he was indicating that he looked similar to what he had looked like thirty-plus years ago, I wasn't going to comment. I glanced back down at the yearbook and flipped the page I'd marked with a straw wrapper, revealing a picture of four smiling students.

"My mom had a sister." I tapped the picture of the girl next to Mom, their features almost identical. While I had been pacing outside of John's office earlier, I had scanned the student section of the yearbook and found that the other woman in this photo was named Victoria Thomas.

"Yes." Mr. Hastings nodded. "It was tragic when she had passed not many years after graduating. She was far too young. They both were."

"What do you mean by *they* both were?" I questioned, and Mr. Hastings merely tilted his head, studying me.

A student practically ran into the desk, breathing so heavily that her long black hair flew away from her face with each breath.

"I left my assignment in here last night, and it's not at the table where I was!" she said in alarm. "Do you know where it is? Can you please help me find it? Please, Mr. Hastings? It's due first class!"

She looked at her watch, her eyes bulging when she realized first period started in five minutes. Mr. Hastings faced me, bowing slightly.

"You are special, Selene. Just like your parents." Mr. Hastings turned and left to help the complaining student, who was already speed-walking off toward a few desks.

My head swiveled in his direction, and I forced myself not to follow suit and demand answers. He had known my *parents*—not just Mom. Who else had known?

Chapter Eighteen

Selene

Two weeks had passed since the *Demonher* rat incident. And almost two weeks had passed since I realized my mom had a twin and that Mr. Hastings had known our parents. To my frustration, Mr. Hastings evaded any questions I threw at him. The other times I attempted to talk to him, Mara had been working or other students were nearby. I dug more into the other boy in the photo with Mom and my apparent aunt, but I only got as far as his name. *Cursed not having internet.* We never had it growing up, but it would have been helpful now.

I let out an audible, frustrated sigh as I headed to John's office. The hallways were louder than usual as students prepared to leave for the day. Most classes were typically done by two on Fridays regardless, but the Winter Ball was tonight. It was held the week before exams. Which meant winter break would start in one week. Apparently, it was an exciting yet nervous time for the typical student.

John's office door was cracked open, so I pushed it open the rest of the way and stepped in. John peered out the window, the sun outlining his silhouette. Despite the room's brightness, many candles were still lit, even next to Aura as she slept on his desk.

"Hello, Sal." John didn't turn around just yet. "I heard you're going to the ball tonight."

"I am." I made my way to his desk. A file caught my attention on top of other papers. The label on top read *Ender Hart*.

"Good," John said as he turned around. I looked at him, averting my eyes from the file.

"Why is that good?" I asked as Aura popped up from her spot on her desk and ran over to greet me, her oval charm dangling on her necklace.

"You should enjoy yourself." John pulled out a small box from his desk drawer. "This is for you—of your own choosing to wear it."

John opened the box and held up a beautiful gold necklace with a singular pearl.

"What's that for?" It was gorgeous—and I had no idea why he was showing it to me.

"Your mother wore it for her senior winter ball. She knew I was one of the few students who had access to the art room and had asked me to help her *borrow* it." He let out a small chuckle. "I ended up helping."

"And you happened to still have it?" That was an odd thing to keep.

"She borrowed it for one night. It's been sitting in the art room closet since." He glanced at the necklace.

I stared at the piece, picturing Mom in a beautiful gown, wearing the gold chain around her neck. I wasn't one for jewelry, but part of me couldn't refuse.

I nodded, snagging the box from him and closing it.

"Why hadn't you mentioned my mom's sister before?" I blurted after a long pause. The only information I could find about her was that her name was Victoria. The past couple of weeks, I had contemplated if I should ask John about her, revealing that I hadn't known Mom had a sister.

"Ah." John lifted his chin, making his narrow nose look even longer. "Mr. Hastings had mentioned you asked about her."

I raised a brow in annoyance. Of course the older man had.

"And he avoids all of my questions about her and Mom," I said.

"You and your sister had never mentioned her before, and it wasn't my place to bring her up. She had been the only relative noted in the academy files. It was assumed a conversation you wouldn't enjoy encountering."

"And you clearly knew her just like you knew my mom," I stated. "You were in their class."

"I was." John nodded. "Victoria and I were acquaintances as well. However, we did not have as many classes together."

My lips pressed together as I studied him. There were so many questions I wanted to ask regarding my mother and her twin. But would he even know any of the answers? Questions could clue him in about my ether magic. I couldn't gauge him or comprehend how this beautiful little fox, currently rubbing against my waist as she stood on the desk, was his. I gave her a quick pat on the head.

"Thanks." I held up the box containing the necklace. It would match the outfit I would be borrowing from Sydney for tonight. I would also be asking Sydney if she wanted to go office sneaking after the Winter Ball and find out why the headmaster had Ender's file on his desk.

Chapter Nineteen

Ender

I WAS VAGUELY AWARE of the cool, hard surface of the stone pillar pressing into my shoulder as I leaned against it. Each time someone exited the west dorms, my heart beat a little faster with anticipation. Crowds made me nervous—not that anyone knew—but waiting for Selene as my date did something else to me. Her cheeks had flushed when I had asked her to the ball during lunch in front of her classmates. It was merely to get a reaction from her, but to my surprise, she had narrowed her eyes in defiance and said yes.

A flash of white caught my attention and I looked over at the dorm entrance again. Selene walked through this time, and my heart stilled. She had ditched her buns and braids combo for loose waves that fell just below her shoulders, and her white pantsuit hugged her curves elegantly and flowed as she walked, her low heels clicking against the stone. The perfect formal attire to still fight in.

I pushed off the pillar, brushing the dust off my black suit and telling myself to stop gawking. Selene stopped in front of me, and I held her gaze. I was about to tell her she looked beautiful, but someone else spoke.

"Are you two just going to stand there and ogle each other all night or are you actually going to make it to the ball?" Sydney started toward the gym. "I'm going to go dance."

I hadn't realized Sydney had come out right behind her.

"Shall we?" I held out my arm.

Selene nodded, slipping an arm into mine, and I steered her toward the gym. A stone path led to each building and the grounds behind the main building were covered in snow, the air a bit cooler than normal. They went the whole nine yards every year for the Winter Ball.

A medium-sized wooden sign was staked by the pathway to the entrance:

NO magic or any elemental use.

NO alcohol.

You must sign in and sign out.

A sign-in book lay open on a small wooden table just outside the entrance. A guard stood next to the door, wearing his typical black garb with his gold insignia jacket.

"Okay." Sydney dropped the elegant wood pen on the sign-in book and turned to face us. "Let's go."

"You signed us in?" Selene strode over to check the book as Sydney took off through the entrance. "Looks like she did."

Selene glanced up at me, and I held out my arm once again for her to take.

Inside, the gym was turned into a winter wonderland, but the temperature felt like a spring day. Small pine trees scattered about, sprouting from low flowerpots, and the walls were decorated in fake cotton to resemble snow—one of the few things not created from magic. The lighting made the ceiling dark like the night sky as snowflakes fell, vaporizing before they hit the ground.

Selene held out her free hand, catching a snowflake in her palm before it disappeared. She glanced around, her shoulders dropping as she took everything in. She was clearly well-rehearsed in elemental magic, but she must've never experienced something like this. The upbeat pop music was a bit out of place, complements of one of my classmates the Winter Ball Committee had deemed fit to be the DJ.

"It's a bit much." I leaned in toward her.

"It is." She looked out into the rows of tables next to the dance floor, her gaze fixating on something. "There's Viv."

We made our way toward the table where her sister, April, Sydney, Denise, David, and Joseph sat, passing Ivy in the process. Gwen stood next to her with Nick's arm wrapped around her waist. I gave him a nod, and he winked in response. Gwen must've finally said yes to coming to the ball with him after all these years. Ivy didn't glance at us, to my shock. Her constant need to follow me around and tell me her melodramatic stories had been nonexistent lately—which was to a relief.

As soon as we reached the table, Vivian began enthusiastically discussing the decorations with Selene. Focusing on the discourse of ornate flowers sprouting from the tables was not easy, and the hum of conversations and thumping of the awful pop music drowned my thoughts. Wanting to slow the rising anxiety in my chest, I concentrated on Selene and the touch of her arm still wrapped around mine. She wore a gold chain necklace with a white pearl complementing her pantsuit. A slight glimmer of gold powder was dashed across her cheeks, matching her eye shadow. The color brought out the warmth in her brown eyes, diluting the fire I'd grown attached to that usually resided there.

Sydney started laughing, which trailed off into a cough, bringing me back to my surroundings. She tapped her chest and I glanced around the table, realizing no one had any drinks.

"If you'll excuse me," I slid my arm from Selene's and rested my hand at the small of her back, "I'll go get the table some punch."

She gave me a nod, her gaze lingering a little longer with mine, before giving her attention to Sydney.

The crowd parted for me as I made my way over to a large punch bowl. I was filling the third cup when Miss Lee joined me.

"What a handsome young gentleman you are. Getting all the ladies punch?" Miss Lee asked. She often chaperoned these events, saying it made her *feel youthful again*.

"I wouldn't say a gentleman, but yes to the handsome." I smiled.

"Ah. Typical Ender." She laughed. "Ruffle any feathers yet?"

"Not yet." I gave her a friendly wink.

Miss Lee glanced behind me.

"I see you finally came—and with a date," she said.

"I did." I turned to look at Selene.

"I'd be careful with that one. She seems to be hiding something." Miss Lee looked down her pointed nose as she tilted her chin up. "Take warning."

"Shouldn't all women come with a warning label?" I laughed, hiding behind the truth of her statement. Selene *was* hiding something, and I wasn't about to share what that was. Miss Lee was an old, sweet lady, and she was very knowledgeable. I wasn't surprised she suspected something even though Selene didn't have a strong scent or multiple scents of each element.

"Just be careful. Enjoy your night." Miss Lee nodded and walked away.

I glanced at the cups that annoyingly lacked handles. Getting them to the table without magic wouldn't be possible.

"Can I help with those?" David walked up next to me.

"Please." I nodded, thankful for his offer. I had doubted his character, but he was always friendly. Still, something about him bothered me. It wasn't that he didn't say anything about himself. I didn't, either. But something bugged me.

We brought the drinks back to the table.

"Aww! Thanks, Ender and David!" April beamed at the sight of the drinks and reached for two of them, handing one to Vivian.

The blaring music and everyone's conversations started to pound against my eardrums, urging me to seek quiet. On top of all the decorations and that fact that the gym rarely held this many students at once, it was overwhelming. The impulse to leave was strong, but what I really found myself desiring was to be alone with Selene.

It didn't take long for Sydney to convince everyone—everyone but Selene, David, and me—to go dance. I had asked Selene to join me for one slow song, but there was no persuading her.

"Do this many students always attend?" David asked.

"This is my first time attending."

"It is?" Selene's gaze drifted from the dance floor to me and I nodded.

"It is very cool." David glanced up at the snow that fell from the dark ceiling.

"Have you been to anything like this at your old school?" Selene asked David.

He shook his head. "I didn't get the option to attend something like this."

I didn't ask questions, not wanting to overstep. Selene didn't comment either. We all had our background, and that story was ours to share if we wanted to.

"I don't bite." David smiled. "Whenever I mention something about my past, everyone goes quiet." He paused before asking, "Can I confide something with you both?"

We nodded and David leaned across the table. "I know you've heard the rumors about me, specifically the one where I may have offed my parents. I'm actually here because the council sent me. I was deprived of any training during my childhood and was a fire mage orphan—not because I did something to my parents, but because I never knew them.

The council believed Fives Academy would be the best location for me because of this. Head Trainer Murphy meets with me multiple times a week. These gloves are enchanted to help contain my magic so I don't accidentally burn things."

"The council made you wear enchanted gloves?" Selene's brows knitted together.

"Yes." He shrugged. "It was a part of my agreement."

"That's rude," Selene said and I agreed. The gloves were almost like nullifying cuffs.

"It's truly fine." He waved his gloves in the air for emphasis. "They provide a sense of security, and I don't mind them. They also add fuel to the rumors—apparently."

"Couldn't they have made ones that weren't leather? They sent you to a school where it's usually hot and sunny," I said.

"They could have given me snow mittens." He laughed and held out his covered hand, catching a snowflake.

"Touché." I took a sip of my punch. "I hope that your training helps. Trainer Murphy is excellent."

He nodded. Maybe that was what bugged me about David. He was friends with Selene. Could he be a potential danger to her if his gloves came off?

Chapter Twenty
Ender

The bass of the music beat through the gym as students danced. It felt like hours had passed by, but one glance at the clock told me I was wrong.

Selene sat next to me, her gaze on the dance floor. Her shoulders were tense and I had a feeling she wanted to leave, just like she had at her birthday party. I didn't blame her. The only reason I had even been here this long was for her.

The only reason I am here is for her, my internal voice reminded me.

"Want to go get some fresh air?" I leaned into her ear, asking over the music.

"Yes." She immediately stood, as if she had been hoping for an invite to step away from the party.

I clasped her hand in mine, leading her to the back where a small sign lit by small torches read *Warm Escape* next to the exit sign. Through the door, trees and flowers made a temporary garden—the only area without snow. The trees opened up, revealing the night sky, and more torches lined a small walkway. The stone path led to a small roofless gazebo where snow fell on the other side. Everyone else was in the gym, so we had the place to ourselves.

Selene's outfit shimmered in the moonlight, but it didn't compare to the soft glow illuminating her cheeks. She walked around, letting her hand softly trail along the flowers. I followed as she told me about each plant. Heat built in my gut, and it felt like I was on some sort of high as I listened to her.

A student came out but froze when he took one look at me and then Selene. He turned right back around.

"Other students are afraid of you," Selene said.

"Are you afraid of me?"

She whirled around to face me, a retort clearly on her lips, but she froze. Her mouth closed and she swallowed.

"I think I should be the one asking you that." She headed over to the gazebo and leaned over the railing.

"I think anyone who makes you angry should be afraid."

"And you don't?" She raised an eyebrow.

"I don't what?" I leaned against the railing next to her.

"Make me angry?" She grinned.

I winked. "Only sometimes."

Her hand flitted to her necklace as she blushed.

"That's beautiful." I gestured to the opaque pearl dangling from the gold chain.

She froze, her hand clutching the pearl. "Thank you." She looked out toward the tree line. "My mom had worn it to her dance. She was murdered, and then we had no choice but to come here."

Not only did I catch a glimpse of pain on Selene's face, but it was like I could feel it drowning her, filling her lungs. She had mentioned she'd lost her mom but hadn't stated she'd been murdered.

"Fives Academy was the safest option for Vivian and me." She cracked her pointer finger knuckle with her thumb. I placed a hand over hers and laced our fingers together. She stared at our now entwined hands but didn't pull away.

"You think whoever killed your mom is the one trying to kill you?" I kept my voice steady, internally working hard to calm the rage at the memory of the bruises around her wrists and neck from a couple weeks ago.

"Not exactly," she said. "It was a dark mage—one who used to be a powerful water mage—that used blood magic to kill my mom. I think whoever is trying to kill me knows what I am. A dark mage wouldn't want me dead without syphoning my magic."

"I'm sorry." I faced her. Blood magic was a thing of nightmares and shouldn't be real. Yet, nightmares exist. "I will help you find whoever is trying to kill you and whoever killed your mom."

"I'm not asking you to do that." She glanced at me, her brow wrinkling.

"Is that worry I see, Selene Thomas?" I joked. "Are you worried about some smug jerk?"

"I mean ..." She let out a low chuckle at my description of myself, the tension releasing in her shoulders. The moonlight hit her just right as she looked out toward the forest, causing her to be more radiant than normal.

I found myself reaching for her cheek and froze as she turned toward me. She didn't pull away, so I continued brushing her skin. The back of my fingers felt like they sparked at the contact, and we both drew in closer.

"You are absolutely stunning," I whispered, trailing my fingers across her cheek and tucking a strand of hair behind her ear.

Her lips parted, like she was about to say something. Despite every instinct telling me to move closer, I lowered my hand and went to take a small step back. She grabbed my wrist, stopping me. Her eyes were wide.

She slowly moved my hand back to her cheek, and she looked up at me. Her eyes flitted to my lips and I leaned in. She smelled like roses with a hint of sandalwood—it was the first time I had picked up a scent from her. And it was enticing.

My lips gently came down on hers, and she welcomed them. Her hands moved to the back of my head, pulling me closer. I could feel her heartbeat against my own chest as if it were my own. My magic swirled inside me, bouncing with joy.

The door to the gym opened. A slight hesitation in Selene's movements told me she heard it too, but we didn't part ways just yet. We kissed one more time before she pulled away, her dark brown eyes searching mine for answers I didn't have.

"I knew you were trouble," she whispered, almost inaudible, and I grinned at her words.

"Now what makes you think—"

"Sorry to interrupt, Sal," Sydney said as she stopped halfway down the path, grinning. "I wanted to see if you still wanted to have that movie night we were supposed to start a little bit ago?"

"Oh. Yes." Selene's cheeks flushed as she looked from Sydney to me. "Bye, Ender."

"Bye, Selene."

One thing Selene didn't excel at was socializing, but that wasn't a flaw by a long shot. Her small amount of social quirkiness amused me. It matched my hate for public socializing.

My hand grazed down her arm as she walked away, slowing at her palm before my fingertips completely left hers.

"I didn't mean to interrupt the you-know-what with the you-know-who that you aren't interested in," Sydney whispered to Selene when she reached her.

I caught enough of a glimpse to see that Selene gave her the classic *Selene Look*, pinning her with a glare. After they were through the doors, I leaned back against the gazebo's fence and gazed up at the stars.

That was the most remarkable kiss I swear anyone in eternity has ever had.

Chapter Twenty-One

Selene

My fingers grazed my still tingling lips and my head spun as my magic danced across my nerves like they were its own personal dance floor. My own thoughts berated me for leaving Ender, especially after that kiss, but Sydney and I had some late-night *research* to do.

A slow song played inside the gym-turned-winter-forest-wonderland, and there was an overwhelming buzz from everyone talking, adding to my inability to focus.

"Did Viv leave?" I asked Sydney as we weaved through students I barely recognized, wishing I could blame it on their formal attire.

"Nope." Sydney nodded toward the dance floor, and my gaze drifted in that direction.

Viv had her arms around April's waist, swaying back and forth, smiling as they chatted. I had admired Viv's beautiful deep-plunged purple dress, and she had curled her hair into long, black ringlets. Now, I admired it in a different light—along with her intense reaction when I had asked her to keep a low profile, which meant hanging out with her new friends less. She had a thing for April—who also looked beautiful with a floral dress and matching flower crown seated in her curled, short red hair. April was very social and always out, which would leave Viv alone in their room.

"Come on." Sydney nudged me as she grinned. "We gotta go."

We had research to do.

My math teacher was stationed at the sign-in and check-out book near the door. She seemed to be holding the attention of a guard as she chatted away. I tucked my head and quickly walked past, following Sydney out the door and disregarding the sign-out book.

We made our way inside the main building, its doors typically unlocked until late at night. But getting in wasn't the problem—it was the locked doors on the inside that would slow us down.

"You couldn't have picked this pantsuit in literally any other color?" I glanced down at the vibrant white that was a beacon in the dark academy halls. Staying in our dress attire was included in the plan in case we were caught—easier to make up some alibi about post-dance shenanigans.

"White is good for the soul." Sydney smiled over her shoulder. "Plus, I like white when I use fire magic. It's a bold look."

It was too bold.

"You seem very casual about this," I whispered as she led the way toward Headmaster John's office. I'd done my *exploration* of the academy at night to become familiar with the grounds, but I hadn't expected Sydney to feel at such ease—but with her skill set, which I would be utilizing, I shouldn't have been surprised.

"Do you know how I told you my parents sent me here to try to strengthen my magic?" she asked.

"Yes." I also remembered April telling me how she would sneak off at night, though now I knew it was due to her panic attacks. Sydney had mentioned she was very good at picking locks—the reason she was coming with me tonight.

"Well, they also sent me here to get rid of me." Her tone dropped, a touch of hurt seeping into it. "They were hoping it would get rid of my *rebellious* side."

"I'm sorry." I didn't know all of her story, but from the pain in her voice, I could tell it was a hard topic, and I wondered if it had anything to do with her panic attacks in the middle of the night.

"Here we are." Sydney knelt in front of the headmaster's door. She pulled two bobby pins out of her hair and went to work.

Ender had believed I unlocked the doors in the library when, in reality, I had stolen the librarian's key and didn't want anyone to know. Every single lock in this forsaken academy was made of tungsten—and I couldn't manipulate it. If we had gotten caught, it would have been better if he had no knowledge of stealing a key or taking part in the thievery.

Stealing the headmaster's key, on the other hand, wasn't a very accomplishable task. The little charm around Aura's neck would immediately be noticed if it was MIA.

"Got it!" Sydney whispered in triumph a few short moments later. She went to open the door, but it wouldn't budge. "That's strange."

"Are you sure you unlocked it?" I asked as she stepped aside for me to try. My hand turned the knob, and it opened just fine.

"Huh." Sydney shrugged. "Must've been stuck."

"And you just loosened it for me," I joked.

Inside, the office was dark, so Sydney lit a small ring of fire. She didn't know I was an ether mage, and despite how close we were getting, I wasn't going to tell her. Not only did it put her in danger, but it also put Viv in danger.

"Thank you for your help," I said to Sydney as I went over to John's desk and began opening anything that was unlocked. She had been eager to help when I told her I needed to see why he had Ender's file on his desk, but she'd declared herself all-in when I said we had to pick the lock.

I assumed Ender's file had been present because of the rock creature incident, but that was a month ago. Then there was the phone I had found, and no one seemed to actually know what type of mage John was. He had a familiar, so was most likely a level four. Of course, the directory had been left with the *Demonher* rats before I could find out and take more than a couple pictures of its pages. I needed to know more.

Inside one of the drawers was a lighter, the body carved from wood. *Interesting choice to make a lighter with.*

I glanced up. Besides the soft glow Sydney's magic was emitting, the room was dark. No candles were lit, and I wondered if they hadn't always been lit with magic.

The file wasn't on the desk, so we started searching the filing cabinets. They were alphabetically labeled but locked. I didn't have to wait long for Sydney to unlock the cabinet marked *H*, so I could look for Hart. After she whistled and muttered something about that being her fastest picking yet, I made quick work, my fingers moving through the files.

"Can you watch the door?" I asked Sydney, and she nodded, taking a guard position.

Once I found Ender's file, I set it on top of the others, opening it. The first sheet had a picture of Ender. His face was narrower, and his hair was a bit shaggier—he looked like a freshman. I wondered if the files for me and Viv had our pictures—we hadn't taken one during orientation.

There wasn't a lot of information besides the mention of a small school he had attended in Canada prior to his arrival, a Priscilla Hart—his guardian who worked for the council—and that his parents were deceased. It didn't even mention his parents' names.

Another paper with a small picture stapled to it lay behind it, and I pulled it to the front. The older woman in the photo looked just like

Miss Lee, the groundskeeper who had given Ender the cupcake. But the name on the sheet said *Bernila Galang*.

Why would she go by a different name? And why would a scant record sheet on her be in Ender's file?

"Someone's coming," Sydney popped back though the partially closed door. "I can hear wheels and think it's the janitor. They haven't rounded the corner yet."

"Let's go." If it was *Miss Lee*, the groundskeeper, I didn't want her to find out I was sneaking into the headmaster's office.

I put the file back and closed the drawer. The letter *T* caught my eye, and I paused. I would love to know what John had in my file—but then again, would it be nearly empty like Ender's? How much did he know?

I guess it didn't matter. Our time was up.

Chapter Twenty-Two

Selene

Winter break officially started four days ago, which kicked off the academy's semester break. The majority of the students had already left after their exams and some had yet to leave. Students were either picked up by family or transported by guards to the closest city as a meeting point.

Guards and few professors remained on campus, including Mr. Hastings. April said they held Christmas in the library and had few events throughout break for the students who didn't—or couldn't—go home. A bit of sorrow balled in my throat, and I swallowed it down. It wouldn't be our traditional small holiday, playing cards and eating a mix of chestnuts and walnuts, but Viv and I would still spend it together.

"Any news from your friend yet?" I asked Sydney as she met me in the courtyard before lunch. Her parents hadn't invited her home for the holiday. She wanted them to reach out to her first, and when they didn't, she opted to stay.

"Nothing." Sydney shoved her phone in her pocket. Since the reception was awful and spotty, she had to go to the front lobby of the academy to check for a response. She had gotten a message out to an old friend a week and a half ago after we snuck into John's office. He was going to look into both names, Bernila Galang and Eleanor Lee. He had found information on Miss Lee. She was an earth mage who had moved from the Philippines. There had been no red flags found. "He couldn't find anything on a Bernila Galang."

"I'll just have to ask her myself." The groundskeeper was hiding something if the headmaster was looking into her, and I didn't have any more time to wait for someone to choke me with plants in my sleep. Her earthy scent was weak, unless she was masking it, which made her my only lead.

"That's a bad idea." Sydney tucked a strand of hair behind her ear. "What if her name is hidden to protect herself from someone? If there had been anything, my friend would have found it that day I asked him to look into her."

"But then why was her picture in Ender's file?"

"I don't know." She shrugged and opened the cafeteria door. "Maybe because they seem close? You did say she brought him a cupcake when no one knew it was his birthday—not even his so-called friends."

"They have similar features."

"And?" she asked.

"And ..." It didn't mean they were related. I was grasping at straws. This conversation would be a different story if I told her someone was trying to kill me.

"Either way, the file is suspicious," I said quietly as we entered. No offense to Syd, but I didn't know her friend and couldn't trust that there had been nothing on the head groundskeeper.

Ender stood when his gaze found me. He was sitting with Viv, April, and David, but the intensity he watched me with told me he'd been waiting for me to arrive. He wore black jeans and a black T-shirt. Typical, bland attire, but he wore it great. His dark brown eyes held my gaze as he strode toward Sydney and me, a small grin tugging at the corner of his mouth. I probably had some smug remark coming my way. And my stomach jumped with excitement at the thought.

I looked away from him and at the student in front of us, who surveyed their lunch options.

Ender came up behind me, stopping so his lips were an inch from my ear, and I froze.

"About time. I'm here for your company," he whispered, his breath hot against my skin. His cedar and bergamot scent were starting to smell like home. "Not to hear about how makeup can be made from dirt."

Something inside me set off, my magic danced along my nerves, and I was stupidly immobilized with no response, even after Ender had straightened, no longer at my ear. We hadn't kissed since the Winter Ball a week and a half ago, and part of me urged to feel his lips on mine again, but I needed to focus on keeping Viv safe and searching for any clues about Mom's killer and my assailant, so I had avoided him when possible. Classes and studying had been my main excuse, but he'd been sitting at our table, and he'd joined me on my runs since finding out about my attacks—the only reason Viv said she let me still run. That, and she hated running.

I told myself it was fine to have a friend besides Vivian ... and maybe Sydney.

The word *friend* felt weird. Ender and I hadn't established what we were, though attending the Winter Ball together had sealed most of the other students' assumptions of us being an *item* or whatever.

"Did you hear me?" Sydney waved a hand in front of my face.

"What?" I swatted her hand away.

"I said ... your stomach's not going to feed itself. They finally made a decision. We're up." Her gaze flitted to Ender over my shoulder, then back to me. She smirked before going up to the counter.

"Didn't mean to fluster you with my presence." Ender moved so the back of my shoulder brushed against his chest.

"You didn't." I stepped forward. "Your breath stinks. It's disorientating."

"Sure." He chuckled, a low, deep sound that had my feelings betraying my last remark.

Sydney and I grabbed our food. There were only a few students besides our table, and there was a lot less background noise. It was more peaceful. We headed to the table with Ender behind me like a tall, muscled shadow. He sat down next to me, leaning back and resting his closest arm on the table and draping the other over the empty chair on his other side, something he did daily at lunch.

"Ender." David wiped his mouth with a napkin. "Are you heading home?"

"No. I won't be." The hitch in Ender's breath was barely noticeable. I had a sense it was because of his parents, and his guardian must've not been available. My chair began to subtly shake and I glanced over at Ender. He was bouncing his knee.

"Sounds like there'll be plenty of us here over break. We won't get bored," I added, placing my hand on Ender's leg under the table. His gaze immediately flicked to me.

"I'll be helping with prep around the academy, but I'll have plenty of time to still party." April shoulder-nudged Viv next to her, smirking. They hadn't declared themselves a couple or committed to acting as one, but I imagined they didn't want to get in trouble, considering they were roommates.

"The guards will need something to keep them on their toes while everyone's gone." Viv laughed.

Ender brought his arm underneath the table and linked his fingers with mine, his leg no longer moving. A light squeeze told me he was thanking me.

"I heard that a majority of them leave to complete academy tasks or something?" David asked.

"I've seen them coming and going a lot this year already." Sydney shoved a spoonful of peas in her mouth.

The conversation continued, but something dark crept along my spine, spanning across my skin. I pulled my hand from Ender's and brought it to my throbbing stomach, which threatened to upchuck my partially eaten lunch. Ender tensed next to me, and I was hit with a foul stench of rotting flesh that had been buried in soil for a long time.

No. The academy was supposed to be safe.

I stood, pushing my chair back and turning toward the entrance, Ender moving simultaneously with me. All chatter ceased as everyone finally felt the dark magic and realized there was a figure standing in the doorway, wearing a cloak that was a deep shade of hunter green. The hood was pushed back just enough for us to see the ghastly features of a woman, grey strands of hair trailing over the collar of her cloak. Her dark eyes were fixated on me.

Yellow lights near each doorway began flashing and an alarm sounded—the alert for all students to shelter in place.

"Sal?" Viv asked, so many questions in one mention of my name. I glanced across the table at her, our gazes meeting, and shook my head. This mage wasn't one of the three dark mages who had attacked us and killed Mom. Her robe and stature were different, and judging by her scent, she no doubt had been an earth mage.

"You need to run," I said to her.

"I'm not going anywhere." Of course she wouldn't listen.

"What's going on?" April asked, but I didn't look away from the dark mage to see my friends. *Friends.* Dang it. I had grown attachments whether I had wanted to or not. And now, that put them—and everyone at Fives Academy—in danger.

The dark mage took a step and Ender moved in front of me.

"Ender. Don't." I stepped out from his shadow.

"I was never one to listen to orders." His voice was playful, but his gaze never left the threat.

The side door to the outside opened and Miss Lee strode through, her gaze landing on Ender. A student nearby escaped through the door behind her as if they had just realized their legs could move.

Before I could make anything of her presence, static filled the air and a sharp gust of wind came soaring toward us. Ender threw his hands upward and turned around, holding up a wind shield of his own. He strained against the pressure but sent the gust upward and over us, only letting a waft filter through.

Miss Lee held out her hands, chanting something under her breath. The wind stopped as vines wrapped around the dark mage—some from a plant nearby, others that Miss Lee created. *A four.* She'd clearly been hiding something or had been deceiving everyone—which was the same thing. The dark mage wrapped long, bony fingers around one of the vines. Black ooze seeped from her pale hand, the ooze trailing down the vine and disintegrating it.

The dark mage chanted something and sent a rush of wind toward Miss Lee before my brain could compute what was happening. Miss Lee was lifted off her feet and sent crashing through the door, its glass shattering. Ender took a step toward her and the broken door but didn't move any farther.

"She's here for me." I rolled my neck and shook out my shoulders. "Everyone needs to go. Now!"

Before it's too late.

But no one moved.

"Yeah. I don't think so." Sydney raised a defiant brow.

April stood tall next to Viv, and I glanced at David, but he only shook his head. No one was going to leave.

The dark mage bared her yellow teeth, revealing black gaps in her grin. I took a step forward, ready to battle with my friends at my back.

Chapter Twenty-Three

Selene

Before the dark mage could advance, I used a combo of wind and earth magic to heave a cafeteria table at her. She easily deflected it to the side with a swipe of magic and started toward us. Ender lashed out with sharp slashes of wind-like whips, causing her to wince but barely slowing her down. Someone flung the flames from a nearby torch onto the dark mage's cloak, catching it on fire.

"Fry, rotten flesh bag!" Sydney shouted.

With my magic, I picked up a wooden chair and sent it crashing into the dark mage, who had to stop and douse the fire burning her cloak. She flinched and staggered but remained on her feet, the fire out. I battered her with chair after chair while Ender continued his attacks, causing her to halt.

Ender pushed with his hands out in front of him, and the air felt heavier. He was attempting to crush her with pressure. I joined him. The dark mage crossed her arms in front of her face like a shield but forcefully brought them down, straining against the crushing air. Tiny sand particles appeared out of thin air and headed straight at us and forced us to halt our attack. I flipped a nearby table, pulling it in front of our small group as a shield against the mini sandstorm. My friends crouched down beside me, taking refuge.

Students who weren't near an exit had taken shelter behind whatever they could find. The noise from the mage's attack had drowned everything else out, but the panic and fear were evident on the other students' faces.

My arm ached from pushing my magic into the table, and my eyes burned from the wisps of sand that had found a way around. Ender had put his hands on the table, using his weight and force to help me push against the sandstorm. Vivian and April joined him, and then David took up the only spot left, leaning in to the table. As soon as the pressure of the attack disappeared, I released my hold on our barrier. Sand had made its way inside my mouth, leaving me tasting grit, and I spat.

Water burst from the top of a bottle refill station situated at the front of the cafeteria and lifted into the air, swarming into a giant ball, and I instantly knew it was Viv controlling it with her water magic. Then she wailed a battle cry.

For the love of all Oreos, please help my sister.

She threw the mass of water at the dark mage, but the dark mage threw her hands up and sliced right through it, the water falling to the floor like a popped balloon. Viv's plan had been most likely to drown her, something I've seen her practice.

The dark mage clapped her hands and stomped a foot. I reached for the sand on the floor, hoping to use it to tear at her flesh and stop her attack, but I was too late.

Her air magic crashed into me, and the ground shook below as her earth magic took root. Rocks and chunks of earth ripped through the flooring, and everyone was sent flying in different directions. My back slammed against an uprooted rock and my breath left my lungs. I fell and looked around for my friends. I couldn't see Ender, but the others were all down. Viv stood and rushed to April's side before meeting my gaze.

I took a deep breath. *Screw it.*

I stood and glared at the dark mage, who was now only ten feet from me. She drew a deep breath in through her nose, her eyes rolling to the back of her head.

"It's just me you want." I felt the heat of my magic rise—the same magic she wanted to siphon from me. "Come and get me."

I melded my magic around the water at the feet of the dark mage and froze it.

"*Ignis uror. Ignis lucidus ...*" I wielded a frozen shard like a knife and managed to slice part of her face. "*Viam reperi, donec accendat.*" I finished the enchantment and flames erupted at her feet. She screeched, the sound laced with more anger than pain. If it wasn't obvious to my friends that I'd been using elements other than earth, it was now.

A black-veined vine wrapped around my hand and pulled it to my side with enough force to nearly snap my hand in two. I lost the fire that was holding the dark mage in place, and she closed the gap between us, her moves choppy but inhumanly fast. Her hand moved to my neck, wrapping her decaying, boney fingers all the way around. My heart beat harder as she crushed my airway, and vines slithered from my toes to my torso like a boa.

My body was pinned, and using magic without movement wasn't easily done, especially with my brain in a state of shock and struggling to keep up without oxygen.

Ender's shadow fell over her from behind and a sickening crunch came from her rotten flesh. The dark mage let out a small cry and released her hold on me. I fell to the floor, gasping for air. The mage glanced down where the tip of a knife protruded from her chest. A second later, she let out a deafening laugh, blood bubbling at the creases of her pale lips.

"How old are you?" I whispered between coughs.

Dark mages were killable; you just had to get close enough. Their magic was strong, but for a dark mage to still be unaffected by our attacks, they had to have been hundreds of years old.

"You missed," the dark mage hissed and turned around, grabbing my makeshift ice shank and stabbing Ender in the shoulder.

"No!" I roared as I got up, but the vines wrapped around me, trapping me once more.

Ender flinched, but moved to disarm her, blood pouring from his wound. He retrieved the knife in one solid motion and landed a kick to her abdomen. Vines grabbed his wrists and ankles, slamming him against a stone pillar and stopping his next attack.

The vines crushed him against the rock, and he grunted. The dark mage cocked her head toward him, her nose pointed upward as she breathed in.

"What a pleasant surprise." She glanced between Ender and me. She thrust her hands to the side, her palms bare of the clan mark, and faint screams came from around me as she pushed the others back with a force of air magic.

A vine with black tendrils shot from her hand and wrapped around Ender's neck. It pulsed against his skin as the veins on his neck turned dark. She was draining him.

Dark mages could only drain ether mages.

And it was going to kill him.

I thrashed against the vines, about to do another fire enchantment, when the dark mage's hand grabbed me by my throat and lifted me into the air, her cloudy white eyes turning to me.

"You're next." Her voice was raspy, like a ghost, and for the second time in my life, I was terrified.

Her hands looked so frail, but they held immense strength as they tightened around my neck. My lungs burned, aching for even the slightest bit of air.

Ender stopped fighting against his restraints, his eyes fluttering shut.

My heart began to crack as if her hand crushed it instead of my windpipe.

The dark mage's grip never loosened, though something felt different. Her hand was a searing brand—but not of fire. It was powerful energy, emitting at me like a beacon. Not just her hand but her entire body begged me to take it. The dark, deadly magic wanted to be siphoned.

It felt slick and greasy, like black goo. A voice in the back of my head told me to take it, but another warned against it. Was this the darkness calling to me? To take the power and take the plunge into the cold void?

The mage's gaze flicked from Ender to me, worry creasing the corner of her eyes as her milky eyes widened. Did she realize her magic had opened to me like a funnel? I slammed the funnel closed, ignoring the powerful sensation to draw her dark energy from her. I didn't want to be her and closing it had been harder than I would've liked to admit.

She suddenly went rigid. Something else happened when I cut off the funnel. The top layer of her skin turned into a hazy, frothy fog, as if something was moving it. Heat radiated from my skin and a burst of energy echoed from me, sending the mage flying into the cafeteria wall. Not only did it send her backward, but it sent Viv and the others, who had been making their way back over, to the ground again.

I dropped to my knees, gasping for air and using my hands to keep me upright, the cold tiles welcome against my sweaty palms. Soft white fur rubbed against my bare arms, providing warmth and comfort and motivating me to look up. Aura's eyes were almost black like her nose before turning a shade lighter. It took me a moment to realize she too was covered in dust, and dark blood stained her muzzle. She shrieked and flitted her gaze to the dark mage.

The mage tried to stand, wobbly in her attempt, as fury flared in her now obsidian eyes. Before she could fully stand, she was engulfed in flames. Her screams filled the room and then ceased as she fell to the ground.

"Sal." A hand rested on my back. "Are you okay?"

I looked up to see David, his brow creased in worry. The hand that wasn't on my back was bare—no glove.

I think I'm okay? But were the others okay ... Was ...

"Viv!" I shot to my feet—too quickly—and the cafeteria began to spin.

"She's okay." David helped steady me as I found Viv in the rubble with the others. They had cuts but overall appeared to be fine as they regained their bearings.

I turned to find Ender slumped against the stone and I panicked at his stillness.

"No!" I ran to him, Aura leaping over uprooted stones as she kept pace with me.

Once I reached him, I found his pulse. I let out a long, shaky breath that helped release a ball of panic that had threated to burst inside my chest. Aura rubbed up against his hand on the ground, her eyes fading to black again. I brushed Ender's hair from his forehead, sand falling from it. He stirred and his eyes fluttered open, taking in his surroundings.

After a moment, he opened his mouth. It took him a second try before coherent words came out.

"I think I like this new cafeteria remodel." He forced a half grin.

My gaze roamed over his disheveled state. His magic *felt* different, almost like it had been awoken yet attacked. Like his magic had been siphoned? And why did I feel so in tune—

Viv crashed into me.

"You're okay." She squeezed me tight, and I winced at the aches across my body.

"You are too." I hugged her back, debating never letting her go.

John stepped into view with a few guards behind him. I wasn't sure when they had arrived, but dust and sand coated the blood and scrapes they wore. I pulled away from Viv and glanced back at Ender, who grunted as he tried to sit up.

"Don't move." I tore a piece of my shirt and held it to his shoulder wound. "You're making it bleed more."

Ender looked at me with a lopsided grin that wavered slightly as he placed his hand over mine. "It's just a scratch."

"Ender?" A worried voice came from the side door where Miss Lee stood assessing the room. Sun filtered through the broken windows, reflecting off the broken glass scattering across the ground-up stone floor.

"Miss Eleanor Lee." John stepped out in front of us.

"Yes?" Miss Lee entered the cafeteria, her gaze on Ender.

"We will be addressing your true identity further." He motioned for the guards to contain her, and they placed enchanted tungsten shackles on her wrists. Once locked in place, the nullifying cuffs glowed green, making her magic unavailable to her. It was the first time I had seen the magical cuffs in person.

"What are you doing?" Ender slowly got to his feet, using my arm to steady himself.

I stared at Miss Lee. Her vines... her show of power... It had confirmed the suspicions I had been hoping weren't true.

"She's the one who's been trying to kill me," I said, glaring at her with new eyes—she was a strong earth mage who—for some reason—had a vendetta against me. Had she let the dark mage in?

"Someone has been trying to kill you inside the academy, Sal?" John turned his attention to me.

"Yes." I didn't want to give him any details. He wasn't on my People I Can Trust List—my really small list.

"She's the one that attacked you?" Ender's brow furrowed as he looked from me to her. "You have it wrong." He waited for Miss Lee to respond, but it never came. I could feel the anger and hurt radiating off Ender at her silent admission.

"Why?" he demanded.

"Her true name is Bernila Galang." John faced him. "She's your grandmother."

Chapter Twenty-Four

Ender

If Miss Lee—Bernila Galang—whoever she was—really was my grandmother, it didn't answer any of the questions. It didn't explain why she had attacked Selene or why she had hidden her identity from me.

I ran a hand through my hair as I paced the sidewalk outside the academy staff living quarters where Miss Lee was being detained. My entire body pulsed with pain, my head threatened to burst, and the wound underneath the bandage on my shoulder was a nuisance. Nurse Adair had given me pain medication and a healing elixir before letting me leave the infirmary with a promise I would return in the morning, which I had falsely granted.

Headmaster John exited through the front door of the staff quarters. His tan dress pants were still covered in dust from the attack.

"You can go in now," he said.

I nodded and entered the building as the headmaster led me through the halls. It was similar to the setup of the dorm except the doors were farther apart. Flowers and plants had been pressed into the bland walls like a book, but there was nothing extraordinary like inside the main building.

We passed a door secured by guards and descended a flight of stairs. Four individual glass rooms were on either side of the underground level. Their glass glowed a faint green—the same as the magic-infused handcuffs that acted as a magic nullifier. I had never been inside the staff quarters and hadn't known an area of this sort even existed.

My supposed grandmother sat on a bench in one of the cells and watched me, her cheeks hollow and eyes dull. I stopped in front of her cell, openly studying her.

"I'll be right outside." Headmaster John stepped outside, where the guards were.

"So, Miss Lee, Bernila ... or should I say, Grandma." I needed to say something to break the silence. "Are you going to tell me why you tried to kill Selene? Was the dark mage your doing?"

Miss Lee didn't flinch at my question, as if she had been expecting it, but her eyes briefly softened and then hardened again.

"No. I had nothing to do with that foul dark mage." *Dark mage* hissed off her tongue with disdain as her voice filtered through the glass. "As far as Selene, yes. I tried to kill her."

My fists clenched as hot anger fueled my blood. The images of Sal's bruised neck and wrists flashed in my mind along with my internal promise that I would tear apart whoever did that to her. It didn't change that Miss Lee had been like family to me or was truly my blood relative—she wasn't my family.

"You had no right." My voice dropped, surprising me with its venom.

Miss Lee swallowed—a short break in her defiance. "I had every right," she said calmly as she straightened. I began to pace, ignoring the sharp throb from the wound in my shoulder. "Selene Thomas will get you killed. Now more than ever. I wasn't sure ..." She trailed off.

"You weren't sure of what? What she was?" I stopped pacing in front of the glass, my gaze pinning her.

"It's not just what she is; it's who she is." She paused, as if calculating what to say next. "Dark mages are an abomination. High-level ether mages are dangerous—it's more tempting for them to turn."

"Selene will *never* become a dark mage." My teeth ground against each other so hard that I wouldn't be surprised if I chipped a tooth. "You wanted her dead because ... what ... she maybe, someday, will turn into a dark mage? Anyone can turn into a dark mage if their soul turns dark enough."

"You don't know who she is."

"That sounds more like a *what* she is reason because you absolutely don't know who she is." I took a deep breath, trying to keep my still healing magic from bursting.

"I do know who she is. I knew the moment she arrived at Fives Academy." Miss Lee stood, moving a little closer to the glass. "She's the reason your parents—my only son and daughter-in-law—are dead. Her mother led them to your parents. Instead of staying to help them, she fled while your dad's magic was siphoned until he withered away. Your mom had hidden you before they gutted her." She stared at me, studying my face. "You have your mother's hazel eyes, you know."

I stood there, confused. "My parents died in a robbery."

"That was the story the news told, which was mendacious. The dark mages were following Anna Thomas. All traces of Anna's existence were hard to find, besides what little remains here at the academy. That day they ran into her, they had also found your father. They must've assumed he was an easier target. Your mother had tried to protect him. She paid with her life."

"My dad was an ether mage?" My heart was pounding in my ears.

"The council sent you to the States with a new name after their death. I thought your new identity would keep you safer than being with me. They had kept you hidden at their Canadian homestead and school. I came to the academy before you would've enrolled, assuming their plan would be to send you to this *esteemed* academy—the same school the person who had killed your parents attended. I kept an eye on you and to see if your magic had or would emerge, but it never did." Miss Lee took another step forward. "Your mother, father, and I lived a quiet life, hiding the majority of the time. I didn't know if Daniel's"—my heart skipped a beat at my dad's name—"magic had manifested in you. It wasn't until the dark mage siphoned your magic that I confirmed it."

"What do you mean?"

Dark mages could only siphon from ether mages. It was the main reason ethers were thought to be extinct. I had believed them to be gone, until Selene. They were rare to begin with, but dark mages had been hunting them for centuries, and about two decades ago, they were to have thought to have been killed off. The only natural enemy of dark mages were dragons—enchantments didn't work on them, and they warded off negative magic like a shield.

They were also known to be extinct.

"You understand what it means," she said.

Deep down, I did. *I am an ether mage.* But I didn't want to process that right now. The entire *kill Selene* overshadowed that thought.

"Even if any of what you are saying is true, Selene had nothing to do with any of it. That was sixteen years ago." I kept the other swirling emotions at bay.

"I stopped once I fully realized what she was to you." She watched me, like I was supposed to know what that meant.

The door opened and Headmaster John strode through.

"One of our guards needs to talk to Bernila." He stayed near the door. "I have to cut your session short."

"Did you know you had a level five ether mage in your academy?" Miss Lee pinned the headmaster with a glare—a side of her I had never seen. "After all, you run the tests. Not only did you let one ether mage slip through, a powerful one albeit, you failed to detect a second one." Her eyes softened as her gaze drifted to me. "You must protect him. They'll only keep coming. Especially now, and especially if *she* is here."

"Miss Lee." The headmaster pinned her with a deadly glare. "You managed to keep your identity hidden in your background check and for the duration of your employment. That alone is a crime. I understand your need to protect family; however, that doesn't justify your lies. The reason you are being transferred to a containment facility under the council and will remain there without release is a result of your attempted homicide. I take the security and safety of all our students very seriously."

Headmaster John pivoted away from her cell and ushered me out.

Chapter Twenty-Five
Selene

I was really starting to hate the fact that my increasingly frequent trips to John's office were allowing me to memorize what was on his shelves.

"Are you alright?" John asked for the third time this evening. Despite his eerie calmness, he hadn't sat since I entered.

"I'm fine."

I wasn't fine. My sister could've been killed. I thought the safety of the academy's dome and trained guards would have been enough. It wasn't even the dark mage who had killed Mom—but it had been someone from the same clan. And they weren't going to stop. As long as I remained at the academy, Vivian wouldn't be safe.

"Would you like some coffee?" He went over to the wooden cart and poured himself a mug, the rich aroma wafting over to me.

Despite the excited zing in my brain and grumble in my stomach, I was only here for answers—not coffee. The migraines from the caffeine withdrawal had long subsided, but not the urge to have a steaming cup.

"Did Ender's grandmother let the dark mage in?" I asked, leaning against his desk. He set the carafe down and strode over to the window with his mug, not showing if it had bothered him that I hadn't answered his question about coffee. He took a sip as he looked outside, the view overlooking the courtyard, giving him a small view of the training fields.

"I have reason to believe otherwise." He smoothed the cuff of his collared shirt with his free hand. "She wouldn't want any harm to come to Ender."

"But she did want me dead." If the stick to the eyeball wasn't obvious enough.

"Dark mages can only siphon from ethers." John turned to face me. "She would never take the risk of exposing her grandson and getting him caught in the crosshairs."

"Because he's an ether mage." I was pretty sure I felt it when we were in the Academy's basement fighting off those *Demonher* rats and again after the dark mage attack.

"At this time, we are unsure how the dark mage got past the barrier and how the *Demonher Rattus* took hold in the academy's basement and escaped into the library." His voice was calm, his lips didn't waver, and his brows weren't creased. The only telltale sign that this entire situation had upset him was the red-tinged whites of his eyes and the fact he had started slowly pacing. He and the guards had been fighting five *Demonher* rats when the dark mage had arrived, so they hadn't been able to get to the cafeteria right away. One guard hadn't made it.

"The dark mage must have had help." The place was like an impenetrable coconut, strong on the outside but malleable from within. "The *Demonher* rats have been in there for weeks."

John's gaze assessed me. "You knew there were *Demonher* rats in the basement?"

I blinked. *Whoops.* In hindsight, I should've shared that information immediately.

"Mr. Hastings had found the secondary door to the basement unlocked and something had tampered with the enchantments. There had been no signs of *Demonher* rats in the basement during its reinforcing. It seems you and Ender had a more exciting trip than we had thought."

"You knew we went down there?"

"Not only was it unlocked once, but it had been unlocked twice." He opened one of his drawers and pulled the hefty staff directory out. "Once, when Ivy had stolen a summoning book, and another when you had gone down looking for this. After we noted the second security breach, this was found on the basement floor. Now we know why it was left behind in that manner."

"How ...?" I had been careful, or so I thought.

"*How* we had learned that three students were able to get into the basement is irrelevant. What is relevant is *how* we ensure it doesn't happen again."

I fiddled with my hands. Not that I cared if I got detention, but how did detention work when it was winter break?

"So ... why would Ender's grandmother want me dead?" I asked, and John took a deep breath.

"She knew you were a level five ether mage." Now John had figured it out too. The back of my neck itched, giving me the inkling he had already known something was different with me.

"How did she figure it out?"

"She knew your mother's background. We assume she had tracked what little she could of your family." He let out a sigh. "A lot of mages believe ether mages are dangerous, and level five is incredibly rare. Some will act to dispose level five mages, as they believe it is the correct course of action. Her grandson is her priority, but that doesn't justify her actions, and she will be transferred to a containment facility."

"So rare, Mom hid my sister and me our entire life," I muttered. "She's not safe with me."

John stopped pacing, his jaw tensing and the creases at the corners of his eyes crinkling—the most serious I had ever seen him.

"I am sorry I failed to keep the academy a safe place. I am sorry you, Vivian, and the other students were put in danger." His gaze never left mine and he took a moment before continuing. "She lives because of you."

I snorted. I'd be the cause of her death or the reason she'd get injured.

"You're planning on escaping the academy." He straightened slightly and studied me.

What? How? How did he know that when I hadn't even decided if I was going to go through with leaving myself?

Liar. Sometime between the attack and arriving at John's office, I had decided that I was going to leave the academy. I just hadn't thought out the escape plan in the middle of a frozen desert.

More lies. I would steal a teacher's car. It would be easy.

"Every single thing you have done since the moment I found you at that cabin in Venezuela was to protect your sister." He must've read the question in my eyes. "The dark mage was after you, not your sister, further increasing the chance that others will come. If you leave, I ask you that you please let me know. There are well-trained guards here who can protect you."

"Well-trained? Where were they when the mage attacked?" I already knew the answer but couldn't help my response.

He sighed, his head dipping ever so slightly.

"You already are aware of this." He paused. "Out there, there will never be a time where you won't be looking over your shoulder. When you leave, please don't go alone."

"You're just going to let me walk out of here?"

"I could stop you today, but there's nothing stopping you from trying tomorrow or the next." He took a breath. "I am not going to throw you in one of the holding cells next to Miss Lee. You aren't a criminal."

"And if I don't go?"

"Then you stay here, with your sister," he said. "I propose that a group of guards join you if you don't choose my next offer. I accompany you, with a couple guards, and Vivian. I'm sure you want answers, and I can help ensure the areas you would like to go are safe, including your home in Dominica."

"Let me get this straight." I tried to unravel his proposal. "You are offering for you and a group of guards to join Viv and me wherever I choose—even where my mom was killed?"

"If you leave, would you not visit your old home?"

"You are the headmaster of the academy," I noted. "You can't just leave."

"It's between semesters. I do not have to stay on the grounds." His jaw set, as if he didn't need to explain any further.

"I will think about it."

"Let me see your phone." He held out his hand, and I handed him my phone. He took it back to his desk, did a few things, and a moment later, he handed it back to me. "I added safety features."

"Like tracking?"

"Please consider my offer," he said. "There's less risk if we join you."

But there's more risk for Viv.

I wasn't sure what else to say, so I simply walked out. I hadn't been expecting him to practically open the front gate for me or to offer his services. As a headmaster, he had a duty to protect the students. I was some mutt who happened to wander in later. But I couldn't help feel the heavy emotion that had charged the air in his office, almost as if he did care about me.

He had a funny way of showing it if he did.

In less than thirty minutes, I had made it to the roof of the east dorms. It was late, but my sister was still waiting for me. I plopped down next to her and let my legs hang off the back as I stared off into the woods. She leaned over, resting her head on my shoulder. I leaned mine against hers. My hair was still damp from my shower and no doubt was making hers wet. The aroma of her lilac shampoo and familiar fresh rain scent caused my stomach to clench. This was going to be tough.

"What do we do now?" Viv asked.

"The academy is still the safest place." I pulled away from her and straightened. "Vivian. There's something I need you to promise me that you will do."

"What is the promise?" Her eyes narrowed.

"I need you to promise first." I swung a leg over the parapet so I could face her more easily.

"I can't make a promise until I know what I'm promising."

I sighed and continued, "I'm going to go home and see if there were any clues left behind. While—"

"I'm coming," Viv stated. "I mean; I don't really want to be where Mom died, but you are not going without me."

"Please let me finish." I looked at her, waiting for her confirmation. She nodded. "While I'm searching, I need you to stay here at the academy. The dark mage that had attacked—"

"No! I'm going with you." At least letting me say a half a sentence more than I thought she would.

"Vivian!" My voice rose. "Please just let me finish and then we will discuss it. I want to hear how you feel and I want to know your desires, but I also need you to hear me out."

"Fine," she huffed. "I should have brought Oreos for this."

I smiled at her and shook my head. *I* should have brought *her* Oreos. It might've helped persuade her.

"The dark mage was only after ether mages. It was after me—and Ender."

"Ender?" she asked.

"Yes," I said. "But that story is for another time. The dark mage didn't know about Ender, but she knew about me. So if I leave, the rest of her clan shouldn't be interested in the academy. While I'm gone, I can see if I can find any information on the dark mages. I need you here, safe, while I'm gone."

"First of all, how will they know you left? Second, why would you think I would let you go alone?" Viv frowned.

I knew she wouldn't like my plan, but I had an idea that might help her.

"I wouldn't know, but the academy and our friends—including April—would be safer with your skills around." I was playing on her feelings, and it was dirty. "Including you. Vivian—you would be safer. I have to go back to where *it* happened. Even if I don't find anything, I need to go home. I need some closure."

"You know about April." She glanced down at her hands, then back up at me. I nodded and she took a deep breath. "You're my sister. I should be going with you, and I don't want you going alone."

"John offered to join both of us, along with a couple of guards. He asked me not to go alone."

"The headmaster approved all of us going together?"

"Yes, but I'm unsure of him. It'll be easier to move around alone. This is something I want to do by myself, and as my sister and best friend, I'm asking you not to go." I grabbed her hand. "Please do this for me."

She took another deep breath and stared off into the night. "If I say yes, do you promise me all the Oreos I can eat and a girls' night?"

"What kind of girls' night are we talking about?" I pulled back and arched an eyebrow. "A party with half the student body or all the cookies we can eat while binge watching a TV series or movies?"

"I should say a party, but I guess a night in would suffice." She grinned.

"That means you'll stay?"

"I don't think I should be letting my older sister go alone, and it's dangerous." Her expression fell flat. "But I want to respect your wishes and I am thankful you are talking to me instead of just acting."

I smiled, even though my heart stung. "Thank you."

"You owe me." She nudged me, then frowned. "I still don't want you going alone."

"If I possibly ask for a guard to join me, would that make you feel better?" After being independent and only relying on two people, it was hard to ask a stranger to watch my back.

"Not really." She shook her head. "When are you thinking about leaving?"

"Tonight."

I knew she'd be resentful for leaving the new life she created at the academy, even if it was for a short period of time. I couldn't take her away from her new friends. There were still questions regarding the security of the academy, specifically how the dark mage and *Demonher* rats had gotten in. I was hopeful my departure would deter any future attacks, and with the majority of our friends together, she would be well-guarded.

Chapter Twenty-Six

Selene

I slipped inside the dark dorm room. Sydney's back was to me as she lay in her bed, her body only moving with her slow breaths. Once the grounds had been cleared after the attack, all students on campus who didn't actively need medical attention were to remain in their rooms. I didn't know what time Sydney had made it back to our dorm. She most likely had a quick visit to Nurse Adair.

Sydney didn't stir as I retrieved my escape pack underneath my bed. Behind the bag was the box safely storing Mom's ashes. Viv knew where her urn was, and we had decided Mom would stay there until we found a more permanent location for her.

Next to my bed was Mom's yearbook. As a last-minute decision, I decided to toss the book in my bag. I slung the grey pack over my shoulders and had almost made it to the door when Sydney's bed creaked and the glow of fire lit the room.

"No goodbye?" She sat straight up in her bed, holding a small ball of fire like it was a candle. Her gaze flitted to my bed. "Not even a note?"

"Sydney." I faced her, unsure of what to say.

"Is Viv leaving too?" she asked.

"No." I squeezed the strap on my pack. "The dark mages are after me, not her."

"Because she isn't an ether mage." She stayed where she was, frowning. Everyone who had been in the cafeteria now knew I was an ether mage, and soon, the entire academy would hear about my existence—and then it would spread to the entire elemental world. "You think leaving will keep her safe? Rubbish. This is the best place for her and *you* to be! All the guards and teachers will—"

"Will what?" My voice rose and my chest started to heave. "Not let a dark mage hurt any of the students? Just like earlier today? We're lucky a student wasn't killed."

Sydney stared at me, frozen in place. I had known a guard had been killed, but I wasn't sure if other students had been informed.

"I'm sorry." I hadn't intended to lash out at her. I was tired and all my earlier composure I had with Viv slipped. "I need to do what's best for my sister."

"Does Viv know?" she asked.

"Yes." *And I should leave before she changes her mind.*

"Will you be back?"

"When it's safe." I wasn't sure of my entire game plan besides leaving the academy, hopefully preventing any further dark mage attacks, and finding a sliver of closure.

Sydney sat a moment before giving me a curt nod of understanding.

"Thank you." I meant it and turned to head out the door.

"Wait!" Sydney hopped off the bed, letting the fire travel to a small wall torch—which was a violation for us to have—and hugged me.

"Keep yourself safe, will you?" Her voice sounded like she was on the verge of tears.

"I will." I pulled away. "You too. Don't let the panic attacks control you."

She sucked in her lips and nodded. I squeezed her arms and left.

I stepped out onto the terrace in front of the dorms, looking out into the darkness of the night. The wonderful scent of cedar and bergamot drifted through the night breeze and my heart beat faster. It was a scent that had begun to get more potent lately.

"Following me?" I spoke to the shadows.

"How do I know you're not the one following me?" Ender stepped out from behind a pillar. His hair was wet from a shower, and I assessed his stance. He didn't seem to be in too much pain from the attack. *Good.* "Last I checked, I was out here first."

"And last I checked, you don't own the terrace to the dorms." I brushed past him, careful not to hit his injured shoulder and ignoring the ache that yelled at me for more contact.

Ender laughed his deep-belly laugh. *Ugh.* I kept going. I couldn't let whatever beautiful thing we had growing between us keep me here.

"Selene. Wait." His hand grazed my arm and I froze at the intense burn there. "I'm coming with you."

"No. You aren't." I didn't bother coming up with the lie that I wasn't leaving. It was clear what my intentions were—it was late, we weren't supposed to be outside, and I had my bag with me.

Ender let out a grunt.

"You aren't going alone." He dropped his hand, but his voice was stern. *Playful Ender* had been replaced with *Serious Ender.*

I faced him and laughed—and not a cute laugh. A crazy, unhinged laugh. All my composure around Ender just vanished. And that was irritating.

"You don't get to choose whether you're coming with me. Plus, you need to recover. You were stabbed less than five hours ago!" *Not to mention a dark mage began siphoning your magic.* A flash of worry flitted across my face before I masked it, and I brought my hands to my hips in a not-so-flattering look. "I am leaving. Without you."

"I can't let you do that." Ender stood tall, ignoring the entire part where he had been stabbed. There was fire in his eyes, but it wasn't hate. It was ... protection? Worry? Lust? Maybe it was just stubbornness.

"Then try to stop me." I took a step forward, daring him. My gaze dropped to his lips and I could feel my anger sizzling out into something else.

Ugh. I needed to get control of myself.

"How do you plan on leaving?" Ender took a small step forward, lessening the already small gap between us. I could stick my tongue out and reach his nose if I wanted to.

Where the heck did that immature thought come from?

"Easily." I planned on hijacking a teacher's car. Options would be limited because most staff were escorted by the guards, but I'd return it—eventually. If that plan went south, I could always ask John if a guard could take me. By halfway through the trip, I should know if I could trust them enough or if I needed to ditch them. Why didn't I think of that before? I debated calling John. Maybe his plan was the best.

The corner of Ender's mouth turned upward into a sly grin, as if he was reading my thoughts—or intentions of *borrowing* a car. "The guards will be on you before you can drive out of here. All the guards' and teachers' cars are alarmed. Even if you manage to take one, I'm sure they have tracking software in them, and they'll be on you by morning."

John had said he couldn't stop me from leaving, but I'm pretty sure stealing a vehicle would put me on some sort of wanted list by the academy. I wasn't worried about the tracking. I believe he had turned on some type of tracking in my phone settings, but I had no clue how to check. He could track me. He already knew where I was headed, and I had permission to leave; I was just supposed to have someone come with me ...

I stared awkwardly at Ender.

"I'll drive." He started walking. "But we take my Jeep."

I watched him for a moment before jogging to catch up to him. "You have a car?"

He grinned and kept walking.

Not many students were allowed to keep their car here, but I shouldn't have been surprised the popular guy had his own car at the academy.

"You're still hurt." I eyed his collar, where part of the bandage showed itself.

"I'm fine," he said. "Do I look ill and like I can't drive a vehicle?"

He actually looked great considering all that he had just gone through. I sighed. I couldn't believe I was doing this.

"Okay. We'll take your car." I told myself it was for his vehicle and his aid, but I secretly also wanted his company. Plus, it might keep John from hauling me back even though I was positive he didn't mean for me to leave with Ender. "It could be dangerous … and you aren't packed."

"I keep a bag in my Jeep." He glanced at me from the side, no doubt reading the surprise on my face. I hadn't expected Ender Hart to keep a ready-to-go bag like I had. "So where are we going?"

I sighed then asked, "Do you have a passport?"

"Yes?" He tilted his head. "It's in my Jeep."

"Good."

"Hey!" a guard shouted behind us. "All students are supposed to be in their dormitory rooms." The guard caught up to us, assessing my bag and glancing in the direction we were headed, toward the staff headquarters and garage. "Where are you going?"

"The obvious. The woods for a midnight stroll and picnic," Ender said.

The guard narrowed his eyes and pulled out his phone, dialing someone.

"Headmaster John. I have Selene Thomas and Ender Hart on campus grounds and out of their rooms. They appear to be headed in the direction of the garage." There was a pause. "Yes, sir." The guard pocketed his phone and looked at us. "I will escort you to Mr. Hart's vehicle."

"What?" Ender blinked. "Can you please repeat that?"

"Follow me," the guard said.

Chapter Twenty-Seven

Selene

It had been a long trip to Dominica. Ender's vehicle navigated through the snow with ease. The guard—Guard Taylor—who had stopped us at the academy followed us all the way to the airport. John messaged me, informing us that he was to ensure our safety until we were on the plane. He was concerned there could've been a dark mage outside the dome and didn't want us to be followed. Surprisingly, I was relieved once it was just Ender and me.

The flights were uneventful, and Ender helped pitch in for costs, even though I had enough money stowed in my bag and the guard had attempted to hand us a prepaid Visa at our boarding gate. I kept John updated through our travels, per his request, and Ender informed his guardian. Though John was disappointed I hadn't accepted a pair of guards to join us, he appreciated that I kept him up to date about our plans and our whereabouts. He seemed slightly relieved I hadn't gone alone.

I stared at the quaint island cottage that I had called home my entire life, part of it in shambles. Our own private piece of paradise, as Mom had called it. It was the only house for half a mile on either side along the ocean.

The door creaked open as I pushed against its cracked wood and stepped through the threshold. The broken pieces of wood, burnt soot trails, and glass shards brought together the disturbing memory of that horrifying day.

Fractions. I hate fractions. That had been my last thought before my world came crashing down. I had been scribbling numbers on my homework, the swaying of the hammock making my writing even messier. Viv's cheers were distracting as she jumped over the small incoming waves like she was a kid again and not a teenager, water dusting her shorts. The heat from the sun would dry them quickly.

"Girls!" Mom had shouted from the back porch stretching over a mix of sand and grass, the alarm in her voice giving me goosebumps. "Get inside! Now!"

I had shot straight up, clutching my notebook. Never had I heard her voice so commanding yet full of alarm. I went to wave Viv to hurry up, but she was frozen in place, her gaze fixed on the ocean. My heart began to race as soon as the pungent odor struck me. Before I could react, the ocean water rushed at us. The water burned as its force knocked me out of the hammock and onto the sandy ground.

I sat up, coughing out water.

"Viv!" I shouted as I blinked away the burn from the salt and sand.

My blurry vision slowly began to focus on the three hooded figures standing at the water's edge. Though I couldn't see their faces, I could feel the one front and center staring at me, as if it were looking into my soul and freezing me to my core.

"Run." Mom hoisted me onto my feet.

Viv had been blown back away from the water's edge and was scrambling to her feet.

"Viv!" I shouted again and she turned. Her face was pale as she ran over to us.

"Now. Selene." Mom never called me Selene.

I grabbed Viv's arm and tugged her up the cottage steps as loud crashes that sounded like thunder boomed behind us. *I have to get me and Viv out safely, no matter what.* That had been the drill if we were ever attacked.

"Mom!" Viv cried out as I rushed her into the living room and led her behind the rocking chair. The same one Mom had rocked us in when we were little.

"Stay here." I placed my hands on her shoulders. "I'll get Mom. If I'm not back in five minutes, take the car and go."

Before Viv could protest, I was running through the living room and toward the back door. Just as I reached for the handle, the door swung open. Mom rushed in, slamming the door behind her and locking it.

"The enchantment won't hold for long." Mom turned to face me, her brown hair astray and clothes soaked and torn. "Get Viv and go."

"But—"

A loud boom echoed through the house as wood splinters and glass shards flew everywhere. Water exploded through the back door, cracking its frame. The rush of water sent me flying backward, parts of my home landing on top of me. I shoved a wooden plank off my stomach and sat up. Dust sparkled in the sun as if time had stopped. A ringing in my ears began to fade, and I tried to calm my overwhelming panic as I stared at a hole where our back door and kitchen cupboards had been.

A hand touched mine and I glanced over to see Mom smiling at me. Why was she smiling?

"Sweetheart. You have a full life ahead of you." Mom brushed a strand of hair from my face that had strayed from my braids. "No matter what happens, you need to take your sister to the safe house. Do not look back. Go. I will always be with you. I love you, sweetheart."

My mom moved her hands in a circle and thrust them out toward me. Her air magic slid me backward, and she began an enchantment. Our house plants grew thick vines as she weaved them through each other, creating a wall and shielding Viv and me.

"Mom!" I slammed my fists against the wall, but it wouldn't budge.

I used a nearby glass shard, lifting it with my air magic and bringing it to me. I began chopping away at a vine, earning a small gash in my hand, but it was no use. Though she was a level four and I was a five, the vines were strong and I couldn't manipulate them. She had used an enchantment and was more skilled.

"Stay away from my girls," Mom gritted through her teeth.

Through the cracks, I could see one of the hooded figures. There was no way I could get to her in time, and running around the cottage would leave Viv completely alone.

Mom went to fight, but her body went rigid and she lifted into the air as the dark mage strode closer. From where I was, I couldn't see her face, but I could hear her pain.

"No," I whispered, the world spinning. "No!"

The dark mage was controlling her by the water running through her veins. Blood magic. It could only be used by dark mages who had been powerful before their descent. Mom had told us stories, but they hadn't existed for centuries.

A red glow radiated over Mom's skin and black liquid floated through the air toward the dark mage who stood only a couple feet away. He was siphoning her magic. Bursts of white light cracked through the red glow, like Mom's good magic was pushing out the evil magic. And it looked like the light was about to blow.

"Viv! Get outside!" I ran over to her and guided her outside.

Once I was reassured Viv would stay, I went back inside, but before I could make it halfway through the living room, white light burst out and I briefly shielded my eyes. The vine wall disintegrated, smoke filling the air.

Once everything settled, I found Mom lying on the ground and the dark mage a smoking heap in the kitchen, their black robe covering them.

"Mom!" I ran to her. Her skin looked like it had been burned, and her tears left clear streaks on her smudged face, but she was smiling at me. "Don't look at me like that." It was the same smile she had given me earlier, except now, it seemed to hold a definite finality. She wasn't coming back from this.

She searched my face—for what? I didn't know.

"Your father, Sal. He—" Blood bubbled from my mom's mouth and she coughed. Once her coughing stopped, her eyes, which were once full of life, faded, her head lolling to the side.

"No ... no. No. No!" The world had ceased just like my mom's heart, and an eerie stillness of magic crackled in the air and then burst outward like an invisible beacon.

I slumped over. My mother was my world. She had been with me my entire life. Not only was she my teacher, mentor, trainer, and mother, but she was the heart and soul that had fueled me. I would be lost without her.

"Sal?" Viv's worried voice came from outside. I could hear her steps get closer to the front door.

"Stay out there, Viv!" I could not have her see Mom in that condition. But I still had to fight for her, fight the empty, dark void that had left a gaping hole inside me. Viv was my motivation for fighting.

The dark mage had moved—or so I had thought. I stared at the still body until the bloodied hand marked with a black circle on its left palm twitched. They were still alive.

One of the other dark mages had entered the enormous hole that had been our back door and part of our kitchen. Before he could attack, I felt for the sand with my magic. The sand at the dark mage's feet rose. A scream tore from my throat as the sand swirled around the dark mage, eating away at each layer of fabric like sandpaper.

"Sal!" Viv hollered from the door. I turned to see her. Broken boards scattered around Mom, hiding the majority of her from Viv's view. I ceased my magic as the dark mage fell to his knees. We had to leave. If we didn't, the dark mage would—

"*Hey.*" Ender's soft voice broke me out of my own nightmare.

I blinked as I came back to the present and my broken home in front of me. Hot tears ran down my cheeks at the ache of the memory. The cottage looked the same as when I had left Mom almost two months ago—except she was no longer lying lifeless on the floor and caution tape that had once sealed the gaping holes in the cottage now flapped in the warm breeze.

Ender grabbed my hand, wrapping his fingers around mine. The pain lessened at his touch, but it still threatened to prick my heart a million times, over and over. I squeezed his hand, glancing at him. His gaze was guarded as he watched me, and he almost looked ... looked like he too was in pain. A phantom pain stabbed my heart—I wasn't used to empathy.

Before losing Mom, I had only ever been in pain from training. Mom had empathy, but she wouldn't show it when she was teaching us to defend ourselves. If she did, we surely would have used it against her when we were younger. She had been so strong. She had taught us to be strong.

I swallowed, letting his hand go. It was time to look for any clues—not that there would be any. The council had probably searched the place, and it wasn't like the dark mages would have left anything behind that indicated who they were. But I needed closure.

My entire life had been inside these walls and on this remote piece of land. Mom had rarely taken us away from the cottage, and usually, that had been to show us how to get to the cabin on the mainland. The island's salty coconut air was all I had ever known.

An hour later, I hadn't found anything. It had turned into searching Mom's belongings among other things, reminiscing. The bedrooms were mostly untouched.

"I think I found something," Ender called from the living room.

I clutched my mom's favorite hoodie. It was white and had a small black outline of a ghost on it. Instead of dropping it, I brought it with me to put in my pack. Mom had loved celebrating Halloween.

"What is it?" I asked as I came down the hallway.

"Did your family have a phone?" He held an older-looking cell phone in the air. "It was under the TV stand."

"No." I grabbed the phone, dusting it off, and pressed the on button. The screen lit up, surprising me that it hadn't been damaged in the pandemonium. "None of us had a phone."

It took the phone a good solid minute to turn on, which felt more like fifteen. I clicked the inbox and a box popped up. My body stilled as confusion slapped me.

There was a message from an unknown number—the same message that had been sent on the phone hidden in John's office.

They're coming.

Chapter Twenty-Eight
Ender

The turquoise water thrummed against the hull of the ferry, and the sun beat down on my back, the hot railing leaving red marks on my arm where I leaned against it. Selene's old home wasn't the ideal spot to stay, considering its living conditions and because the dark mages had already been there once before. The plan was to travel to her family's safe house and stay there for the night. The dark mages hadn't known its location.

The text on the mystery phone had apparently come from a phone in the headmaster's office, and Selene had questioned if staying at the safe house was the best option. She had gone tense at the topic. Headmaster John had been keeping secrets and clearly kept in contact with her mother. He had warned them that the dark mages were coming and it appeared that his intentions were good, so we decided to stay on course and continue updating him with our plan—though she had been less detailed and had delayed her updates.

The warning wasn't the only secret the phone contained. We had found a single photo of an old *for sale* flyer of a house somewhere in

Croatia. The home would be our next destination after a night at the safe house.

Wind wisped at the loose strands in Selene's hair as she leaned over the railing and looked out toward the mainland. She seemed so careless and free, but I could sense her apprehension.

"That's your thing, isn't it?" She looked over at me, her eyes hidden beneath the sunglasses she had gotten at the small airport when we had first arrived in Dominica.

"Watching a beautiful woman stare off into the vast ocean?" I tilted my head, not hiding my smirk. "It most definitely is my thing."

She scoffed, but her smile gave away the small amount of joy that overcame her annoyance.

"Your shirt." She waved at my bare chest. "You have a tendency to be shirtless."

"Ah." I straightened and slung my shirt over my shoulder. "Just when it's hot. Besides, there's a lot of shirtless men on this ferry."

"Well, it's going to be even hotter on our trip to the cabin, but you'll want a shirt on in the jungle."

"Can't we just use our magic and fly?" I joked, mostly.

"And risk being seen flying over treetops or the ocean, and drowning because we got too tired?" She raised her sunglasses so they rested on top of her head. "We'll get a ride most of the way to the cabin. I'm not worried about the headmaster knowing we're there. Apparently, he was Mom's ally. The only question is why. She always told us to trust no one."

"You said they were friends at the academy—could they have been more than friends?" I leaned over the railing next to her.

"More questions and no answers." She sighed.

I slid over and reached my arm over hers, sliding her hand into mine. She tensed and I waited for a sign that she wanted me to move, but it never came. She relaxed and rested her head on my shoulder.

After a minute, something cool inside my veins stirred—my magic. Something pricked at my fingertips. Small water droplets rose from the ocean and stuck to my free hand. They clung to my fingertips and then popped, the water trickling back down into the ocean and the frosty prickling sensation disappearing with the droplets.

I spared a glance at Selene—she hadn't noticed. It was water magic, and it felt like my magic. We had to be careful—we didn't want to attract attention and magic had a scent, though I could barely scent Selene's. I had never done water magic before, and I hadn't even been trying to use it.

I am an ether mage. Great. Something I still wasn't sure what to think of.

Selene was right. *More questions and no answers.*

The ride on the ferry was long, but it could have been longer. I didn't mind the time with Selene, enjoying the ocean—and more—my view. Once we arrived in Venezuela, she talked a local into driving us part way before we made the trek through the jungle, arriving at the cabin right at dusk. I knew little Spanish, but she apparently was able to speak it fluently. And I thought Priscilla's training had been extensive. The thought of her hurt. Was everything Miss Lee had said about my parents true?

Selene had filled me in on the mechanics of the safe house, and I helped her turn on the generator and alarms. The place had a musty odor—which wasn't as appealing as the smoky cinnamon smell of the woods—but honestly, I wouldn't mind staying there for a while. We needed a safe place to stay for the night, and she wanted to search the safe house.

I showered and headed to the room I was going to stay in. It had twin beds, so I'd left my bag open on one. I went through it and pulled out a pair of boxers. Selene had offered the room with the queen-sized bed to me, but I refused. I imagine that was where her mom would have slept if they had ever come here together.

"Ender." Selene's soft voice came from the other side of the door. "I'm going to bed. Knock on my door if you need anything."

Like a foolish teenage boy, I rushed to the door and hastily opened it before she could leave, though I didn't have anything to actually ask. She went to say something but froze, her gaze traveling down my body. Her cheeks flushed and my gut instantly tightened into a ball of fire. I didn't need to glance down or back at the bed where my boxers lay to know I had just answered the door in my towel.

Did I care? No. Did she? I wasn't sure if *care* was accurate, but by the look on her face, she felt something. And I felt a little bad—tiny bit bad—for the situation.

She composed herself quickly ... then her gaze landed on my unbandaged shoulder and she frowned. Nurse Adair's repulsive healing elixir had worked its magic and my wound had healed enough that it would suffice without a bandage.

"One moment." She ventured off. "You and your cursed shirtless abs," she mumbled under her breath as she disappeared down the hallway. To my delight, she returned in thirty seconds with a first aid kit.

"Here." She set the box down on the dresser and I remained quiet as she got to work redressing my wound. "That should do it," she said when she was done. "Was that what you needed?"

"No." I leaned against the doorframe. "I just wanted to say goodnight."

"Oh." Her cheeks reddened again. "Goodnight." She turned and started down the dimly lit hall.

I grinned as I watched her walk away. She wore loose joggers and a baggy shirt and still managed to look great. I thought of what Miss Lee had said when she was in the cell: *I stopped once I fully realized what she was to you.* There was an internal part of me that had wondered if she had been referring to soul-bounds. The trip had only made me consider it more. In school, elemental bonds, called the soul-bound, were a brief topic that was only mentioned in history class. It was something I was eager to explore.

Closing the door, I put on my boxers and joggers, then propped the bedroom door back open. The security system should pick up any anomalies, but I wanted to be able to hear better if anything happened.

Despite the jet lag and lack of sleep, I wasn't ready to sleep. So I lay there for what felt like hours, ignoring the desire to walk down the hallway and just sit outside Selene's door. Eventually, I fell asleep.

Sometime in the night, a scream tore down the hall and my feet hit the floor before it ceased. Although my eyes were adjusted to the dark, I still wanted clear vision but didn't waste time finding the switch to the hallway light. Sprinting down the hall, I threw open Selene's door, not bothering with a knock. I felt a cool breeze, and a candle on the dresser lit. My hands were already out, prepared to fight, but the room was empty except for Selene sitting up in her bed. The covers were thrown off her, and her chest heaved.

"Are you alright?" I slowly made my way closer, examining the sealed windows and surroundings for any sign of entry.

"Just a nightmare." Selene's breathing slowed as she calmed herself down. "I thought the dark mage was here… I thought Viv was here and…"

"I'll go check the cabin and outside." I went to leave when her pause turned into the end of her sentence.

"No. Don't waste your time." Selene rubbed the back of her neck, brushing her silky brown hair out of the way. "Seeing where it all happened brought back bad memories."

I nodded. "Can I get you anything?" I asked after a few moments of silence passed.

"No, thank you." She covered her legs back up with the blanket, and I took that as my cue to leave.

"I'll be right outside your door." I stepped through the doorway and grabbed the handle, going to close it.

"Wait," Selene called.

"Yes?" I turned to see her drumming her fingers along the hem of the quilt.

"I don't want to be alone."

It took me a split second to realize she didn't want me to leave. I nodded and entered the room again, closing the door behind me. I made my way over to the foot of the bed, grabbing a blanket slung over a chest. Tossing it on the floor, I made myself a makeshift bed on the rug between the door and bed.

"You don't have to sleep on the floor," she said.

"I don't say no often to a beautiful woman asking me to join her in her bed," she rolled her eyes, "but I think it would be best if I stayed near the door," I said.

More like I didn't trust my uncontrollable desire to feel her lips again.

Selene nodded, and my gut dropped at the disappointment in her eyes.

"Thank you," she said.

I lay down on my back with my hands beneath my head, staring at candlelight flickering across the ceiling.

"Want me to put your flame out?" I asked.

She didn't answer right away.

"Yes. That's fine."

I swirled one of my hands, sending a burst of wind toward the candle and putting out the flame. It wasn't enchanted, so it could be diminished with a small gust of wind.

Minutes passed before the bed moaned as Selene shuffled. It sounded like she rolled over.

"Ender?" Her voice was soft.

"Yeah?" I stayed lying on my back.

"I didn't light the candle," she said, and I looked at her as realization hit. Her face showed no traces that she was being dishonest. I didn't say anything, accepting the truth. "How long have you known you were an ether mage?"

"Probably as long as you have." If Selene hadn't pieced that together when the dark mage started siphoning my magic, she had now. Though, it had taken the conversation with Miss Lee to fully realize it.

"Who did your testing?" she asked, and I laughed at her blatancy. "What?"

I just smiled and answered, "Priscilla, when I was a child."

"And at the academy?"

"Headmaster John." He had done it when I first arrived.

"And they never said anything? You didn't know?"

"Nope." I held my sigh.

"So the tests were altered or someone hid your magic so well that it didn't show. The scent of your magic isn't strong either." She was thinking out loud and I let her talk, unbothered by it or her questions. "That night in the academy basement ... did you feel ... different?" she asked.

"I felt ... yeah ... I guess different is a good way to put it." I stretched my upper back and shoulders, leaving my hands tucked beneath my head. "But it's not every day a girl takes you to a secluded basement on a secret mission."

She was silent and I rolled over to face her as she watched me from the bed. I wished the candle was still lit so I could see her more clearly.

"What are we?" Selene asked after a minute.

"What do you mean?" I asked casually while my heart started to pound. Did she know we were soul-bound? *Are* we soul-bound?

Her face remained neutral. "We went to the ball together, we hang out, you're here with me..." She paused. "We kissed."

I grinned. "Are you asking me if you're my girlfriend?"

"No, I—" She fumbled for words. "I ... don't know."

Her phone buzzed, interrupting her cute, scrambling ramble.

"You have service?"

"John did something to my phone before I left. I'm assuming whatever he did was to help track me or reach me." The light from the phone lit her face, and her lips flattened.

"What is it?" I asked.

"It's John. Miss Lee escaped the new facility."

Chapter Twenty-Nine

Selene

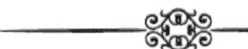

Our trek across the ocean started the next morning. Over thirty hours of traveling later and a six-hour time change, we made it to Croatia in early afternoon of the following day. The flight was expensive and we had an overnight layover in Madrid. Spending an abundance of one-on-one with Ender was very ... different. Surprisingly, I didn't get the urge to throw him out of the plane's emergency exit. The more time we spent together, the more I was comfortable with him.

A bus took us to a local town near the sea, and we walked until we arrived at the address found on Mom's mystery phone. The sun brightened the dated pale blue stone the home was made from. Though the house appeared to be older, it looked like it had been updated, especially compared to the rest of the block. The overgrown flower beds that lined the home had seen better days. I worked up the courage to knock on the door, unsure of who I would find living there, and took a step back on the cracked patio.

The door slowly creaked open until a middle-aged woman took up the doorway, peering down at me. She stared at me expectantly, and I struggled to find the words I needed to say—in Croatian. It was one of the languages Mom had never taught Viv and me.

I gave it my best to pronounce, "Hello. Do you speak English?"

Her thick brows narrowed and she closed the door.

"Either your Croatian was perfect and she doesn't like us, or you just asked her to lick your toe." Ender had a toothy grin. "Probably the latter because that was the look she gave us."

Despite the sinking feeling in my gut, Ender managed to help my spirits. He had a way of—

"Did you see that?" I asked. The curtain at the home next door moved, and I swore I saw someone. I started back down the sidewalk, hiking my pack up by its straps. "Maybe they'll know something."

I walked down the street to the neighboring house which was much brighter in contrast. A small wrought iron table with four matching chairs sat in front of a window of the home. Before we made it to the house, the front door opened.

"Hello!" An elderly woman dressed in casual wear and white fluffy slippers that seemed too hot for this weather greeted us.

"Umm, hi," I said as I reached her, my eyebrows knitted.

"I could tell you were American from a mile away—not that my eyes can see more than ten feet without these glasses." She nudged her glasses up on her nose. "My name is Noretta."

I was at a loss for words. She was the complete opposite of her neighbor.

"Thank you for such a warm welcoming." Ender nodded in greeting, saving me from my inept social skills. "We were curious about the history of the neighborhood."

"Ah." The lady leaned against her house. "You're interested in that house." She pointed back at her neighbor's house and tension crawled up my spine. "You've come because it's haunted."

I glanced at Ender. The only sign that he thought the situation was odd was that he glanced at me too. My nose twitched. No signs of elemental magic filled the air or came through the threshold from her home.

"There are stories, then?" I asked.

"Oh, my." A short, delightful laugh came from the lady but ended with a touch of ... sadness? "You are much like her. You better smooth those wrinkles of yours so they don't become permanent."

She nodded to my forehead, and I went to un-furrow my eyebrows, but they raised instead, still causing wrinkles. I wasn't helping my situation—*wait*. Back on track. *You are much like her?*

"What do you mean?" I tensed, even though the lady casually stood in the doorway, smoothing her ruffled white blouse.

"How about you two come in for tea?" She stepped aside. "It appears we have much to talk about, if you are who my old brain is remembering."

Remembering? She had to know something. Common sense told me not to go in, but my gut told me it was safe, and I wanted information.

"We're rather comfortable out here," Ender said before I could take a step, putting on his charming smile. "It's a beautiful day. No need to waste it inside."

"Very well, then." The lady waved to the wrought iron chairs. "Let's have a seat. My old legs aren't very trustworthy these days, and you'd think these new knees would make them sturdier."

Ender and I headed over to the table. The lady hobbled after us and nodded at Ender as he pulled out her chair.

"What a charming young chap you are." She nodded in thanks as she sat, the sun brightening her dark grey hair. We sat as she continued, "So what does that house mean to you?"

"I'm not sure." I absently cracked my pointer finger's knuckle with my thumb and chose to be more straightforward. "I was hoping you could tell me not only about its past, but who had lived there."

"Yes," she hummed. "There was a family that lived there many years ago. A very nice family. It was such a tragedy the home became a haunted attraction."

My spine went stiff at her words and Ender's hand slid over mine underneath the table.

"What happened?" I cleared my throat, my voice calmer than I had expected.

"Only those that were involved know what happened, but I have my surmise." Her shoulders drooped. "They had two beautiful little girls—one a baby and the other barely over a year old. The family mostly kept to themselves but would still wave and say hi to their dear neighbor over the years they lived there."

I assumed she was the neighbor in her story, and my guess was the two little girls were me and Viv.

"One horrible night," she continued, "someone broke into their house. I could hear screams, but by the time I was able to get outside, the house was engulfed in flames. The back gate creaked and I was able to make out two figures, both holding two little girls. The young woman looked right at me, horrified, before they ran. I had a feeling something horrible happened. It was later that I had found out she had lost her sister and brother-in-law."

"Her sister?" I recalled Mr. Hastings mentioning Mom's sister had died.

"Yes," she said. "Her twin sibling. When they left with her sister's child, I could only assume the baby's parents were gone. The fire was so intense, I had to back away. No one could've survived that fire. There was so much pain in the young woman's eyes." She glanced back up at me. "I venture you're here to ask what happened that night—what happened to your family?"

"How do you know who I am?" It felt like the fire was still next door; sweat dripped down my spine—and not just from the hot weather. "And the baby and the little girl weren't sisters?"

Her brow furrowed slightly at my question, but she continued, "You look just like your mom but have your dad's nose and cheekbones. I remember your mom always smiling, working in her gardens while pregnant with you. You look just like her." She let out a gentle laugh as she clasped her hands together. "The baby, on the other hand, looked more like her father than her mother, with her head full of black hair. Her mother would walk down the street and back every night while she was pregnant with her. I distinctly remember each couple having one baby."

I gaped, and it took me a second to put the puzzle pieces together. An idea hit me as I remembered and I pulled my mom's yearbook out of my backpack, flipping through the pages until I found the one with Mom, John, her twin, and some other guy named Nathan who I had suspected was a possible father candidate. Now, though, it was clear he wasn't the father of both me and Viv.

"Are you referring to her as my mother, her as the sister, and him as the youngest girl's father?" I turned the yearbook over to her, pointing to each one. Even though the picture was black and white, it was clear that the boy had ink black hair—just like Viv's.

Ender casually glanced at it. I hadn't shown him yet, but he looked on in silence.

"Ah." She adjusted her glasses as she leaned closer. "Yes. Such lovely young couples they both were. They look the same as when they lived next door."

"*Couples? They?*" I squeaked. "As in ... this man was also involved?" I pointed to John.

Her forehead wrinkled as her frown came back. Clearly, she didn't expect me to not have known this, but what she was referring to was that Headmaster John was my father and Viv was not my biological sister.

It couldn't be true. This entire time...

"Dear..." She held out her hand and I blankly stared at it, unsure what to do.

I glanced at Ender, who shrugged—a movement I doubt the lady could've seen. I gave her my hand, hiding the small bout of unease at touching a stranger.

"If you don't know any of this and are going to a stranger about your family's history, that must mean you lost your parents?"

I gulped and nodded, not wanting to give any more information away. She didn't need to know about ... *my father*. To me, he was gone.

"The baby?" Her eyes became watery as she squeezed my hand tighter.

"She's okay." I squeezed her hand, then pulled mine away, feeling awkward. "If they kept to themselves, how did you know so much about them?"

"I didn't." She shrugged. "Just the regular waves and observations from friendly neighbors. I didn't even know their names—I don't even know yours."

And you aren't going to.

"Would you like me to get the tea?" Noretta offered after silence fell between us.

"No. Thank you for the story of the haunted house." I grabbed the yearbook and stood there awkwardly as I glanced at Ender, afraid if we stayed any longer, one of the many emotions bubbling inside me would burst.

"Thank you for your hospitality, but we best be going." Ender stood, following me as I began walking away.

"Miss?" the elderly lady called after me, and I hesitantly looked over my shoulder. "I may not know what danger was after your parents, but evil leaves its marks. Take care of yourself now."

She nodded at both of us, but I continued to the road, not saying a word as hot pressure built inside my veins.

"Hey, Selene." Ender's hand softly fell on my shoulder once we were a block away. "You don't have to face this alone. Confusion, pain, hurt ... are all okay to feel."

I stopped to face him. "It's just..."

"It's a lot." He finished for me when I couldn't. "But you aren't alone."

I wrapped my arms around his waist and his arms engulfed me. Some of the smothering pressure released from me, and after a few moments of silence, he spoke.

"What's the next step, Captain?" His voice vibrated in his chest.

"Time to make some calls." I gritted my teeth and pulled away.

This was *not* what ... I tensed. Ender must have realized and turned, following my gaze behind him ... where my *father* stood next to some woman with black hair in a short bob. Something about the woman was familiar, but I couldn't place it.

Aura pranced down the road, looking happy to see us.

Chapter Thirty
Selene

"So tell me again why we had to travel down the coast of the Adriatic Sea to grab a bite to eat." I stood behind John—*my father*—in line at a small window carved in between other stone buildings. The ride in John's rental car had been quiet.

John twisted so he could see me, merely giving me a look and turning back around. Aura didn't receive any glances, even though she was cradled in John's arms.

Ender's arm brushed mine, and I leaned into him. The woman standing behind us who had come with John was Ender's guardian, Priscilla. They boxed us in between them, and I didn't like it.

The couple in front of us grabbed their food and walked away. John placed an order—in fluent Croatian—and walked off to the side. He set Aura down, much to her dismay, and waved for us to follow.

"She's camouflaged. Similar to how the academy is." Priscilla leaned in. When I raised an eyebrow, she nodded toward Aura. *Oh*. Now the lack of stares made sense.

Wind rustled the leaves as animals and insects hummed, and the ocean waves crashed against the shore somewhere behind the stone buildings and through the trees. It reminded me of my island life growing up—even though we had rarely left our home. Minus the quiet chatter among the few others eating, it would have been serene, but the silence among our group was stiff.

The man behind the counter handed four cardboard containers to John, and we headed to a nearby table.

"I'm trusting you're not trying to kill us with food from a stone window." Ender grabbed the box John held out and took a seat in one of the metal chairs.

"Opposed to the fast food restaurants with greasy, frozen food in America?" John sat and passed out the rest of the food as I joined them. "I have not been to this specific area, but all of these places are quite good."

"Did you go to *these places* with my mom?" I spun the box around, flipping the lid open. The smell of fresh sweet dough and Italian dressing wafted out. Two different types of deli meat and sliced-up veggies were stuffed inside a flaky loaf of bread next to a sliced-up apple. "And what makes you think I like whatever this is?"

"Your mom loved *burek*." John's lips naturally curved upward as if a joyful memory tugged at the edges.

So, you did go to these places with her. I shook away the image of them walking along the uneven stones through small cities.

"We have food now," I said. During the ride here, he had said he would explain everything, but first we needed to get food. "Explain."

"You haven't eaten." He frowned.

"I'm not hungry." The only question he had answered was why he had shown up when he did. Ender and I were already aware our phones could be tracked, but why show up at that moment? His answer? Noretta. Apparently, he knew that Noretta, the very kind neighbor, had still lived next door and figured his strong-willed daughter—like my mother—would figure it out, and he apparently wanted to be there for me when I did. His words. Not mine.

A grumbling noise came from my belly, and I glanced at the sub-looking thing. Mom had made Viv and me large sandwiches all the time growing up. John laughed at my stomach's betrayal, his normal professional headmaster demeanor gone.

"I will talk, but you need to eat." *He sounded like Mom.* "Noretta gave you the story, but I'll still give you your background. Anna, your mom and I separated—not our marriage—physically from each other to protect you and Vivian." John rubbed his empty ring finger. "Your mom had a twin sister who was also an ether mage."

I spared a glance at Priscilla, waiting for her reaction. Something about her hollowed-out cheeks and strong jawline, straight black hair, and tall, athletic build was familiar, but I still couldn't place it. While I didn't know her, Ender seemed to trust her.

"She knows everything." John folded his hands on the table, his thumbs grazing their pads. "No one at the school knew your mom and aunt were ether mages, but we heard the rumors of ether mages being hunted. So we fled shortly after graduation. We were young and in love. We thought it would be perfect to create a quiet life in a different country. With magic, it was easy to find local jobs where we could stay hidden. Nathan, your uncle, and I knew *of* the dangers dark mages presented, but we didn't *know* the dangers. We weren't careful enough." He sighed. "We eloped at the same time, and shortly after, your mom became pregnant with you. Then Victoria became pregnant with Vivian after you were born. A dark mage—one of the strongest—found us. We weren't expecting the attack, though; we had been so careful." He rubbed his eyes, his short blond hair falling over his forehead, making him look uncharacteristically disheveled.

I continued to slowly chew. My mouth felt numb as my brain processed everything even though I had gathered most of this from Mom's old neighbor.

"Victoria and Nathan—your aunt and uncle—didn't make it. Your mom was able to push back the mage, allowing us to grab you and Vivian to escape. We moved around until we came up with a plan to keep you girls safe. The previous headmaster of Fives Academy was trustworthy, and her health had been declining. She proposed that I take her position. so I stayed away from my family, becoming headmaster and joining the council to help keep track of the dark mage covens. We kept your true identity hidden and hid who Vivian was so there wouldn't be a connection. That night in Croatia, the dark mage had seen you—*smelled you*. We knew he wouldn't stop. And that same night, the dark mage became stronger."

Yeah, by draining my aunt's magic and soul. And John became headmaster to have leverage. At the safest school in the world.

Ender placed his hand on my thigh. My emotions bounced around inside me but seemed to stayed tethered, and I couldn't help but think it had something to do with him.

"And now that same dark mage is the one after Selene," Ender said. During our travels, we had talked about the dark mage who had attacked the school. I told him how that wasn't the same one who had killed Mom.

"We believe so." John nodded.

"Who is *we*?" I asked.

"We." He pointed between him and Priscilla. "The council doesn't know who you and Vivian are."

"So we basically don't exist?" I took another bite of my sandwich, sinking my teeth in the fresh-baked bread. "But our last name is the same as Mom's."

"Essentially *you* don't exist. Your level, capabilities, and ties to your full family lineage has been wiped clean. Your mother's identity was also hidden. Though it is only a matter of time." John glanced down at his sandwich, and I wondered how much there was that he had done to keep Mom and us a secret. "There is so much to talk about, and it is a lot to take in. Let's finish our food and find a place to stay for the night."

"No." My voice was hard, causing others around us to look over at our table. I leaned across the table. "You let me travel across seas when you had the answers this entire time!" I whisper-yelled.

I stared John directly in the eye—they bore a resemblance to mine—as he stayed quiet, sitting there with his hands clasped together on the table like we were at a stupid conference meeting. My anger boiled as my normal composure began to crack.

"Why did you let me come all this way—when you said it yourself—it's not safe? To let me find out on my own?" I demanded, not caring if he was my father or the headmaster of the school I was currently enrolled in. I swung my pack from my shoulder and fished out the cell phone Ender had found at my old home. Once I retrieved the small phone, I slid it across the table at him. "Your warning was too late. Mom is dead."

John stared at the phone. His Adam's apple bobbed as he swallowed. After a few moments of blankly staring at the phone, his gaze flicked back up. A part of me felt sorrow for him—he had lost someone too—but he hadn't told me the whole truth.

"The academy's wards were intact. Someone let the dark mage inside." John glanced at Ender, who had tensed at the topic of the attack. "Even though Miss Lee seems like the most plausible suspect, I believe she is telling the truth. She has stayed hidden for years to protect Ender—I don't think she'd jeopardize his safety by letting a dark mage inside the academy wards."

"So you think there is someone else inside the academy who's still a threat to Selene?" Ender drew his shoulders back as if he wanted to take on that person right then and there.

"Possibly." John looked between us.

"Wasn't that already suspected prior to our departure?" I asked.

"Yes. Priscilla and I haven't been far from both of you since you left the academy, and the internal investigation at the academy is still being carried out," John said. "You planned to leave regardless of what else I would have suggested. I wanted to ensure your safety."

"You've been following us?" I laughed and went to ask how close they had been to us when Ender and I were at the cabin in the woods but stopped myself. They would have had to camp in the middle of nowhere, and the cabin's surveillance covered a wide range. The cameras had never picked up anything—then again, he had known we were there. I had wondered how the academy guards had originally found me and Viv so easily. He knew the cameras' whereabouts. Heck, he probably had set the cameras up himself. "You helped Mom secure the safe house." I stared at John. "You had been so close to us but never visited."

John swallowed again, the only display that he felt any emotion.

"We've been in public too long. Let's go." Priscilla stood. I couldn't get a scent from her, and John's belief that we were safer with the two of them following us made me wonder what her element was.

"Wait." It clicked—where I had seen her before. I reached in my pack again, pulling out the yearbook. I skimmed through it until I found the picture I was looking for: my aunt, standing next to a tall woman with defined cheekbones. Ender's guardian. She looked more youthful, and her black hair was long.

I shoved the yearbook toward her. "That's why you look so familiar."

"Yes." Priscilla nodded at the yearbook. "I was close friends with your aunt and mother. We need to leave." She glanced at Ender and turned, making it clear that we were leaving right then and there.

John pocketed the phone with a gentleness of handling something delicate and stood.

It was time to go.

CHAPTER THIRTY-ONE

Ender

FLYING IN A PRIVATE jet was much more comfortable than flying economy, though economy put Selene practically on top of me, and there was no complaining on my end. I had recognized the smooth beige seats and speckled carpet when we boarded the private jet at a small airport near Croatia. This was Priscilla's jet, and though it was older, it was luxurious—perks of working for the council.

Growing up, Priscilla had taken me into the cockpit and taught me how to fly. She was one of their top agents and had left on missions when called, and I guessed the council had thought it was worth her having her own jet and private hangar in her backyard. Living in the middle of Canada with a few hundred acres of land surrounded by more uninhabited property allowed us to go unnoticed.

A part of my gut twisted at the recollection of home. During Priscilla's missions, Mr. Scott, the elderly man who had cared for the house in her absence, had also been assigned to babysit me. I always teased him for getting stuck with me, but I could tell he secretly enjoyed my mischief. He had taught me a lot, and his passing a year before I started at Fives would not erase away the memories.

I glanced at Selene. She had fallen asleep in the chair next to me. I leaned forward, gently brushing a stray lock from her face, fully aware—and not caring—that the headmaster was facing us in the next row. A smile tugged at my lips. She looked fierce, even in her sleep, with her soft, plump lips, the color of a seashell, subtly parted—not firmly pressed together as usual. There had been a substantial amount of convincing involved for her to board the jet. Headmaster John had reassured her we were not traveling to Fives Academy but to another location and that it wasn't safe to stay in one area for too long. She wanted time to weigh the benefit of staying away from Vivian versus going back to the academy.

I brushed her arm, her skin soft under my fingertips, and stood. I didn't want to leave her, but I had to talk to Priscilla. Not only did I have questions about my parents and entire upbringing, but I had questions about the bond. She would have answers, and there was no way I was talking to Headmaster John about this, nor was I going to bring it up in front of Selene. The entire time in Croatia, I could feel Selene's anger, pain, and sadness as I sat next to her, listening to the headmaster explain that he was her father and why they had kept her and her sister hidden.

I didn't look at John as I passed him, unsure if my anger toward him was my own or Selene's. His actions were understandable and well rationalized. I could see that. I could also see that at some point, Selene had inadvertently crawled into my life. I would do anything to protect her.

The cockpit door was partially cracked and I snuck inside, closing it behind me.

"Nice of you to join me, Ender." Priscilla didn't look up, her gaze fixed beyond the windshield at the night sky. "I was hoping you would."

"I have a lot of questions." I sat in the first officer's seat on the right.

"I'm sure you do." She flipped the autopilot switch and faced me, her chair creaking as she twisted. Her headset was put up, and I assumed she had already been expecting me.

"We aren't blood related." I looked directly at her, her face not wavering.

"No. We aren't," she confirmed. "But that doesn't change how much I care and love you."

I believed her. We were always direct with each other, and our relationship a mix of an aunt and nephew, mother and son, and trainer and apprentice—despite my understanding that we had been distant cousins.

"Why take me from Miss Lee?" I asked.

"We didn't know you had any surviving relatives. There were no records, and I assumed your parents had kept your family lineage hidden as much as possible. No one had come forward."

"Is Ender my birth name?" In the cells, Miss Lee had told me she thought I'd be safer with a new identity.

"Yes." Priscilla tilted her head to the side, a sign of her endearment. "But your last name was Galang. We changed it to mine and created the story of your parents dying in a robbery—my cousin and his wife."

"But you don't have any family that I've met." I took a breath, keeping my calm.

"None in my life." She shook her head, and I understood the meaning of her words. She didn't have any family she was close with.

"And who is the *we* who helped you make all these decisions about me?" I asked, a lot like Selene had asked Headmaster John.

"The council and me," Priscilla answered. "The plan we drew up was the best we could do to keep you safe and with me—in case anything changed. I could sense a mix of all the elements in you, but you tested negative for ether magic and only positive for air magic. I believe your parents had paid for an enchantment to dampen your other elements, so you weren't easily found, and I had Mark Hastings hide your scent."

"The Librarian Mr. Hastings?" Earth mages were the only ones who could hide a mage's scent. With their array of herbal and flower creations, a stronger earth mage could use an enchantment to create or dampen a specific scent.

"Yes." Priscilla nodded. "He had been a good friend of the previous headmaster. Just like John had later on trusted the headmaster, I knew Mr. Hastings would be a trusted ally. He would also be able to monitor your safety at Fives Academy should you have attended."

Selene's mother must've kept her daughter's scent masked, and the thought of her rose and sandalwood essence made me want to brush my lips against the smooth skin on the nape of her neck.

I shook my head, trying to focus. "And what did Selene's mom have to do with my parents' deaths?"

"Your dad was an ether mage—which you already know from Bernila. Your mom was an air mage," Priscilla said.

I hadn't told her about the conversation I'd had with Miss Lee, but I imagine there had been cameras in the cell area. I wanted to hear it from her, along with more details. "Anna, Selene's mom, and your parents were in Singapore at the same time. Anna was there to meet someone for a healing spell. Victoria, her sister, was sick, and Anna needed to be the one to meet with the mage." Priscilla straightened. "A dark mage found Anna by awful luck, and she ran. She hadn't immediately realized the reason she had lost the dark mage was because they had found your father. It was too late once Anna realized, and your parents were already gone. She fled, to keep Selene and her sister safe. I was called to the scene, and it was then that I found you hiding behind a food cart less than two blocks away. You were so little." She sighed. "I consulted with the council, and the plan was made. John made contact with me on behalf of Anna. He knew of my position with the council, which was concerned for the family that had been attacked in Singapore—yours. I promised Anna and John I'd take care of you. Since John took the position as part of the council and headmaster of Fives Academy, he's been observing your safety and care ever since."

"So the headmaster felt guilty for the deaths of my parents?" As much as I didn't want to remember the events in Singapore that day, I wished I could.

"The guilt weighed heavy on Anna, and John had said he should have gone with her, that he could have done something. He had stayed back to help Nathan with Victoria and watch over Selene. Since Anna and Victoria were twins and shared similar genes, Anna had to be the one to meet the contact." Priscilla took a deep breath. "I am sorry, Ender. The truth is hard, but you deserve it."

"Someone should have told me. You should have told me." I bit the inside of my cheek, causing it to bleed. "I don't blame Selene's mom. It wasn't her fault. It was the dark mage."

The betrayal of being lied to stung—I had been old enough to know the truth long before now. I gave myself several minutes to digest the information, the hum of the jet's engine filling the cockpit.

"We are on our way to where your parents lay at rest," Priscilla said after some time, giving me my much-needed moment. She turned back toward the front and hit the autopilot switch, turning it off. "They are in Singapore. It's heavily populated, and there's a rare chance the dark mage who's after Selene will suspect we are going there."

I nodded, though she wasn't looking at me. She was giving me closure, and I wondered how much she'd had to push the headmaster to approve the detour. The entire situation infuriated me—not at Selene's mom or the small amount of betrayal I felt toward Priscilla, but toward the dark mage for destroying so many lives and taking my parents from me.

"Why hadn't you told me the truth?" A small amount of disappointment seeped through my words. I needed to know why she hadn't told me if she thought I had deserved the truth.

"We didn't want you to go digging into your past and be found." She glanced at me. "Dark mages have become resourceful."

Which meant they could find us wherever we went—which also meant it did not matter if we went to Singapore. They had already attacked Fives Academy.

The thought of Selene and the urge to be next to her and keep her safe tugged me to leave the cockpit and head back into the main cabin, which led me to my next question.

"What do you know of the elemental bond?" I casually asked, as if my gut hadn't clenched at the words. Priscilla sharply glanced my way and then back out the windshield.

"It's rare and is formed between two mages with the same element. It's a strong emotional and physical connection." She stared straight ahead, and I could feel her wanting to ask more.

"Do they have to share the same birthdate and year too?" I had done research while in the airport before Selene and I had left. It was hard to find information regarding soul-bound.

"From what I know, not always, though it is believed to be more powerful if they do." She glanced my way again. "Some strengths of certain elements are rumored to not emerge until the mage meets their soul-bound. It might even be powerful enough to break a strong elemental magic dampening enchantment."

I rolled that thought around in my head. I had felt something different with my magic during the demon rat attack when Selene and I made contact. It could be why my other elements had emerged if my parents had put a dampener spell on me. Selene and I shared the same birthday, but we were a year apart.

"What does the bond feel like?" I asked.

"I wouldn't know, but I heard it's like you are one with the other person. Your souls are aligned. It's also the reason that soul-bounds are not able to create a familiar. There is no part of their soul left to give; it would cause the mage to die or become dark."

Priscilla eyed my bouncing knee. What I felt for Selene wasn't quite *aligned*, but it was close. During our kiss at the Winter Ball, it felt as though my soul wanted to merge with hers, but it hadn't and was being kept at bay. I had never wanted to give part of my soul to a familiar. Maybe the bond was why? Regardless, there was no doubt what Selene was to me—what we were to each other. She hadn't just become a part of my life.

"Selene is my soul-bound."

Chapter Thirty-Two
Ender

The headmaster and Priscilla had decided a night in an actual bed instead of the plane chairs would do everyone some good before we left Singapore. I had been sure we would be headed back to Fives Academy, but I imagined that was a conversation Priscilla and the headmaster would have had—and then they'd had to persuade Selene.

The four-star hotel's floor gleamed of marble, but I wondered if it was real. Wood panels lined the walls from the floor to the vaulted white ceiling. We were quiet as we headed to the front desk with our bags. Headmaster John spoke to the concierge—in Mandarin. Turning to us, he explained that I would be staying in a room with him, and Selene would stay with Priscilla—undoubtedly because Selene would be uncomfortable with her newfound father.

Glancing at Selene next to me, I tried to read her expression. Her lips were pressed together as she watched her father face the reception desk. I leaned over her shoulder.

"You know," I whispered, "we just traveled alone. You'd think he wouldn't be so concerned about splitting us up."

A hint of a smile formed on her lips and she blushed, sending my heart into a frenzy. I wished we weren't in separate rooms.

"We have our keys." The headmaster turned around and held up two matte grey rectangular cards.

While everyone's backs were turned, I took a deep breath. Prior to arriving at the hotel, I had visited my parents' grave and Selene had made her dreaded phone call to her sister, filling her in on everything. The image of the smooth headstone of my parents' shared monument had imbedded itself in my brain. Someone had been taking care of the grounds, and the grass had been cut around their stone. *Daniel Galang* and *Maria Galang* were each engraved in cursive writing with a knot underneath, along with their birthdates and day they died.

Priscilla had shown me a picture of my parents—the only one she could find—but it didn't feel real until we were standing in front of their grave. Growing up, I had been told my parents were not into photography and hadn't kept photos, even their own. At the time, I thought I understood. I was a child who didn't care much for his picture being taken, but now, I realized it had been suspicious. There might have been a subconscious part of me that didn't want to ask questions that had answers I didn't want to know.

After a quiet ride in the elevator, we found our connecting rooms. I tossed my bag onto the queen bed closest to the window, and it landed softly on the comforter. The headmaster's familiar had already claimed the bed closest to the hallway. I frowned at the locked latch on the adjoining door to Selene's room.

"The lock will be unlocked, but the door will remain shut at night." The headmaster didn't look up as he glared out the window, the setting sun turning his hair a slight orange. He didn't need to explain the reasoning—if his daughter was attacked, he needed to be able to get to her.

"Sir," I said out of respect, "I still don't understand. Why did you let her leave the academy if it's the safest place for her?"

"Have you ever had a dog?" He faced me, closing the curtains as he turned.

"No?" Priscilla didn't have time for a dog, and my training kept me far too busy—though I would've made time and asked her frequently for one. I internally laughed at the thought of Mr. Scott frowning at all of the dog poop in the yard and muddy paw prints next to my own shoe prints on the kitchen floor.

"If a dog wants to run but you don't want them to run, what do you do?"

"Put the dog on a leash." If he was going to say Selene was a—

"Yes." He clasped his hands in front of him. Despite his dress pants, collared shirt, and relaxed posture, he radiated power—not magical power, but power in knowledge. "You then walk the dog outside and it pulls and pulls, causing itself to choke. If you take them off the leash, they'll run, but they are no longer choking. They now face the challenges of the weather, traffic, hunger, but they will acquire new knowledge and do not feel restrained. Most of them come home."

"Selene is not a dog." I narrowed my eyes at his comparison. "Your *daughter* is not a dog."

"No." The headmaster shook his head. "Sal most definitely is not a dog. But keeping her at the academy would ensure her own chaos and internal struggles. Sal was the initial target. In her mind, keeping her distance from Vivian would keep the dark mages away. If she wanted to leave, she would, unless I put her in a holding cell. She is brilliant and would do anything to keep her sister out of harm's way."

I looked at the small flat-screen TV. His use of the word *sister* threw me off. Knowing the truth, it was hard to hear him say it.

"And now that she knows what happened, you think she'll go back?" The truth didn't change the danger following her.

John glanced at the carpet, then back at me. "I think she's torn. While the dark mage after her could give chase, it could also go for a target that's not hiding."

"Vivian."

"Yes." John nodded. "Out here, Selene could be found by dark mages. They can find you too." He paused, letting that information sink in. I still didn't believe I was an ether mage. "But if it is the dark mage who killed her aunt and uncle who is after her—which we have reason to believe—the better tactical plan would be to go after what she treasures and would do anything for, if it is an easier target. A dark mage may have a dead soul, but it does not mean they have lost their intellectual capabilities.

"Plus," the headmaster continued, "we believe there is someone inside the academy after her."

I glanced back at him. "You mean someone my grandmother may or may not be involved with."

"Possibly."

"She escaped," I said.

"Yes—once she was out of our custody." He nodded. He started to say more but there was a knock on the door connecting our rooms.

The headmaster strode over to the door, unlocking the silver latch and opening it—the heavy wood would not keep a strong mage out. Priscilla stood on the other side with Selene behind her. Selene clutched her mom's white hoodie in her hands, the ghost visible.

"Sal would like to see you, Ender." Priscilla's gaze landed on me. She had taken the news about us being soul-bound surprisingly well and vowed not to disclose the information to Selene. She had, however, encouraged me to tell Selene soon, and there was no doubt the look she was giving me now was indicating that tonight would be as good a time as any. She had said bonds like this were sacred and rare, and leaving the other half in the dark could end badly.

"What?" Selene asked the headmaster, who had been smiling at her.

"I gifted that hoodie to your mom in good fun. She was essentially a ghost to the world." His expression softened and his eyes glistened as if he were somewhere else; another memory perhaps. "She adored it."

"Oh." Selene held the hoodie tighter, shifting her weight from foot to foot. "Can we walk the hotel?" She asked, changing the topic.

Headmaster John looked at her.

"Do not leave the building," he finally said.

"Not that I plan on running, but you let me travel across the world and now you're tightening the restrictions?" Selene put a defiant hand on her hip.

"You were never alone." The headmaster's expression didn't change. "You have two hours, and Aura goes with you."

Chapter Thirty-Three

Selene

Aura trotted along the hideous blue and green checkered carpet. The few people we passed in the hallway didn't spare a glance at her. A small amount of magic tickled my nose when she was near, but that could just be because she was a familiar or from the spell hiding her.

"Here." I abruptly turned and pushed open a door so Ender could enter.

Aura spun around, tilting her head slightly to the side.

"Come on." I waved, and she bounced on through after Ender.

"This hotel does have elevators." Ender's smile turned smug. "And if you wanted somewhere private to kiss me, I can think of at least five other places inside this hotel with a better view."

I rolled my eyes and nudged him as I passed, my shoulder tingling at the contact. My cheeks flushed at his comment and I was thankful he couldn't see my face as I went up the stairs. Though he was joking, something inside me urged me to do just that—kiss him.

Aura wove between my feet and climbed the stairs, taking the lead.

"So where are we going?" Ender asked as we passed the next floor and kept going.

"You asked for a better view." I waved to the next level, where a door led outside.

"I didn't peg you for breaking the rules." He raised an eyebrow at me and then glanced at the locked door. "Are you going to pick this one too?"

I flinched. I had let him believe that assumption.

"Yeah. I didn't pick the lock that day in the library. I just stole a key." I shrugged and strode over to the door.

"I lied," Ender said. "I definitely peg you as a rule breaker."

"I can't manipulate any of the locks at the academy, but this is steel, not tungsten. Plus, my dad said to not leave the building." I froze. I hadn't meant to call John my dad.

I swallowed, ignoring the pain in my chest, and hovered my hands over the metal box where the lock was. I closed my eyes and concentrated. Metal was the hardest for me to manipulate and was draining. My magic's warm sensation slid from me into the lockbox, searching for the release. Once I found it, I closed my hands, opening the lock with a click.

"Why am I not surprised you can manipulate metal?" Ender's smile fell as he stared at me. "You continue to amaze me."

Little spirals of fire went up my spine at his gaze, and I swallowed. The admiration in his eyes told me he wasn't lying—and it wasn't just a fascination. I had unknowingly taken a step toward him or he had taken one toward me—I was unsure of which. The closer we were, the more—

Something warm moved around our legs, and I glanced down to see white fluffy fur. Once Aura got our attention, she trotted toward the door.

"Someone must be excited to go outside." I let out a small laugh.

"Or doesn't want us to kiss." Ender took a deep breath as he ran a hand through his hair, then waved me onward. I couldn't get a read on his expression, as my own nerves confused me.

I pushed open the door and stepped onto the roof. Even though it was winter, the warm air was fragranced with jasmine and burnt sugar. It was too warm for my hoodie, so I had left it in the room. The fact that the man who had pretended to be only the headmaster of my school and not my father had given the hoodie to my mom didn't make it any less special.

The newly dark sky was clear, and the stars were visible even with the lights from the city.

"Careful," I told the little fox as she jumped up on the chest-high parapet overlooking the city. Clearly, she wasn't afraid of heights.

The hotel wasn't the biggest building in the city, but it wasn't the smallest either. I leaned on the cool cement parapet—avoiding the growing moss—next to Aura, who began nuzzling my arm until I rubbed her chin.

"Now this is a view." This was a first for me. I had never been to a big city like this.

"It is." Ender's voice was raspier than usual, and I turned to see the corner of his lip turned up into a sexy smile, warmth crawling up my spine.

"What?" I asked.

His gaze held mine. Wind swirled around my head, sending loose strands of my hair flying. It softly trailed across my neck and stopped below my chin, pushing it upward. I looked up at him; his magic was like his own caress as he stepped in close.

And we stared at each other just like we had in the stairwell.

"What is this?" I blurted out.

"This is called a rooftop." Ender's grin was cocky, and I snorted.

"You had told me that there's something else between us, and that I feel it too." My teeth gnawed at my lip, my heart racing at its own will. "What did you mean?"

"When you first arrived," Ender's expression softened, "I was drawn to you. I thought it was the fascination with how you avoided people, especially me, but you also did everything to protect your sister. You looked like you hated sitting at that lunch table, but that's where your sister sat. I found similarities between you and me—we both hate crowds and socializing."

"Okay, Mr. Popular." I rolled my eyes.

"Not by choice. Magic likes power and tends to be drawn to it." Ender shook his head. "The night I passed you coming out of the woods, something stirred inside me. I couldn't shake that feeling or the urge to just be near you. But there was still something more than my own desire to get to know you and my want to spend time with you. The night in the basement at the Academy, I felt it again."

He paused before taking the back of his hand and grazing my cheek.

"Do you know what an elemental bond is?" he asked.

I stopped breathing, unable to say the word *no* out loud, but when the words came off his lips, my heart suddenly had a mouth and wanted to say *yes*. I couldn't speak and awkwardly stared up at him.

"It's a bond between two mages where their souls connect. They have to be of the same element and may or may not share the same birthday. That part is unclear." His hand moved from my cheek and down to my sleeve, then trailed down my bare arm. "Like us."

He was quiet, letting the reality dawn on me.

"Same day. Not year," I thought out loud while internally admitting that he could possibly be very right. "You're one year older."

"There isn't much I could find on elemental bonds and soul-bounds." He dropped his hand.

"We're soul-bound," I affirmed and he nodded. "What do you know about ... it?"

"Their souls are more of a connection that mirror each other. It's different from a familiar, where you give a part of your soul away. The bond can't be created, either—it's natural."

"Can it be denied?" I asked before thinking of the repercussions of my wording, and his face fell, the vein in his neck pulsing.

"I'm not sure." He swallowed, taking a step back. "If this is something you don't want—"

"No. I ... it just caught me off guard." I shook my head, attempting to clear it. "I'm sorry."

I spared a glance at Aura, who was lounging on the parapet, her back facing us. I felt *happy* when I was around Ender, and not like how it was when I was with my sister. My stomach fluttered and my body hummed happily. But with everything going on, I didn't have the time to explore it. Mom's killer was still out there, my sister was in danger, and Ender could also be hunted by dark mages.

Something else popped into my head.

"If an elemental bond has to be accepted or denied, do you think..." I stared at him, wanting to see his reaction as I blurted out the next part uneasily. "Does that mean we would have to—"

A low growl came from Aura, snapping my attention away from Ender. Her hackles were up as she stood, staring off behind us. I turned to look, but nothing was there. My nose twitched. I thought I caught a different smoky scent—one of vanilla and cinnamon rather than Singapore's flowers.

"Aura. What is it, girl?" I walked over to her, but she growled again, glowering in the same direction.

"Whoa." Ender's voice was full of shock, and my magic came to life before I could finish whirling around.

Beyond the arm Ender held out, shielding me, a sleek black dragon perched on a pipe sticking out of the hotel's roof.

Chapter Thirty-Four

Selene

The dragon was twice the size of Aura—small for a dragon—but its round, feline-orange eyes made it look fierce as it bounded off the pipe and to the rooftop. White specks sparkled like the stars above on its black scales. Its white horns matched the spikes lining its tail and claws. It looked like a baby dragon, but it carried itself like an adult as it stared directly past Ender and at me.

Aura hopped off the edge and prowled over in front of us, the dragon not even sparing a glance at her. Elemental Creatures class was in the spring semester, but I knew enough from my prior schooling to know that you never stared directly in a dragon's eyes.

This was impossible—dragons were extinct. Yet, we still learned about them. Their powers were random, usually consisting of scorching fire, but some could create water or air. Some could even manipulate the earth around them. But they were thought to have been killed off by the dark mages because they were natural enemies.

The dragon shifted, sitting straight up. It relaxed as it bounced on its front feet, tail giving a slight wag, like a happy dog. Its eyes shined as if it was excited to see me, and I naturally dropped the defensive magic that stirred as new, symphonic magic flitted under my skin.

"Ender." I reached a hand out, lowering his arm. "He's friendly."

"I know." Ender lowered his arm and glanced at me. At one simple glance, his acknowledgment was my own.

Somehow, I *felt* that he understood my natural reaction to this dragon—that he wasn't a threat. *To us.*

Aura let a low growl escape and scampered back to us. No sooner had she sat at my feet than she yawned like she was ready to sleep.

"So." Ender still stared at the dragon hesitantly. "How do we explain we went for a walk and came back with a dragon?"

"Maybe my dad—John," I quickly corrected myself, "has an explanation. He seems to have a lot of secrets."

"This dragon seems awfully fond of you," Ender said as the dragon held my gaze and stretched his neck toward me.

"I'm not sure why." A symphonic hum of magic lightly brushed along my skin. I stepped forward, reaching out a hand.

Suddenly, the hair on my arm stood on end and the dragon swirled around, growling. Aura jumped to all fours, hunched, and hissed toward the door. Dread struck my gut as I got a slight, awful whiff of burning skin.

"Get to the edge!" Ender shouted and we took off toward the opposite side of the door.

Movement caught my eye as vines wrapped around the ends of the parapet in front of us, and we froze. Someone's hands grabbed the vines and pulled themself over the edge and onto the roof. Miss Lee stepped away from the ledge, brushing off her casual blue pants and blouse like it was just an ordinary day and she wasn't a fugitive of the mage council.

"That proved to be quite difficult in my old age." Miss Lee's gaze fell on the dragon. "That's peculiar."

The dragon looked back, growling at her, but he must have decided whatever was behind that door was more of a threat because he turned his attention back toward it.

"What are you doing here?" Ender cautiously angled himself between Miss Lee and me, somehow keeping his eyes on the door too. As much as I wanted to wrap my own vines around her neck to see how she liked it, I needed my attention on the door.

"Making sure you stay safe," she said. "I see you decided to come home."

"This isn't my home." There was some pain behind Ender's voice.

"Well, in the Far East. Much closer to the Philippines." She took a step closer. "Did you figure out what you are to each other?"

There was a brief pause.

Ender glanced at me but looked away when the door to the roof swung open and a dark mage stepped through wearing a burgundy cloak.

The little dragon jumped, taking to the air as he spewed fire toward the intruder. A scream came from the dark mage as they pulled the cloak farther over them. Once the flames died, the dark mage lowered their cloak, undamaged.

Okay. So this mage had a fire-resistant cloak. *Great.*

The movement of their cloak revealed a shadowy face with wide eyes fixated on the dragon. The dark mage's skin looked pale and crinkled, but nothing compared to the one who had attacked the academy.

The dark mage gained his composure and shot fire, the flames outlined with dark shadows, toward the dragon. The rooftop became ten degrees warmer, but the dragon merely shielded himself with his wing. Once the fire dissipated, the dragon shook his head, his obsidian scales shifting on his neck as he let out a low roar of annoyance.

"I've never seen fire—that level of fire—barely leave something untouched." Ender stared at the dragon in wonder.

"One of the many reasons dark mages fear dragons," Miss Lee said, still eyeing the dark mage whose narrowed gaze shifted between the dragon and us. "Even the little ones."

"You brought a dark mage here." I took a step back, keeping Miss Lee in my peripheral.

"No." Miss Lee shook her head. "I merely followed them here. I would never harm my grandson."

Ender cracked his neck and released an annoyed breath as he prepared to fight. A foreign anger touched with resentment filled my chest. I clenched my fists, fighting the urge to bring that emotion forward to examine it. Now wasn't the time.

"Them?" I asked. "Is there more than this one?"

"Inside." Miss Lee nodded.

My stomach dropped. My dad was inside.

I charged toward the dark mage.

"Selene!" Ender shouted, but I tuned him out.

The dark mage at the school appeared to have been more decrepit, which meant this one was less powerful but not to be underestimated. They had patches of withered skin and narrow black veins but was not as decayed as the one at the academy. How could they still be so powerful yet their body was dying?

I circled my hands around each other in a fluid motion as I ran, charging my air magic. The black eyes of the mage greedily watched my advance. *Idiot.* I wasn't going to get close enough for him to touch me. I sent my air magic across the rooftop and it slammed into the dark mage, knocking him to the side.

The dark mage attempted to stand, but I honed in on the moss growing near his feet. My magic absorbed into its rhizoids, rapidly growing their size and strength. The false roots sprouted, wrapping around his ankles and legs, pinning them to the rooftop.

I went to run by him so that Ender and I would surround him, but he incinerated the vines and lashed out with a powerful blast of heat. Before I could use my magic as a shield, the fire soared around me as wind pushed outward. Ender held out his hands, creating an outward funnel encasing me like a domed shield—something that took practice and energy.

Black obscured my view as leathery wings flapped in front of me. The little dragon landed on his hind feet, expanding his wings so I was hidden behind him. He turned his head, glancing at me over his shoulder. I stared at him in disbelief. He was protecting me.

He shrieked and flinched as a rust-colored dagger pierced his scales, smoke trailing from the wound. He reached for it with his mouth but couldn't quite reach. Without hesitation, I stepped forward, pulling the knife from the him and tossing it away from the dark mage. If I recalled correctly, there once was a weapon that could be created to harm dragons more easily.

I turned to face the dark mage, but thick emerald green vines wrapped around his torso as Miss Lee worked her magic.

I really despise those vines.

Aura stood at Ender's feet, hissing, and Ender flung his arms forward, sending air magic at the mage. It sent the mage crashing into the parapet and down to his knees. Summoning my fire magic to my palms, I went to incinerate him, but the little dragon beat me to it.

The dark mage was unable to shield himself and the flames licked at his cloak, this time slowly melting it away until the fire reached the rest of him. I briefly wondered if the entire block could hear his screams, and I scrunched my nose at the nauseating smell of burnt flesh. I looked away.

Once the flames dispersed, I turned back to the dark mage, surprised to see his extremities weren't as burnt as his core. There hadn't been a noticeable mark on his hands during the attack, and he hadn't been as strong as the mages who had attacked Mom, Viv, and me, but I had to check. I walked closer to the smoldering body, his face unrecognizable, and kicked his hand over. Nothing. I held my breath and walked over to his other hand, pushing back the smoking cloak with my sneaker.

His palm was free of a black circle.

"Are you okay?" Ender came to my side, studying me.

"Yeah." I cleared my throat. "Just checking to see if it had the same mark as the ones that killed my mom."

Ender nodded and put a hand on my shoulder, the small gesture somehow comforting.

A cross between a whimper and a grumble came from behind us, and we turned to see the dragon trying to reach the wound on its shoulder.

"Hey. Hey … it's okay." I strode over to the dragon, resting a hand on his snout. He nuzzled into my hand, and I smiled.

Less than a second later, the dragon backed up, swaying his head in apparent agitation as he turned toward Miss Lee, who was picking up the dark mage's dagger from the ground.

"It'll be okay." Miss Lee examined the dagger closely.

"What will be okay?" I put my arm out, trying to calm the dragon.

"Your dragon." She nodded toward the dragon as she slowly set the dagger down, kicking it away from her.

"He's not my dragon," I said.

"You can tell yourself that." She straightened. "The dagger was made with a dark mage's familiar's blood and not the blood of a dragon. It burns and harms them, but it doesn't seep deadly toxin into their bloodstream."

"What do you mean by that?" Ender walked over and stood between Miss Lee and me, his shoulders still tense.

"The familiar to a mage who becomes dark slowly dies, but if it's sacrificed, its blood can be mixed with iron and forged into a weapon. It's destructive to a dragon, but one nick doesn't kill. A weapon mixed and enchanted with dragon blood would."

"Ender, we need to go." I nodded at the door. John and Priscilla were in danger if there was another dark mage.

Before we could leave, the door to the stairs swung open and John and Priscilla ran through, their concerned parental gazes scanning the rooftop.

"Sal." John's gaze landed on me as his chest heaved and brow wrinkled. He glanced at the lifeless body of the dark mage and ran over to me, resting his hands on my shoulders as he examined me. I tensed at the contact. "Are you okay?"

"I'm fine." I studied the rips throughout his shirt, but he appeared to be okay. As he lowered his hands, I noticed black soot on his palms. *Huh.* Was he a fire mage? Normally, magic didn't leave residue like that on your palms.

"That will need an explanation," Priscilla said as she looked behind me. She had run over to Ender while John assessed me.

I turned, expecting to see Miss Lee, but she was gone. There was only the dragon, who stood on all four limbs with Aura at his feet. Aura's tail swatted the dragon in the face before she trotted over to John. The dragon snorted, a white fluff flying away, and then dipped his head toward me before taking off into the air.

Did the dragon just bow to me?

CHAPTER THIRTY-FIVE
Selene

PRISCILLA HAD LANDED THE jet at the airport Fives Academy utilized and joined us for the ride back to the academy. She planned on staying for a short while to assist with the security of the academy upon our return. Guard Taylor, the same guard who had caught Ender and me the night we left, met us at the hangar and escorted us back to the school. The moment we arrived, I met Vivian on the east dormitory's roof and began filling her in on everything. And of course, I had brought the Oreos I had picked up on the way back to the academy.

She ate the filling of a cookie as she contentedly swung her legs over the roof, the grounds quiet. The sun had set, but the days were starting to get longer again.

"So we technically have Mom's last name?" She grabbed an Oreo from the package and split it in half.

"We do." I smiled gently, happy that she still called Mom her mom despite now knowing that she wasn't her biological mother.

"And her sister's last name—my real mom?" Viv glanced at me, and I nodded. "That doesn't seem very smart if they were trying to keep our identities hidden."

I shrugged. They probably had thought it was a very common name, though she was right.

The last forty-five minutes had been story time about everything that had happened during the trip and what John had told me. The briefing I had given her over the phone had lacked details, and after the mage attack, John had successfully convinced me to travel back to Fives Academy. Ender wouldn't go back without me, and Vivian was still in danger at the academy.

"That was the only Double Stuf Oreo package in the store. You might want to eat them sparingly; I'm not sure when we'll be able to get more." I glanced at the half-empty pack.

"I've been out, and we both know I get hangry without them." Viv grinned, but it wasn't her full, joyful grin. "Maybe we can convince the academy to add them to their food pickup."

"It's been, what? A few days without them? You had enough to last you weeks when I left," I teased.

"It's called stress eating." She glanced down at her half-eaten Oreo. "I regret that I said it was okay for you to go without me."

"I'm sorry." I glanced up at the stars, sighing, then faced her. "It wasn't fair for me to ask you to stay. But I am not sorry for keeping you safe. I will do anything to protect you."

"I know," Viv said. "I'd do the same for you, and that is why I should've gone."

"Viv." I softened my voice. "It's not your responsibility to look after me."

"So you only protect me because it's your responsibility?" she asked, her voice edged with doubtfulness.

"No." I bumped her shoulder. "It's more than that. We're family."

Even if we are technically cousins and not biologically sisters.

"Exactly."

I nodded in understanding. But I would still protect her even if that meant upsetting her. That would never change.

"So." Viv's voice lightened as she truly grinned this time. "Ender is your soul-bound?"

"Yes." I glanced over the academy grounds. "We have an elemental bond."

I had casually slipped it in while talking about our trip and why Miss Lee had stopped trying to kill me. Viv didn't let it slide and told me we would circle back to that and go over it in great detail.

I had hoped she would forget.

Chapter Thirty-Six
Selene

It was Christmas morning, two days since we had gotten back from Singapore. Viv had spent the nights in my dorm while Sydney stayed with April. We caught up, watched movies, and ate snacks. She went back to her dorm to freshen up before brunch at ten thirty.

"How did Viv take the news?" Sydney's voice was muffled as she popped her head out of our adjoining bath, toothbrush in hand. I had just given her a very brief summary of my trip with Ender, telling her John was my father, and that I really, really liked Ender.

"Besides initially stopping her from going all magic and blazing after John, she took the news well," I said. "I think she had time to process it before we got back."

"Yeah." Sydney popped back into the bathroom, talking in between brushing her teeth. "Time is usually your mind's worst enemy, but in some cases, I guess it can help."

"I guess so."

After a moment, she strode out of the bathroom, toothbrush no longer in hand, and grabbed her snow boots. Snow covered the grounds for the holiday, but it would be gone by the end of next week when classes started.

"Hey. Have you seen Ender around?" I hadn't seen him since we'd gotten back, but I'd only left the dorms a few times to grab food. I wanted to spend this time with Viv and make sure she was okay with everything we'd learned.

"Actually, no. He hasn't been with his old posse either." Sydney grabbed her coat. "Are you ready?"

"Yeah." I donned my own academy-supplied boots and coat. "Did you just brush your teeth to go eat?"

"Yes?" Sydney glanced at me. "Why wouldn't I? It's not likely we'll come right back when we're done."

"Usually people brush their teeth after they eat or as soon as they wake up." I laughed, but she was right. I'd had almost a full semester to get used to brushing my teeth before breakfast, but it was still odd to me.

We headed out and I paused at the stairs. Ender's room was on the third floor, and I thought about taking them. Instead, I followed Sydney down the stairs and out of the dorms. He should be at the brunch.

We had made it to the courtyard when someone called our names. I turned to see David.

"Welcome back, Sal," he said when he caught up to us. "It's been less exciting without you."

"Hey!" Sydney swatted him on the shoulder. "Are you saying that I'm boring?"

"No." He smiled. "But it's been very anticlimactic."

"Isn't that a good thing?" I asked. "That's why I left."

He laughed. "I'm not talking about dark mages attacking."

I was confused and stared at him.

"He means he missed you!" Sydney said. "We all missed you. We missed Ender too."

"Oh." I blushed, not used to having friends who miss me. It turns out, I had missed them too. I'd gotten used to Sydney's company every morning and her showing me the progression of her art every evening.

I turned to go into the cafeteria but slipped on a patch of ice and fell on my butt. The ground was harder than expected, and I internally cursed at the cold weather. I missed the beach.

David grabbed my hand and helped me up. I froze, and so did he. My magic stirred, fighting against itself like a tug-of-war. I wanted David's magic. It was strong. A pit formed in my stomach as tension and something else crept along my spine.

Sydney glanced between the two of us and he dropped his hand. I stepped back, feeling uncomfortable. I felt his power and wondered if he had felt mine.

"There you are." A strong arm wrapped around my shoulders. "I was looking all over for you."

I raised an eyebrow at Ender though I welcomed his timing. "Such blatant lies already this morning?"

"I will never stop seeking you out," Ender said, leaning down so his lips brushed against my ear. Goosebumps rose on the back of my neck. Good goosebumps, despite the built-up tension. "Merry Christmas."

David cleared his throat, then looked at me. "I'll see you both inside."

"I'll join you," Sydney said and they headed in.

"Are you okay?" Ender kept his arm draped over my shoulders. "I sensed you were uncomfortable."

"You ... what?" I looked up at him. "Through the soul-bond?"

Ender dropped his arm and pinned me with his gaze. He didn't even have to say *what else would I be talking about?*

"Yes." I nodded, some of my tension disappearing. "My magic did something weird when David helped me up. I think he sensed it too."

"Weird?" He glanced at the door behind me.

"I don't know." I shook my head. "Sometimes I question what we can do as an ether mage."

"You are a level five." He nodded. "Your full capabilities are unknown."

I shivered, from both the thought and the cold air.

"Here." He noticed and pulled me to his chest. A moment later, he said, "We should head inside."

"Are we..." I pulled away and pointed between the two of us, then let my hand fall. I was well aware the cafeteria had windows to the courtyard and the students inside could see us.

"Are you asking again if you're my girlfriend?" He looked amused.

"What do you think—" I stopped, realizing the tension had completely vanished. And it hadn't been entirely my own. "That was your tension."

"Alright," he said. "Now it's my turn to ask. What are you talking about?"

"When I was with David, you felt my feelings, but I think I also felt yours." If he was inside, he most likely had seen David and me standing there awkwardly.

"I think David—or any other guy—being that close to you would certainly cause you to be tense." He frowned.

"Alright, now you're just being rude."

"That was pretty rude of me," he agreed. "But the important part of this conversation is what you and I are." His grin was back.

"Ah. Yes. Girlfriend. Boyfriend. Acquaintances—"

"Acquaintances?" He let out an exaggerated humph. "No." He leaned in close. "You are my soul-bound." Ender stepped away, his warmth leaving with him. "And you are my girlfriend—with your approval, of course."

There was a bond between us—I couldn't deny it. I had mentioned I didn't have time for a relationship, but I couldn't ignore this. I didn't want to. There might be a lot going on and I wasn't sure what was going to happen, but one thing I was certain of was that I wanted to pursue the bond between us.

"I do."

Chapter Thirty-Seven

Selene

THE GYM WAS A Christmas dream. While this morning, the cafeteria was decked out in Christmas decorations, the gym was decorated similar to the Winter Ball, except it looked like Santa's elves had visited. I didn't think I could eat any more after brunch earlier in the morning, but the food smelled delicious and I had worked up an appetite after a short but brisk run with Ender.

"Why did we stop here?" Viv asked, staring at the dessert table, where we stood with our friends. "We have thirty minutes until they said dinner would be ready. The chocolate fudge brownies are taunting me."

"Fifty dollars that Viv goes straight for the dessert table before getting food," Sydney said.

"That would be a losing bet." April pointed at Viv, who was still eyeing the dessert table.

"No takers?" Sydney glanced at everyone else but April.

"I don't think you have any takers," David said when no one answered and Sydney sighed.

"April, you did a good job with the decorations." I glanced at the tall pine tree. Poinsettias were perfectly placed along its branches.

"Thank you!" She smiled.

"Come on." Sydney waved. "Let's go grab seats."

"Hey, Sal," David said. "Can we talk outside?"

"Yeah. Sure." I spared a glance at Ender.

"I'll grab us some drinks and meet you at the table." Ender nodded and strode toward the drink table.

I followed David outside, the cold air stinging my face. It would be good for us to talk after what happened this morning, but it didn't mean I wanted to, especially outside in the cold.

"I'm sorry for pulling you out here. I didn't want to speak about this in front of everyone, but I didn't know if we'd get the chance to talk later." David led me around the side of the gym. "Remember when we talked about why I'm here?"

"Yes." I recalled that the council had sent him here to help teach him how to control his magic.

"I still haven't been able keep my gloves off. That might be because I'm afraid to remove them, but when I touched you earlier, it was like I knew my magic wouldn't hurt you. Even through the gloves."

That was not what I'd felt; at least, that was not how I interpreted what wanting to take his magic felt like. I thought he was going to ask me ether questions and then I would apologize for earlier.

"Trainer Murphy is great, but I never had that feeling with her. I get nervous and lose control. I think if a friend were to help me, I would be calmer." He swallowed. "You're probably the only one here who could handle my magic."

Understanding hit. He was asking for help.

"What do you need me to do?"

"Can we meet before classes start up again?" he asked.

"How about we try now?" I could tell this was bothering him and we still had some time before dinner. I knew the feeling of needing an outlet before it emotionally dragged you down.

"Are you sure?"

I nodded. "Take off your glove. Let's see what you can do."

He sighed and grabbed his right glove, holding it there.

"They're enchanted." He eyed his glove but didn't make the move to tug it off.

"I'll be fine," I promised.

He removed his glove and sandwiched it between his opposite arm and side. His jaw set as he held out his hand, focusing on his magic. Less than a second later, fire lit.

"I can create it and manipulate it with ease." Light from the fire flickered in his eyes. "It's when my emotions are elevated that it explodes."

"That's very common." I stared at the small flame in his palm. He had control of its size. "Is it phantom fire?"

"No. I'm inept in phantom fire." He shook his head. "Trainer Murphy has tried a few times, but we've been focusing on de-escalation techniques."

"Let's start there." Phantom fire didn't harm others. It was what created mage lights. Spells could be added so the flames would last but also not burn down their surroundings.

I moved my hand to hover over the warmth created by the small fire, but it immediately disappeared as David pulled his hand back.

"This is what you wanted. I can't help you if you don't let me." I glared at him. "Now do it again." He swallowed and reached his hand out once more, lighting the flame again. "Good."

I lowered my hand closer, the flame almost licking at my palm, and David paled. He was truly afraid of his fire, even with such a tiny flame.

"Close your eyes," I instructed. Once they were closed, I continued. "Now, focus on something that makes you happy. Once you have it, hold on to it and do not let it go. Take that happiness and protect it. Protect it from your fire. Will it to not harm it." I gave him a moment. "Is it safe?"

He nodded.

"Good. Now create a safe cast over that happiness and keep it there." A part of my heart squeezed. I was teaching him the same way my mom had taught me. "Keep your light on and don't drop the magic, but steadily project that safety cast."

I gave him a moment longer. "Open your eyes."

He did, lines edging the corner of his eyes as he looked at me and then glanced down. He gasped but didn't tug his hand away from mine. I rested it on top of his palm. Fire breezed around my hand, no more than a mere warmth smothering it.

"You did it," I said.

"I did." He grinned, this time fully. The darkness surrounding his irises didn't vanish, but they lightened. It was small feat with a small flame, but a huge step. "Are you able to help me once or twice weekly?"

I nodded, agreeing to help him control his fire magic.

"Thank you." He sighed.

"Now let's head back inside where it's warm."

Chapter Thirty-Eight

Selene

My backpack sank into the ivory comforter. Today was the first day of the spring semester—which I thought was odd since it was still winter—and all the students were back from break. It was only a little over a week since Christmas and a few days since the start of the new year, but the snow had already melted and the weather was warmer. The days had been spent hanging out with my friends, running with Ender, and helping David with his magic.

Sydney grabbed her leather jacket from the back of her desk chair. It was fire red, almost matching the tips of her blonde hair. She had asked me to help her dye it the other day before classes began, and it reminded me somehow of the little dragon in Singapore, even though he'd been black, not red. I hadn't seen him since.

I loaded up my bag with the books I had picked up from the library the day before and slung it over my shoulder, ready to go.

Sydney chewed at her bottom lip, then glanced at me, her brow quirking upward as she assessed me from head to toe. "Is that your outfit for your first day of your last junior semester?"

I tugged at the hem of Mom's hoodie and glanced down at my parachute pants. The outfit was comfortable despite being slightly on the warm side.

"Yes?" I donned my bag and headed for the door.

"Only you could pull that style off." She nodded at my clothes, then followed me out the door. I didn't object, as I could not care less about what I looked like—I only looked in the mirror when I brushed my teeth. Meanwhile, Sydney rocked jean shorts and a black halter top, finished off with her red jacket.

As soon as we stepped into the dormitory hall, it was like my first day all over again. The stares, the hushed whispers, and the tingling sensation that went down my spine as words were exchanged behind my back. The only difference was everyone cleared out of my path, smashing themselves against the walls.

I scanned the grounds as we made our way to class, searching for Ender, but I didn't see him. The small hum of chatter stopped as we stepped inside the main academy hall, each student's head swiveling to face us.

"Whoa." Sydney paused at the entrance.

"Is this what it feels like to be popular?" I joked, squirming in my skin.

"What?" Sydney raised her voice, spinning in a circle. "You've never seen an ether mage before?"

Everyone glanced away, the chatter slowly picking back up.

"Hey." I nudged her arm. "Was that necessary?"

"It worked, didn't it?" She shrugged. "It's not like no one knows what your element is by now. Will you be okay?" She looked at me, and I nodded in response. "I'll see you later in class."

She headed off toward her locker, and I pivoted toward mine. At the beginning of last semester, I was glad that her locker wasn't next to mine;

now, I wished it was. Sydney had become an unexpected friend I could trust.

The hinges on my locker door let out a short screech as I opened it and I tossed my backpack inside, grabbing the books I would need for my first class, English. *Boring*.

"Good morning." Ender leaned on the locker next to mine, his hands shoved into his jean pockets. "Care for some company?"

"I would love some company." I closed my locker door and I could *feel* the other students looking in my direction once more. Something itched at the back of my neck and the weight of their glares suddenly grew heavy. A sudden rush of anger rose inside me, but it vanished, replaced by a dizzy spell. The hallway blurred and I pressed a hand against my locker.

"Hey." Ender grabbed my books with one hand and set the other on my shoulder. "Are you okay?"

I drew in a deep breath and held it for three seconds before letting it out.

Ender's jawline—and the rest of his handsome face—became less blurry as my vision cleared.

"Yes." I straightened but he didn't release me. "I'm okay. That was weird."

"You look pale." He assessed me, his brows still knitted. "Are you sure you're okay?"

"Yes." I nodded. The world finally steadied around me, and the haze in my head lifted. I glanced at the other students in the hallway. High school still wasn't for me. "Let's go."

His gaze shifted to where mine had gone.

"Ignore them." He swung an arm over my shoulders, the books still clutched against his chest. "Where are we headed?"

"English." We started walking.

"That doesn't sound like fun."

"Not at all," I said.

"I am meeting you at your door tomorrow morning before classes." He stared at each person who looked our way, causing them to avert their gaze.

I nodded, thankful he was there.

Chapter Thirty-Nine

Ender

Morning classes breezed by, and I was eager to get to lunch to see Selene. Telling her that I would never stop seeking her out hadn't been a lie. I knew where she was, but I was giving her space so she and her sister could process the new information together.

My mind drifted to the hallway before first class and the way Selene hated how the other students kept glancing at her. I'd make sure I was there for her tomorrow from the start.

I made it to the entrance of the cafeteria, but before I could, my name was called.

"Ender." Priscilla strode toward me. "Headmaster John is waiting in his office for us."

"Now?" I glanced in the cafeteria, spotting Selene with David sitting next to her.

"Yes, now. Come." Priscilla stopped right in front of me and waved.

I hesitated, staring at the empty seat on Selene's other side. I took a deep breath and followed the order. Priscilla didn't question my silence as we made our way to Headmaster John's office.

"Good afternoon, Ender." John nodded as we entered, Priscilla sitting across from him. "Please shut the door and have a seat."

The door shut with a heavy clank, and I sat in the chair next to Priscilla and leaned forward, giving Aura chin scratches before settling back. The little fox was adorable.

"Miss Hart and I have consulted with the Mage Council and have decided that she is going to stay at Fives Academy for the spring semester." The headmaster shifted forward, leaning on his desk. "She is going to work on finding the defector."

My gaze shot from him to Priscilla. "It's confirmed that someone inside the academy let the dark mage in?"

"Not confirmed, but there's a reasonable suspicion that someone is helping a dark mage clan and there may be multiple clans involved," Priscilla answered.

"Not just a single dark mage, but an entire clan? Two clans?" My eyebrows almost went through the roof.

"The dark mage who attacked was ancient." Headmaster John opened a folder and turned it toward me, scans of translated scripts neatly organized inside the three-holed prongs. "We found a burned scroll with a blank ink circle inside her cloak. The marking is of a clan that has existed for quite some time. What we are unsure of is if she belonged to that clan and why she attacked alone. Our belief is that she was from a different clan since she didn't bear the mark on her palm."

I read the first page. It contained a copy of a script in what appeared to be Latin. The next page showed an ink-black circle with a short, handwritten line underneath.

"*Immortale Daemonium Tenebris*," I read aloud, transcribing the little Latin I knew. "Immortal demons in darkness."

"That is the clan mark." The headmaster nodded at the page. "During their initiation into the clan, it is said that the mark is permanently burned into their skin, a sign of their enchantment linking them to each other."

I stared quizzically at the dark symbol. "Can they see what the other dark mages see?" That would put us at a huge disadvantage.

"Not quite." Pricilla leaned forward, flipping to another page full of script. "This makes it sound like it is more of a sense or feeling."

"What does that mean?" I asked.

"We don't fully understand it or know if these articles are entirely accurate. They are believed to be a copy of a dark grimoire." Priscilla shared a look with the headmaster. "There's something else."

"This is the clan that killed Sal's mother and Vivian's parents." The headmaster straightened, his jaw tense.

"That was already a given, based on their hunt for Selene." I slid the folder away from the edge of the stone-slabbed desk. "Why isn't she here, being shown this?"

"She will be." It was Priscilla who answered, an uneasiness I had rarely seen settling in her eyes. "But we wanted to give you what answers we could about your parents. It's the same clan that had accidentally found Anna in Singapore."

My brows knitted together as my brain sorted out its thoughts, revealing what this information meant.

"This black circle clan killed my parents." It only made sense. A powerful clan after Selene's mom had coincidently found my father, killing both my ether father and air mage mother, who had tried to save him.

"We are going to find the dark mages responsible." Headmaster John's voice was laced with vengeful guarantee, a promise that struck close to home.

"And my other elemental magic?" I glanced at Priscilla. "You said you thought my parents had somehow dampened my other elements."

"Yes." She nodded. "It can't be undone unless it is removed by the mage who created it or you, yourself, break it on your own."

I laughed, full knowing that the only ones who knew who could have created the enchantment were my deceased parents. Miss Lee hadn't truly known I was ether. "And how exactly do I do that?"

Silence—which meant they were not going to enlighten me about what they did or didn't know. It didn't matter. The enchantment most likely was being stripped by the bond Selene and I shared. That was probably why they didn't want to say anything. Priscilla had mentioned it was a possibility when we were flying to Singapore.

"There's still time for lunch." Priscilla stood, motioning for me to follow her to the door, and I did.

"I want to thank you, Ender." The headmaster called. "For protecting my daughter and your concern for her safety. I am indebted to you."

I nodded and started to turn back toward the door, unsure of what to do with a statement so personal.

"And Ender," he called, "your own safety is high priority. Do your best to remember that as well."

I pursed my lips and nodded once again before exiting his office.

Four hours later, small, sharp evergreen branches scraped against my bare arms as I attempted to dodge the thicker ones. A slight breeze passed through the magically warmed forest, and the faint whoosh of water thrummed somewhere close by. I slowed, nearing the edge of the dome boundary that sat upon the mountains.

The endorphins from my run had heightened and I stopped, attempting for the third time to try to summon any of my other elemental magic. I caged my air magic, straining to call forth my hidden earth magic. I held out my hand, focusing on something that should be as simple as moving the small heart-shaped leaf in front of me, its color faded due to the time of year.

The leaf twitched.

I stilled.

Excitement brewed but ceased once a breeze brushed my skin. It had been the wind.

Needing to relieve unwanted tension, I twisted my head side to side and was awarded with a satisfying crack. I would try again tomorrow. It was about time I headed back to shower before dinner, though it was tempting not to, leaving me with more time to see if I could rile up Selene with my ... smugness. I'd barely had any time with her by the time I had gotten to lunch, and after classes, she and Vivian planned to train.

A twig snapped underneath my foot, but the echo of another branch breaking came from my left—not from me. Nothing was visible in the thick brush, though the sun peeked through the treetops. I crept forward with deliberate steps, debating if I should run. If it was a dark mage or the traitor from inside the academy, it would be best if I was sturdy on my feet in a defensive position.

Both the birds and crickets had stopped chirping, and the only palpable sound was the forest breeze and the flow of the water in the nearby creek. Something was out there.

I waited, not taking any chances and turning my back to run.

Minutes ticked by until glowing orange eyes revealed themselves between two trees. As the eyes approached, black scales with iridescent white tips along a sleek little dragon body appeared. Though his body was a little larger than the size of a big fox, he was fierce and intimidating.

"Hey there, buddy." I held my hands outward in a non-threatening way. "Remember me?"

A growl rose from the little dragon, its lip pulled back, baring sharp white teeth. His nostrils flared and then he sneezed, a small flame firing out of his mouth and disappearing into tendrils of smoke. He visibly relaxed and crept closer.

"I won't hurt you." I shrugged. "Not that I truly think I could. I saw you with that dark mage."

A low grumble erupted from the dragon as if the mention of his foe upset him. He shook, his scales lifting as he did. Once he finished, he trotted over to me slowly and began sniffing my shoes, then my hands, hanging at my sides. His hot black nose brushed my palm, causing my finger to twitch. He jumped backward, poofing up like a cat before calming down.

"You're alright." I chuckled.

Those orange eyes regarded me a moment longer until the dragon trotted past me and into the forest on my other side. When I didn't trail him, he merely cocked his head over his shoulder at me.

"You want me to follow you?" I asked. A huff left the dragon's mouth, and I swore if dragons could roll their eyes, this one just had.

I followed the dragon through the forest until we reached a stream. The water was plenty high and shadows of fish below the surface zipped by. Despite it still being a frozen tundra on the outside of the dome, the nice weather in here allowed life to thrive. It had been this way for a century, the animals becoming accustomed to the magically controlled atmosphere.

The dragon dove in, water splashing, and emerged on the other side, landing on the bank. It looked over at me, fish in mouth. His nose lifted toward the sky and he swallowed the fish whole. With a giant leap, he took off, flying over the stream and landing next to me, standing on his hind feet so his large catlike eyes were level with mine.

I held my breath and waited. The dragon's pupils dilated and I relaxed. As I did, he cocked his head, more like a curious animal than one that was going to attack. I followed his movements, unsure of what he was trying to communicate. He settled back on all four feet. He curiously watched me before leaping into the water again.

I didn't think fire-breathing dragons would like water.

Chapter Forty

Selene

My head lolled back against the chair, giving me a glimpse of the beautiful, domed ceiling in the library, torchlight flickering across the shadows.

"Why did we have to get a packet of homework for Algebra on the first day?" Vivian's angry scrawling screeched against the papers as she wrote.

"You're already on the last two questions. I'm still on the first page!" April waved at her papers.

That didn't surprise me. Just like me, Vivian's studies with Mom had been advanced for the grade level we were in at Fives Academy.

"I could help you." Viv leaned closer to April. I couldn't see Vivian's face as she looked at April, but I could see the small tug on April's lip—until it vanished. They both jolted upright.

"Yeah." April cleared her throat. "Thanks, but I think I should try this on my own first."

Huh. *What was that about?* It had been clear to everyone here that they had feelings for each other. I'd have to talk to Viv later.

"Yeah." Sydney said. "I remember Professor Eaten. Good luck"

"Didn't I hear she eats sophomores alive?" David laughed.

"Yes." Sydney nodded, grinning. "Hence her name."

"She's not that bad so far." Denise swatted at an invisible fly. "If you don't mind watching others suffer."

"Just wait," Joseph said. "You haven't even had her for an entire week yet."

I tuned out the conversation, glancing at my last text to Ender. After training with Viv, I realized I had a missed call and a message that said everything was okay and that he would meet up with me. I sent him a message asking if he was meeting us at dinner, but he hadn't replied and never showed. After messing around in the halls and an hour in the library, I messaged him again. It had only been fifteen minutes since I'd told him where we were, yet I kept finding myself checking for a response. Sighing, I went to put my phone back in my pocket, but it buzzed before it got there.

SOS in the Kitchen. Just you ... please. **—Ender**

My internal alarm went off. Ender said please? It sounded like a trick he would pull, but the mild panic I felt argued otherwise.

"Hey, I'm going to go." I stood, putting my phone away as casually as possible. "I'll catch you all later."

"Mm-hmm," Sydney hummed. "Off to see your boyfriend?"

I raised a sole eyebrow at Sydney, and the others laughed.

"Goodbye." I waved, turning my back.

Once I reached the hallway and was out of sight, my walk picked up into a steady run.

The oak tables in the cafeteria were bare and there were no flames lit, the black stone ceiling making the vast space even darker. It was two hours past dinner, and I hadn't passed anyone on my way here. The majority of students were back at the dorms, gym, or in the library because it was a school night.

A small sound came from the kitchen, light creeping underneath the white-swirled marble door. Nothing in the academy building was conventional. I called my magic, its warmth tingling along my fingertips as I pushed open the surprisingly light door. The last time I had been on the other side of these doors was after the rock creature attack.

I stilled, standing straight as I disarmed my magic. My hand instantly went to my mouth to smother a laugh at the scene before me. Ender waved his hands while whisper-yelling at the black dragon, who was jumping from the racks hanging from the heightened ceiling. Pans clattered to the floor and Ender rubbed his hands down his face. The normally clean stone countertops and marble floor were littered with cutlery and dinnerware, and across the kitchen, the fridge doors hung wide open.

The dragon paused, looking back at me with what looked like a piece of chicken dangling from his mouth as the rack he dangled on swayed.

"What's going on?" I suppressed my laugh and swore the little dragon smiled at me.

"Good question." Ender sighed. "I found him trailing me on my run, but I left him in the forest. After I showered, I was on my way to find you, but the next thing I know, this little guy was following me again."

The dragon growled, as if he didn't like being called little.

"I see why you sent an SOS." I nodded at the mess. "This is why you missed dinner?"

"Yes. Then when he showed up outside the main building, I was trying to keep him hidden, but he kept trying to go find you—at least that was what I thought—until he found his way inside and found the kitchen."

Ender winced as a utensil clanked to the floor and the dragon turned himself around.

The dragon tilted his head back and swallowed his meal before leaping off the rack, landing on his feet and bounding over to me, sniffing at my feet with a low grumble before relaxing. He jumped, using his wings to guide himself, landing on my shoulder—which almost caused me to lose my balance—and nuzzling his cool scales into my neck. The weight on one shoulder was heavy, but his cool tail draped at the back of my neck and across my other shoulder mildly helped with dispersing his weight. Regardless, he was *not* meant to be a shoulder dragon like the Labrador Retriever in *Marley & Me* thought he was a lap dog...

It took a good five minutes of frozen shock as the dragon adjusted itself before I could even think about speaking, and given Ender's blatant stare and hanging jaw, he too was in shock.

"I didn't hear my phone earlier," I whispered, not wanting to disturb what appeared to be a now sleeping dragon, his body now wrapped around my neck from shoulder to shoulder and his tail dangling to my feet. My shoulders throbbed, but I didn't dare wake him.

"I figured as much." Ender looked around, finally taking his eyes off my new dragon scarf. "It is utter chaos in here."

"*Chaos.*" I grinned and stroked the dragon's chin, its body warming as it snuggled closer. "It suits you."

Chapter Forty-One

Selene

"You can't exactly keep him in your room," Ender called as I exited the kitchen and entered the cafeteria hall.

"Why can't I?" I paused, glancing at the still sleeping dragon on my shoulder. There was something about him that felt familiar.

"I doubt our teachers have ever seen a dragon. Imagine how the students will react." Ender came to stand in front of me, taking my hands in his. "It will not go over well with everything else going on. It may even put a bigger target on you." His touch was welcoming, and his contact sent warm vibrations to my core.

My brain spaced as I began thinking about how the touch of his cool hands burned and I almost forgot what we were talking about. *Dragon*. There was a dragon on my shoulder. A very *heavy* dragon. I blinked, collecting my thoughts. It was wild how Ender's simple touch could throw me off track.

Sydney wouldn't tell anyone, but he was right. There would be more disorder than what was left in the kitchen. Speaking of ... we'd have to clean it up so we wouldn't raise suspicion. I had just been about to leave, excited to bring Chaos to my room.

"Where did you say you found him in the woods?" I walked back into the kitchen, Ender seeming thankful I had stopped my hasty exit. As if on cue, Chaos woke and hopped off my shoulder, landing on the island.

Ender revisited his encounter as we started cleaning while Chaos ate another piece of chicken and watched us like a cat observing his servant humans clean up his mess.

Things cleaned up easily, seeing how the place had basically been created for ease of being wiped down. Our air magic helped with efficiency; it looked like a wizard shop with the utensils flying around in the air. Besides gathering the fallen utensils, pots, and pans, we had to scrub the sole trail of chicken Florentine from the fridge to the island. Something about doing something so trivial with Ender squeezed my heart—in a good way.

Chaos eventually perched himself back on my shoulders and slept quietly during the rest of our magical cleaning frenzy. I would need to do shoulder workouts if this was going to be a habit. Once everything was back to how it was, besides the missing chicken, we left.

"What if someone is looking out their window?" I stared at the exit to the courtyard, now suddenly nervous to leave the cafeteria. We had agreed to take him back out to the woods where Ender had found him.

"Here." Ender grabbed the hem of his T-shirt and pulled it over his head, revealing those smooth abs that took me entirely too long to look away from. "Wrap this over your shoulders."

"Umm... I don't think Chaos will want to don your sweaty shirt, nor will it cover all of him." I took the fabric between my pointer and thumb, holding it out as if it was contaminated. "What makes you think *I* would want to wear your sweaty shirt?"

"Hmm." Ender flashed me a smile. "Here I thought you would want my sweat on you?"

I blushed. He was too much with his stupid grin and naked abs.

"Fine." I draped his black T-shirt over Chaos's body, causing him to stir in his sleep. The majority of the fabric covered him, but it did nothing to conceal the end of his tail sprawling down my chest. It'd have to do. "Let's go."

We snuck across the courtyard. No one was out on this beautiful night, and the shining stars reminded me of the white speckles on Chaos's scales. The monotonous temperatures—besides the few scheduled rain and snow days—were getting tediously boring. We at least had storms on the island.

Something hit one of my tightly knotted buns, and it took me a moment to realize it was Chaos unraveling himself. A low growl emitted from him as he leapt onto the grass and prowled in the direction of the library.

"Chaos!" I whispered, grabbing Ender's shirt, which had fallen, before giving chase. "No! Come back."

"Good luck with that." Ender huffed, picking up his pace. "He doesn't listen well."

"You can't go in there!" I reached for Chaos, but he evaded my grasp. Slippery little fellow. I couldn't use any magic on him—it would ruin the trust we had just built.

Using more command in my voice, I tried again. "Chaos. Stop."

This time, the little black dragon turned abruptly. His narrow nose was in the air, sniffing, but in the direction of the dorms. A sneeze came from the dragon before he looked back at the library. He twirled once, sniffing the ground, and plopped his belly down before looking at me. One glance at Ender told me he was just as confused.

"Did you decide to listen to me, or did you lose whatever scent you had?" I knelt next to Chaos and stroked the top of his head, trailing down to his body. His neck was long and narrow, and his hard scales were smoother than expected. He chirped, and based on the complacent closing of his eyes, that told me it was a happy noise.

A door clicked shut somewhere and laughter floated on the night air. The courtyard was empty, but that didn't mean for long. Ender nodded at me and we strode toward the gym—away from the dorms.

Chaos followed contently until we veered off from the gym, and he seemed to realize we were going in the woods. He flew to a nearby lone tree and sat on his rump.

"Hey!" I waved him down. "What are you doing up there? We need to keep you hidden and away from the main part of the campus."

The dragon stuck his chin in the air, like a queen on a throne, and Ender laughed.

"Someone's stubborn," I mumbled.

"Much like someone I know," Ender commented. I whirled to face him, and he held his hands up. "I didn't say who that someone was."

I rolled my eyes and faced the dragon. "Do you not want to go for a walk?"

Chaos chuffed, not making eye contact. *Okay. Let's try again.*

"Do you want to go back to your spot in the woods?"

Another chuff.

"Do you want to stay here at the academy with me?"

Chaos gave me some serious side-eye but did not chuff. I turned to Ender. "It looks like he knows what he wants."

"Yeah." Ender studied the dragon. "I can see that. He's a smart creature."

"So it's settled." I rubbed my palms together. "He will stay in my dorm room, and we will tell Syd." Ender merely looked at me, and I knew it was a foolish plan. "What? Do you have any other ideas to get him down and on board with going into the woods?"

"Yes!" Sydney shouted as Chaos blew fire from his mouth, chasing the short burst of fire that had come from Sydney's palm. My palm tingled slightly with magic as I created water, dousing their flames and creating steam before it had a chance to create smoke.

"Knock it off before you two burn down the west dorms." I waved a hand in the air, dispersing the steam.

"You still think having him in your room is a good idea?" Ender raised an eyebrow at me.

I gave him a small shove with my elbow. Instead of that pushing him away, he stepped closer—and I couldn't help the small trill inside me as my arm brushed against his now covered stomach.

"What? This is the best idea ever!" Sydney moved her exuberant gaze off Chaos and to me. "Why didn't you tell me about him sooner? You can't keep a dragon hidden from a fire mage!"

Sydney had arrived shortly after we did. At first, all she noticed was that Ender and I were alone in the room; that was, until we stepped aside, revealing Chaos. I explained we had just been made aware of his sudden arrival, and after Sydney's initial awestruck dialed down so she could speak, the little dragon and she hit it off quickly. All it took was a dancing fireball from Sydney, and Chaos decided it was playtime.

After filling Syd in and getting Chaos acquainted, Ender left—having to sneak up to his room. He would have been in trouble for entering a girl's room, especially because it was so late. I made Chaos a makeshift bed in the closet, but the little dragon insisted on curling up next to me, his tail tapping with contentment over my face.

Hiding him was going to be a challenge, and I wondered if telling John would be easier. Dragons were known nemeses to dark mages—I didn't see him objecting to having one around, and he already met him in Singapore.

Then again, *my father* had kept a huge secret from me.

Time to play hide the dragon.

Chapter Forty-Two

Selene

Coaxing the little dragon into staying in my room did not go well.

Chaos defiantly held up his head, purposely glaring off to the side when I told him he had to stay put. I promised him that if he was a good boy, I would take him for a run at dusk. He had chuffed at me again but didn't move, so I took that as something.

The day would tell.

Ender met me at my room as promised and escorted me to first period. I had skipped breakfast, not wanting to leave Chaos any longer than necessary. The first two classes dragged, and in third period study hall, I sat near the window, keeping an eye on the dorms.

"You're not in your normal spot." David sat at the desk in front of me, turning so he faced me.

"Just needed a change of scenery," I lied. The window seats were closer to the front of the classroom—I always preferred staying near the back and near an exit.

"The window seat is definitely an upgrade, though it might have made someone upset." David glanced toward the other side of the room, and I followed his gaze. I couldn't remember her name, but she was in a few of my classes. She was staring at me but glanced down at her notebook, her fear almost palpable when my gaze met hers.

"I didn't mean to take her seat," I mumbled, feeling slightly guilty—not for taking her seat; that's inconsequential—for the obvious fear she had of me.

"Nah. I wouldn't worry about it." David smiled, giving me view of his dimples. "Oh. I got something for you." He turned around, grabbing a book from the bottom of the stack on his desk. "I found this."

He set a book on my desk. Its cover was black leather with gold etching the edges. It was untitled and lacked an author's name.

"What is it?" I stroked the old leather. Something about it *felt* foreboding. My finger moved to the flap to open it, but David covered my hand with his gloved hand, stopping me.

"I wouldn't open it here." He glanced around before moving his hand. Goosebumps rose along my arm when the skin of his exposed wrist brushed me when he pulled away. "It's an old grimoire that belonged to a lineage of dark mages."

He grabbed my useless English textbook and placed on top of the leather-bound book, concealing it.

"How..." I gave him a questioning look—how did he know I had been searching for this type of information?

"I pay attention. Sometimes." He lightheartedly chuckled. "You've been searching for anything on dark mages since you arrived."

"Where did you find it?" I had searched the entire library.

"Let's just say I got bored while you were gone." David's smile turned mockingly mischievous, then solemn. "I wanted to find out more about the control of my abilities and if there is anything naturally dark about fire magic. I heard about a basement below the library with forbidden books and figured it wouldn't hurt to look. I saw the book and knew it was something you should see—you know, after the dark mage attack and all. I should have given it to you sooner, but I had hidden it in my closet and forgot it was in there. It would have made for an interesting Christmas gift."

"You went in the basement?" I leaned forward, keeping our conversation quiet though no one appeared to be listening. "Wouldn't it be locked?"

"I know a few things. Plus, I don't think they take the security of the basement seriously." David's brows furrowed. "You don't seem shocked about the academy having a basement."

It had sounded like John took the security of the basement *very* seriously. Maybe something was tampering with the enchantments again, but how did I tell John without getting David into trouble?

"Did you..." I wasn't sure how to ask if he saw ginormous, venomous demonic rats. "... see anything?"

"Yes." His eyes widened. "An abundance of dusty books and an exorbitant amount of stairs to climb back up. Descending had been less strenuous."

I rolled my eyes but also understood. It was a lot of stairs—that's why we didn't have time to take them when Ender and I were running for our lives.

"Your expression is telling me you've been there?" David asked.

"Yes." I nodded. "It was uneventful, but I ran out of time."

David didn't seem to buy it, as he slowly shook his head.

"Yeah," he said. "I will be shamefully honest—it's quite spooky and I didn't last long."

Someone moved to the desk next to him.

"Hi, David." The student smiled, and David gave her a polite nod and gave me a knowing look.

"Too bad you don't have that delicious liquid courage this time," I said, remembering the Halloween party we'd gone to right after we'd each arrived. Though, this time, I welcomed the conversation. I was curious and David had become a friend.

"That is certainly too bad." He gave me a wink before turning to the girl, who had still been talking. I applauded him for his inability to be rude, even when it was apparent he didn't want to have a conversation with her. I was positive that had to be the contributing factor as to why the girls wanted his attention—it couldn't have been because of the *he offed his parents* rumor.

I clutched the grimoire closely to my chest and walked to my locker. I tasted the bitterness seeping from it, unequivocally justifying why it was locked away in the basement. It sent chills down my spine.

A bright white rose was elegantly taped to my locker, complete with a tasteful black ribbon tied in a bow. I leaned in, taking in its fresh floral scent, but another aroma was hidden amongst its pedals and stem. An earthy oil scent?

Exciting awareness alerted me before I felt Ender's breath against the bare skin on my neck.

He took a slow, deep breath through his nose. "The smell of roses and sandalwood. And a rare, beautiful rose. Like you."

I turned to face him. He held a bouquet of white roses, his hazel eyes entrapping my gaze, making my heart flutter. This was a new gesture. A man had never brought me flowers—though there had never been any men in my life before Fives. He had matched my scent—according to him.

"What professor did you charm to have these made, or have you been practicing?" I asked jokingly. In time, he would be able to create them himself. They were the rarest natural occurring rose—blue was the rarest, but they did not grow by natural occurrence.

"Charm?" He gave his best one-sided grin. "I don't have any of that."

I laughed. If it hadn't been him giving me the roses, I would've been uncomfortable. Instead, him knowing my scent did something wild to me.

I shifted the books I held, needing to unlock my locker. His gaze dropped to the books, his lips instantly turning down. The imaginary enamored bubble surrounding us popped, overtaken by questions and fear.

He glowered at the book. "What is that and why does it feel like death?"

"It's a grimoire from a dark mage line." I finished opening my locker so I could shove the books inside. "David gave it to me."

I felt Ender's anger as I shut the door, hoping to leave the stagnant, dreadful feeling emitting from the book.

"Why would he give you that?" He scowled, the flowers still in his hand. Somehow, he looked dangerous when upset ... and hot. *Ugh.*

"Because he knew I was looking into dark mages. I assume after the attack and when everyone found out what I was, he understood why I was looking, even if he doesn't know about my mom." I shrugged. "He probably thinks I'm just trying to defend myself against dark mages but not the entire story."

Ender physically relaxed, but I could still *feel* his anger. He didn't like that I had been given a dangerous book. It didn't need to even be opened to know it held dark secrets.

"Be careful, Selene." He stepped closer, the flowers creating a small barrier between us. "That book doesn't feel right."

"I know." I swallowed. "But it might have answers that could help prevent someone else from dying."

His expression lightened and he wrapped me in a hug, careful of the flowers and protecting me from getting prodded by the thorns. I sighed, leaning into his chest. He understood.

He pressed a light kiss to my forehead as he handed me the flowers and left, heading to the men's locker room. It was too bad I couldn't follow him.

Chapter Forty-Three

Selene

In my training session, no one wanted to spar with me. Head Trainer Murphy moved Vivian into my group, and Priscilla was going to work with us.

Mage lights floated in the air surrounding the training field. The sun was setting even though it was only two o'clock in the afternoon. They illuminated the area well, but I wouldn't be surprised if training would be moved to the gym next week. It was the start of an eight-week snow period this weekend.

Priscilla gave Viv and me the go-ahead and we started our match. We trained just like we had at home on the beach, not holding much back but staying in control of our magic and bodies. The students knew our levels now, and that I was ether, so there was no point in hiding it. That felt good.

Viv knew how I fought—the product of training with each other since we could walk—so it was a fun fight. We started our fights without magic; something about a good fight with no magic soothed my soul. It reminded me of the time with Ender in the gym. I had needed to get my frustrations out that day. It had been when Miss Lee had come after me with her vines, and after that, I'd had that breakdown in front of Ender, so it had been therapeutic.

I kept my magic at a lower level, knowing it could be dangerous. It took more focus to create smaller fires than explosive ones. The day had been exhausting, and I didn't like the adjustment from break. Though I had friends, I knew a lot of the other kids considered me a dangerous, unknown liability.

"Good work," Priscilla said when the timer finished.

Head Trainer Murphy popped over to speak with Priscilla before heading back over to her group. She called out Ender and David's name next. I tensed. I doubt Ender would take anything out on David for giving me the book, but a small part of me was apprehensive.

I caught sight of Gwen and Nick at the other match. He frowned and whispered something to her. I wondered if it was about the match. If I was closer, I might've been able to make out what they were saying.

"Ender and David are going against each other?" Viv took a swig of water.

I didn't say anything.

"Oh, that'll be good." April came over, pointing at the other training match, and Viv gave her a shove. "What? They're both good fighters. It'll be good for David to fight someone with power and skill. He could use it."

I tried to focus on the next set of girls to fight, but my gaze kept wandering to Ender and David. It had been a minute of back-and-forth sparring with no magic yet. It was clear I wasn't the only one watching them. The majority of the students in my group kept glancing over at the match, hushed whispers and appreciation in their eyes.

The sparring picked up, and I wondered how David was going to fight with his gloves on. I hadn't seen him fight yet.

"Now that's hot." Sydney came over, nodding in the direction of the other match. April gave a light smack to the back of her head. "What? I'm just repeating what I heard while walking over here."

"Did you find your shorts?" I asked Sydney, who knew very well I wasn't asking about her shorts.

"Yes. Right where I had left them." It had been Sydney's turn to check on the contraband hiding in our room.

"It's nice to see you're back in time for the last fifteen minutes of training." April gave Syd a disapproving dip of her head.

David sent a quick kick at Ender's stomach—a kick I barely registered—and Ender only deflected part of the blow. He didn't show if the kick had phased him as he spun into David, taking him to the ground. Hoots and hollers came from the students surrounding them but ceased once Ender stood, his shirt in flames.

How?

David, his hands still gloved, pushed himself off the grass.

Ender grasped the hem of his shirt, his air magic helping snuff out the flames as he moved, and dragged it over his chest, heaving it to the side. Smoke trailed from the material on the ground as the sparring continued.

"David's been holding out on us," Sydney commented.

"Not holding out, but holding back," I corrected. Level fours could use their element on any part of their skin. The rumors of David's power had been accurate. "Remember the dark mage he incinerated?"

"Right," was all Sydney said as her gaze never left the match.

Tension prickled at the base of my neck, and I rubbed at it. Something dark flicked in Ender's eyes as he stepped away from David, momentarily faltering. His gaze flashed to me, and I narrowed my eyes in question, but he didn't acknowledge my gesture. Internally, I reached for our subtle but growing connection, but there was nothing.

Ender was panting, like he was battling to get control of himself. In the momentary distraction, David's elbow collided with his face, whipping Ender's head to the side.

"Watch it, David!" Trainer Murphy shouted from the edge of the circle. Face shots were not allowed.

"Sorry, mate." David held his hands up in an apologetic motion.

Ender straightened, his nostrils flared and his dark gaze locked onto David, whose eyes widened. Panic set low in my stomach. That look ... Ender never had that look, even when we fought dark mages.

The ground shook. Ender's own fire whipped from his hands and sailed toward David. David dropped, dodging the fire missiles that struck dirt and grass, sending them up in flames. Ender hadn't been able to wield fire like that. Priscilla's full attention was now on the match next to us—everyone's attention was.

All the students were about to learn they now had two ether mages enrolled at their academy.

David scrambled on the ground, getting his feet under him, but an invisible force knocked him back down. *Wind*. It held him there as Ender climbed on top of him.

"Ender!" Priscilla shouted and stepped toward the pair, but he shoved out a hand, pushing her back with a rush of category three hurricane winds. That was a warning to stay out, but for added measure, the winds continued swirling around them. Trainer Murphy tried to cross the wind barrier, but her arm was wrenched backward and Flame hopped off her opposing shoulder and to the ground.

Beyond the swirling gusts, I could see Ender raising his fist and striking David, who reached out, hands fumbling over Ender's bare chest and neck.

Ender was not going to stop.

I rushed forward, putting my hands up to the wind barrier. Attempting to create my own barrier, I sliced into Ender's wind, only to get thrown to the side.

"Sal!" Vivian ran to my aid, helping me up.

"That didn't work." I straightened myself.

"Obviously, Sherlock." Viv rolled her eyes.

I was powerful. I should be able to break through if I attempted again and tried another method, but the way Ender was not letting up on his assault told me there wasn't time. I closed my eyes, reaching for the bond he and I shared. A small fluorescent string trailed into a bright abyss. I reached for it, mentally tugging on it.

Ender, I whispered to myself more than anything. *Let me in.*

I opened my eyes. Ender had his arm cocked in the air, but he didn't bring it down. The small hurricane surrounding them had lessened ever so slightly. Had he heard me?

I'm coming to you, I mentally said but immediately felt embarrassed and was glad no one could hear my thoughts. The soul-bond must help us deduce our intentions through our feelings.

Cautiously, I edged closer to the gusts and began making my way through the storm, wind grating against my skin and own magic. Inside, Ender had retreated, standing as far as he could from David, who lay still on the ground.

"Ender?" I reached for him, putting a hand on his heaving chest. His revulsion of his actions and confusion ached in my own bones. "You're okay."

His eyes finally met mine, wide with disbelief and horror. He glanced back at David. Beating him to a pulp in an unprovoked training match was anything but his normal.

The storm surrounding us ceased; the training field had gone completely silent. His expression became indecipherable as he stepped away and turned toward the woods, all emotions pouring from him cutting off.

"Ender." I started to follow but he held up a hand.

"I need a moment." He continued, not really walking or running, more of a speed walk—if there was such a thing as a graceful speed walk.

My brain knew I needed to respect his space, but my heart wanted to race after him. I went to move in his direction, but Priscilla strode past, motioning me to stay while also giving me the universal nod that meant *I got him*. At least that was what I thought the tilt of her head meant.

So I stayed, watching him retreat into the woods and ignoring the pain in my chest and the alarmed gazes on both of our backs.

Chapter Forty-Four

Selene

It had been a little over an hour since the fight. My stomach grumbled, echoing across the empty triage room. The protests my stomach put up didn't match my actual appetite, and it was furious I had skipped on a predinner snack to head to the infirmary. I stared at a majesty palm tree across the room. It, unlike many of the other trees sprouting from the academy's floors, grew from a ceramic planting pot. Its long silk leaves fluttered in the absence of a breeze as if it felt the scrutiny of my stare.

"Sorry," I mumbled to it like it understood. Ender's break in restraint and control during his match with David was aberrant. I glanced at the closed door, which Nurse Adair was most likely treating David.

Taking a deep breath, I rubbed my temples and sighed, then rested my arms on the metal armrests of the green shamrock chair I was sitting in. The space was grotesque, with sleek white marble floors, white walls, and two medical chairs for triage that matched the vibrant green exam room chairs. It was migraine-inducing compared to the dark ambience of the rest of the academy—excluding the kitchen.

Thud. Thud. Thud.

I straightened, glancing at the back of the room, where the nurse's office was enclosed by a glass wall. Surprise froze me, and then I abruptly kicked into action. I made my way to the glass door, which was thankfully unlocked, and through the standard-sized office.

The floor-to-ceiling window cracked open with ease, and hot dragon breath instantly greeted me as his long, sharp white claws gripped the sill.

"Chaos," I hissed. "What are you doing here?" Thankfully the infirmary windows faced the woods on the southwest side of the academy, but if someone happened to look just right from the gym...

"Sorry!" Sydney whisper-shouted, out of breath, as she caught up to Chaos. "He was sitting on your bed one minute, made a displeasing noise, and was slithering out the window and flying over here. Thank the entire academy and my well-being, no one has seen him, but I'm sure the other students thought I was crazy, running and yelling at the sky." She wiped the sweat from her forehead. "He's fast."

"You have to stay hidden." I shook my head at Chaos, thankful it was already dark despite the days supposedly getting longer.

He chuffed in my face, dampening my cheeks. His worry for my raised adrenaline and increased anxiety was clear.

"I'm fine," I responded.

He let out a low, grumbling chortle.

"I know. But you can't expose yourself, Chaos. *You* will cause chaos," I warned.

"You speak dragon?" Sydney open-mouth stared between the two of us.

"No." *Not really.* "I'm picking up on his noises and emotions." That was the truth or, if not, close to it. Just like I had with Ender... *I think*?

"Aww." Sydney let her mouth close. "He did seem upset. When I got back to our room after ... the match ... he seemed a little distraught, but I was able to calm him."

Chaos nudged my chest with the hard scales on the top of his head, his sharp opaque horns avoiding me. I ran a hand down the smooth scales along his neck, reassuring him. They reminded me of tungsten: strong, beautiful, and glossy black with opaque white speckles. It would take something strong and sharp—or the blade made specifically for dragons—to pierce through them.

"You need to head back, Chaos." I glanced out the window, making sure the coast was still clear. "We'll go for a long walk tonight."

He dropped his head and shook it side to side.

"We can share my Flaming Hot Cheetos?" Sydney offered with a small grin, her eyes betraying the sadness in surrendering her beloved snack. We had learned that not only did he enjoy meat, but he loved snacks. I had no clue what havoc Cheetos and potato chips would have on his stomach, but he loved them, and if they got him out of here, then so be it.

Chaos swiveled his neck to look at Sydney, snuffed, then turned back to me in a clear *no*.

"Fine." Syd's shoulders dropped. "You can have *all* of them."

That got Chaos's attention. He raised his head, chirped, and turned to face her but didn't give her the affection he clearly showed me.

I cocked my head at Sydney, raising a brow.

"What?" She pursed her lips. "I can learn to move beyond sharing and give the most precious, cheesiest, crunchiest snack to a dear friend." She leaned in closer, her eyes narrowing. "You didn't tell me Ender was ether!"

"That wasn't for me to tell."

"Fine. Fine." She turned on her heels. "Alright, fiery dragon. Let's go."

I watched them retreat until Chaos bounced and took off in the air, Sydney hollering after him and trying to keep up. Shaking my head, I closed the window and turned, resting against the glass. I needed to get out of the office in case someone entered.

Moving quietly, I was careful not to knock over the various plants, each having their own medical purposes. I recognized aloe, which was great when a student accidentally burned themself or another student. Thyme and parsley weren't only for cooking but helped create antibacterial and antifungal tonics; and sage, which helped with inflammation, arthritis, and gout—the latter was hopefully one the students wouldn't be diagnosed with.

I made my way back to the chair. No sooner than my butt hit the cushion than the door to room two opened. Nurse Adair's tall, lean frame filled the short, wide hallway, clipboard in hand. He was in his late twenties, with auburn hair and green eyes. He came from a strong line of earth mages. April idolized him. Due to earth mage enchantments, herbs, and elixirs, level 4 and higher mages could be trained to be magnificent healers. The previous Nurse, Helen... or Hulga... something like that ... took him on as an apprentice while he was just a sophomore. He was her prime protégé to help care for the academy after her demise.

When he saw me, he tucked the chart under his arm, giving me a warm smile.

"Ms. Thomas." He nodded as I stood. "Are you feeling alright?"

"Yes." I glanced at the partially shut door behind him. "How is he?"

"David is doing well." There was a pause as he assessed me, no doubt checking for any injuries from walking through Ender's hurricane or from my own match. The head trainer had most likely filled him in. "Would you like to see him?" He asked after he must have assessed I was uninjured.

"Please." I nodded.

The crowd on the training field had been instructed by John to leave. April, Denise, and Joseph wanted to go with David to the infirmary, but the headmaster informed them no one was allowed to go, and they could visit him after he'd been treated. I overheard him telling them, but

I snuck away anyways. The others besides Sydney and Ender didn't know John was family to me and Viv, and Sydney had promised to not tell April. Not that he would have excused me to go to the infirmary because I was his daughter...

Adair stepped aside, gesturing toward the door. "I'm sure he will be elated to see you."

I nodded and silently walked past him.

After three small knocks on the door, I quietly pushed it open.

"Sal." David sat up but groaned and pressed a hand to his temple.

"Don't sit up!" I rushed to his side, helping him settle back down.

"I'm fine." He waved me off with a gloved hand. "Nurse Adair's medicine is magic. Literally."

"Wow." I studied his face, swollen and with hues of green and blue around both eyes, nose, and cheeks. His face should have still been red with signs of bruises forming, but they appeared to be a couple days old. My mom had taught me many things, healing elixirs included, but nothing on this level. Nurse Adair had a talent for healing, I'd give him that.

"Yeah. If I'd known how good his elixirs were, I would have faked a couple injuries after training to help with hangovers." David's blue eyes perked up with his joke.

"You haven't had hangovers." I narrowed my eyes accusingly. I'd never seen him with a hangover, and I saw him almost daily at lunch and dinner.

"You're wise." He laughed, immediately wincing after.

"I believe, last time, you referred to your drink as horrid," I jested.

"I absolutely did." He smiled, but it didn't reach his eyes like it just had.

I swallowed, not knowing what to say. I had wanted to make sure he was okay on behalf of being his friend and for Ender. Now that I saw he was okay, I was ready to leave.

"How is Ender?" He asked, his features turned downward, not in anger but in concern.

"Umm." The truth was that I didn't know. A small part of me felt disgust, sorrow, and bitterness at the incident, but two of those were not *my* feelings. "I haven't seen him yet."

That was the truth.

David nodded, glancing down at his stark black gloves that contrasted with the white sheet of the hospital-style bed.

"Sal." The serious tone in his voice caused me to still and abruptly look up at him. He was about to ask something personal or have an emotional conversation. I wasn't prepared for either. He took a moment to collect himself, slowly sitting up. "I know Ender is in a fragile state."

"What?" I said out loud.

David searched my eyes for a moment. "Most of the academy hadn't known he was ether, and the others that were at the cafeteria that day might not have seen anything, but I saw the way the dark mage tried to siphon his magic. They can only do that with ether mages."

Viv had learned that same day as me what Ender was, but no one else had said anything. They either didn't see what had happened with all the destruction and disorder or had chosen to be quiet. Sydney hadn't known at all.

"It didn't look like he knew." David's tone dropped. Sadness. Understanding. "Going through that change and learning about that power mentally and physically takes a toll."

We stared at each other for a moment. I never said that David wasn't smart, but he was just as vigilant as I was.

"I don't want that to happen to me."

The grief and fear in his eyes tugged at me. I felt his pain. Ender felt his pain. We had a powerful, destructive magic. But it could be beautiful too.

"It won't," I said.

He gave me a grim smile. "Thank you for helping me learn to control it."

"No problem."

Chapter Forty-Five
Selene

It was late that same night. I couldn't sleep. Sydney couldn't sleep. And Ender hadn't wanted to see me tonight. So I opted to skim through the dark grimoire.

The moment I had partially uncovered the grimoire, Chaos's scales rose along his long neck, steam emitting from his mouth as he hissed. The book radiated a sickly feeling to the point that Sydney had retrieved a thick cloth for preserving books. It didn't just preserve books. It dulled the effects of this one.

"It's okay, Chaos," I said in a soothing voice. "It gives us the creeps too, but I need to read it to help find the dark mage clan that killed my mom and is after me."

Sydney finally knew about Mom. I just had finished telling her a brief summary of how we ended up here. After Ender and I got back from Singapore, I had told her John was my father, but I didn't indulge in the exact *how* we got here and our upbringing, just that we lost our mom and he had found us. She had sat there and listened... and it appeared Chaos had also.

The little dragon hunkered down, and I wondered if he was more sensitive to the effects of the grimoire.

"I agree, Chaos," Sydney said from her desk. "I don't like that big black book either." Her gaze shifted to me. "Should I take him for another walk?"

"I think he would like that." Even though I had just taken him for a short stroll through the woods, he always had energy. And this late, even the stragglers I'd seen wouldn't be out. This tiny dorm room wasn't doing him any good. I'd have to figure out something soon. "But he might need some convincing to go."

Chaos was still hunkered down, his eyes in narrow slits as his glare pierced the book.

After some convincing—and potato chips—Chaos left with Sydney.

Finally free of hot dragon breath and death glares, I opened the grimoire, immediately becoming entranced by its contents. Its pages were thick but fragile, with a little amount of dust coating the edges. I frowned. The basement had a preservation spell to protect its belongings. I imagined the dust had to have come with the book prior to its arrival at the academy. Viv would've made some comment regarding how old this dust must have been if she were with me.

But she didn't need to touch or be near this book. I didn't even let Sydney get close to it.

The majority of the grimoire was in a language I didn't recognize, which was upsetting. After flipping through some pages, I found a couple words in Latin that stuck out. *Circulus obscurus*. The Dark Circle. Translating took some time, as I wasn't as fluent in Latin as I was French or Spanish. And I really hoped I wouldn't have to speak any of this.

A section on the first page had a few Latin words with reference to a clan called The Dark Circle. Its members wore a dark circle on their palm, indicating some sort of link between them. The clan leader's name wasn't mentioned, just that they had been powerful and had been a level four ether mage in their previous life.

My dorm room door flew open, Chaos barging in with Sydney pressed against the doorframe, her hand resting on the handle. He jumped into the air, using his back claws to grab the grimoire from my hand. The grimoire dropped to the floor and fire spewed out of Chaos's mouth at the leather-bound book.

"Chaos!" I shouted, jumping off my bed. "What are you doing?"

I spared a glance at Sydney, but she just shrugged. "He was very adamant about coming back."

The flames disappeared, leaving a burnt circle around the unharmed grimoire. The smell of burnt fibers filled the room, leaving me astonished that an alarm hadn't gone off. I grabbed the cloth and tossed it over the book, not wanting to grab it until it cooled off.

Chaos growled at the book, but I was able to coax him away now that the cloth was over it. Once enough time had passed that I felt the book was no longer scalding, I tucked it safely away under my bed. Surprisingly, the fibers of the cloth had not been singed. The book was truly evil.

Chapter Forty-Six

Ender

That wasn't me.

That was what I told myself for the millionth time throughout the night. That was what Priscilla had told me and what Selene would have told me if I hadn't avoided her after the fight yesterday. I had control of my magic. Very good control.

I sat upright, no longer able to stare at the ceiling in my dorm room. Nick had checked in on me last night and offered me space, which I appreciated. I was sure he appreciated it too, as it gave him an excuse to sneak into Gwen's room and stay with her.

My pajamas were soaked in sweat, and I decided to shower. Nothing would help the blame I carried for the extensive punches I had thrown at David, but a shower was a good place to wash off last night's sleepless sweat. Nick had said David was being treated by Nurse Adair and would make a full recovery. I would have to find David today and apologize.

The shower was cold. I spent extra time under the water. I grabbed a pair of joggers and a T-shirt, thankful it was Saturday.

Not that I would have attended classes today.

Someone knocked hard at my door as I finished pulling the hem of my shirt down. I opened the door, expecting to see either Selene or Priscilla, but it was Guard Taylor. He had escorted us to and from the academy when we went to Dominica. I recognized the majority of the guards but wasn't familiar with all their names, as they didn't typically introduce themselves or wear a name badge.

"The headmaster would like you to meet him in his office." He stared at me.

"Now?"

He nodded and left, not waiting for me.

Okay. I thought he had delivered the message because he was my escort, but he was already gone.

Sighing, I threw on a pair of sneakers and headed to the main building, keeping my head down. At eight in the morning, not many students were out. The sun wouldn't rise for a few more hours and the paths were lit by mage lights.

One knock and I walked into Headmaster John's office, the door already cracked open. He sat behind his desk, going through papers. Priscilla wasn't present, which surprised me. She had followed me into the forest last night, but I had asked to be alone when our conversation had gone nowhere—much from my own doing.

"Have a seat." The headmaster waved to a chair. Once I sat, he shoved a piece of paper in front of me. From her spot on the corner of his desk, Aura stirred slightly. "You are receiving a formal write-up for your actions and behavior yesterday. This is your first formal write-up since enrolling at Fives Academy. Three results in expulsion and losing a diploma. If an action of this type occurs again, you will not receive two more write-ups. You will be directly dismissed from the academy. Do you understand what this write-up is for?"

Nodding, I stared at the paper but did not read any of the words. I could be the occasional burden to the staff at Fives but never had received a formal disciplinary action.

"Good," Headmaster John continued. "Now is your chance to tell me what happened and give your side of the events yesterday."

I swallowed. David did not deserve what I had done. I should never have lost control like that.

The headmaster gave a curt nod at my silence and placed a pen on top of the paper. "You need to sign the bottom of the paper with today's date. You will attend detention with Professor Eaten in place of training the next two weeks," he said. I stole a quick glance at him. His features were stern, but the edges of his eyes were softening. "By signing this, you agree and take accountability for your actions."

"Yes." I cleared my scratchy throat. "I accept any and all consequences for my actions."

After I signed the paper, he crossed his hands on the desk in front of him. "Ender. If there is anything you would like to tell me, please know that you are always able to."

He didn't prod for information, which most likely meant he knew Priscilla hadn't gotten anywhere with me. There was nothing to say. I was disgusted with myself.

The door opened and Selene walked through without a warning knock. Her pants had many pockets, which differed from the leggings and jeans the other female students wore, and her loose T-shirt looked beautiful on her.

It made me internally smile—*she* made me smile.

"Selene." Headmaster John dropped his voice to a scolding tone. "We are currently in a meeting."

"Yes. I know." She took up residence in the seat next to me as the headmaster sighed. "Please continue."

The headmaster sat back in his chair. Warmth encased my hand and I glanced down to see Selene's hand over mine.

"Ender shouldn't be kicked out of the academy. He's idolized by many of his peers. This behavior was an isolated event and will not happen again. I believe that with everything happening and his magic emerging, it—"

"Sal," her father interrupted. "He is not being dismissed from the academy." His gaze moved to me. "Not unless it happens again."

She let out an audible sigh.

"Is there anything else, Headmaster?" I asked before she could begin rambling again. My heart warmed at the thought of her fighting for me to stay at the academy.

"No." He waved toward the door. "You are excused."

I stood, Selene following suit. Her presence had taken off some of the weight on my chest.

"Sal," the headmaster called when we reached the door. "Meet me tomorrow morning. There are some things we need to discuss."

Chapter Forty-Seven

Selene

Chaos blended surprisingly well with the bare treetops, dark sky, and fluffy snowflakes falling from the sky. In less than thirty seconds, he was no longer in view as he took off to stretch his wings, leaving Ender and me on the ground. We typically didn't run into guards when we went on our runs and hoped we wouldn't now with Chaos.

The fresh snow crunched beneath our boots—mine compliments of the snow attire in my closet, the sizing based on the forms filled out upon on arrival. Sunday wasn't until tomorrow, but the snow had begun to fall this afternoon, leaving a couple inches for our post-dinner Saturday night walk. Our plan was for Viv to meet Chaos somewhere other than my dorm room. She and Sydney were going to meet us shortly.

Ender swung an arm around me, pulling me in close as we walked, Chaos somewhere in the sky above. The moon wasn't full, but it lit our path up enough for us to see.

"You seem to be feeling better," I commented.

Ender's steps barely faltered, but it was enough to know I might have made that notation entirely too soon. It had only been a little over twenty-four hours since his incident with David and just this morning was his talk with my dad. "I suppose taking our dragon for a fly would make you most happy," I added, trying to deflect.

"*Our* dragon?" The corners of his eyes crinkled as he smiled. "Is Selene Thomas saying that we share parentage?"

I couldn't help the ugly, short burst of laughter that escaped. "Don't let him hear that. He might think you're implying he's a pet."

"Pets are family." Ender pulled me closer. "Well, he is a mama's boy. He only listens to you."

"Mama's boy?" I laughed. "And listens to me? Yeah, right." I waved off his false statement.

He grinned as we continued walking. The stars glistened above and it took me a solid minute to spot Chaos in the distance.

"Has that book helped with your hunt for the dark mage after you?" Ender pulled back to look at me.

"Uh, not really." My stomach turned inward. "Just minor things regarding the dark mages' mark with their clan and that they have a powerful, no-name leader."

"The mark links them," Ender said, not as a question.

"How do you know that?"

"The copy Priscilla and the headmaster have is probably from the book you have." Ender stopped walking. "They met with me and gave me information about the clan with the dark circle because it's the same clan that killed my parents. It's the same clan after you. I assume that's why the headmaster wants to meet with you tomorrow, to relay what information they have."

"I'm sorry." I swallowed. "It hadn't crossed my mind that the clan after me—and now most likely you—is the same one that had done that to your parents."

"Neither had it crossed mine."

The link regarding the dark clan's mark had been in the dark grimoire, which I had marginally been able to decipher. The revelation regarding his parents should have been obvious, and it stung. Without a second thought, I stepped into him, giving him a hug.

"Want to grow some flowers?" I mumbled into his chest after a long minute had passed.

"What?" His breath was warm against the top of my head, a warm welcome from this cold. I wasn't used to snow and had only donned a coat, gloves, and boots—no hat.

I pulled back and summoned my fire magic. After spelling a bright flame, I let it hover above us, lighting the area. "Do you want to use your magic to grow flowers?"

"Grow flowers?" He raised an eyebrow and waved at the lightly snow-covered ground.

"That's what I said, isn't it?" I took a step back and knelt, the snow melting into my pants. I removed a glove and placed my hand in the snow, the cold biting at my fingertips. I felt dirt that still held some warmth and let a small amount of magic flow. Concentrating, I sent the magic flowing through the ground at our feet. About fifty yellow daisies sprouted, the snow falling off their petals.

"Okay." Ender nodded, looking around at the flowers. He clicked his tongue and knelt in front of me.

I stood, giving him some space.

His brows furrowed as he concentrated, but nothing happened.

"Relax. Focus on the different threads of magic calling to you. Hold onto the one that resembles dirt, grass, life..." I offered.

The furrow lessened and a singular purple wildflower sprouted in front of his hands. He reached out, plucking it from the field of yellow, and stood.

"It may not be as beautiful as you." He gave me a smoldering grin as he held out the flower.

I rolled my eyes, gently taking it. When I glanced back up at him, he no longer wore the grin as his gaze searched mine. He brought his hand to my cheek, brushing the pad of his thumb down my jaw. His hand moved to my neck, cradling it with a soft touch, his gaze dropping to my lips.

I wanted to kiss him. I swore I did. But I stood still, waiting to see if he would bring his lips to mine, which, much to my delight, he did. This kiss was soft, warm, but it started to become more intense. I dropped the flower and wrapped my arms around his neck as he pulled me closer, his cedar and bergamot scent filling my senses. A cold zap tingled my lips, and I could taste a sharp tang of citrus—his magic.

My stomach tightened and I deepened the kiss, harder, faster, until I was the one demanding more. I could get lost in him, but something else drew me in—his magic. The tension in my stomach coiled even more as a slick feeling crawled against my neck. He had a lot of internal power waiting to be played with. The—

"Selene," he said sharply and abruptly pulled away, staring at me.

There was a small drop of blood on his lips, and I brought my fingers to mine, feeling for a cut that wasn't there. *Did I bite him?*

I took a step back, the snow feeling different under my boots, and glanced around. The flowers around us had withered into grey husks and the phantom fire I had created had been extinguished. I looked back at Ender, confused and hoping I had imagined whatever had come over me. His concerned expression only confirmed there were, in fact, dead flowers surrounding us, their life drained by me.

"Viv should be on her way." I swallowed and quickly left the flower circle of death, brushing past Ender and heading deeper into the woods.

CHAPTER FORTY-EIGHT

Selene

"You've been keeping a dragon in your dorm room since last Thursday?" Priscilla swiveled her head in my dad's direction.

John slowly turned from the window overlooking the academy grounds, smoothing his beige sweater.

"It's the same one from Singapore?" she continued.

"Yes." I nodded once, still standing behind the guest chairs in John's office—the same spot I had stood for the last thirty minutes as they informed me of the facts I had already gathered from the grimoire about the dark clan. "It was apparent he wasn't leaving, so we've kept him hidden. Plus, he was helpful against the dark mage in Singapore. It can't hurt to have him around."

"*It can't hurt,*" she mimicked my words.

"I greatly appreciate your forthcoming and honesty, Selene. However, we wish you would have informed us of this the night you had found him." John went over to his chair, finally sitting and taking a moment, looking as though he was contemplating. "I believe this dragon will increase the safety of our students should there be another attack and outweigh the hysteria in regard to a dragon on the premises."

Priscilla nodded.

"Selene." John waved to the chair in front of me and I obliged this time. "You had an ancestor on your mother's side with a dragon familiar. It was thought to have died when he—your great, great, great-grandfather—died. Your mom had told me about it when we were teenagers." A longing smile formed on his lips. "She had thought having a dragon as her familiar would be the most incredible thing."

Aura's face popped up from her fluff curl on his desk, glowering at him.

"Besides you, of course." He reached forward, scratching her chin until she settled back down.

Hold up.

"Having a dragon as her familiar—besides Aura?" I nodded at the white fox, who was happily asleep again. "Aura is Mom's familiar?"

I held my breath until John's confirmation came with a nod. Tears pricked my eyes. Forget my however-many-great-grandpop having a dragon as a familiar. Aura had been Mom's. I had never seen her before.

"Why was she with you?"

"Your mom had sent her with me to keep me safe." John's smile was sad as he stroked the back of Aura's neck. "She created her the day after our wedding as a gift to show that though we weren't soul-bound, we were still bound together. We hadn't known of Aura's minor healing capabilities until a later date. It's an unspoken projected ability of ether magic."

Tears silently fell, trailing down my cheeks.

"She can heal?" My voice came out quiet.

"To a certain extent, yes. She cannot heal the dead. Her eyes darken as she heals." John's gaze seemed distant. "Though they also darken when she is concerned or angry."

Aura's eyes had turned black when she rubbed up against Ender after the dark mage attacked him. Had she partly healed him? Maybe it had been more than Nurse Adair's famous healing elixir. Ender had recovered surprisingly quickly from the attack.

I stared at the little fox. Pain threatened to tear at my chest at the thought of Aura being created by Mom.

"How come you mentioned an ancestor of mine having a dragon as a familiar?" I asked, steering the topic to something a little more comfortable.

"Because I believe the dragon currently in the forest with your sister and Sydney is the same one." John's gaze focused, no longer somewhere in the past. "That's the most probable reason it's drawn to you. There have been old texts noting it is possible for a familiar to live past its creator, and if so, it may be summoned by someone from the same bloodline. Aura is an oddity. She was made with part of your mother's soul for me, but she resembles a version of those notations. Familiars can survive after their mage dies, but they typically do not have a high quality of life and often die of heartbreak sooner or later."

"Summoned?" I had never summoned a familiar. "I would have known if I summoned a dragon."

"When a person goes through a traumatic experience, their controlled and uncontrolled emotions are amplified, and often their own soul is momentarily disembodied from themselves." John's smile was understanding and full of empathy, like the one he had when I first met him in the jungle. Not one of pity.

Had Mom's death triggered me to summon Chaos?

"If that is the case, why has he only found me now, when it's been months since Mom's death?" I asked. "And why didn't he find Viv? She's from the same bloodline."

"Fives Academy's wards are strong and may have blocked his ability to locate you. It would explain how the dragon was able to find you once you left. I wouldn't be surprised if he had been waiting near Dominica for your return," John answered. "As far as finding you, you must've been the one who unknowingly summoned him."

I thought back to when I watched Mom take her last breaths. There had been an outburst of magic, but I hadn't realized it had come from me. And somehow the little dragon had gotten through the academy wards. Animals were able to pass, but I believe familiars were unable to unless their mage was welcomed.

Mischievous little thing.

The academy was eerily quiet, even for a Sunday evening. The snow and lack of wildlife made the grounds feel hollow. I sat behind the parapet of the west dorm roof, using it to shield some of the wind against my back. The gloves I wore protected my fingers from the chill but didn't help turn the pages of the dark grimoire.

I had to orchestrate a third walk for Chaos today just so I could lug this thick book out from under my bed—keeping it stored far away from Mom's ashes. Sydney and Viv protested at having to *fly* him a second time in the cold, but I told them I had wanted some alone time with Ender and that Chaos was restless despite his walk with me earlier.

Only one of those was a lie.

After some more digging and translating, I found that The Dark Circle had a leader who appeared to be immortal and the dark mages of the clan could all possess immortality. They were basically dark demon witches.

The hatch to the west side dorms creaked, and I pushed a little bit of air magic to send the grimoire skidding behind a nearby vent, the magical cloth resting over it. Unsure of the sudden increase in my heart rate, I waited to see who was intruding on my alone time. The tension in my shoulders released when Ender emerged through the hatch, climbing onto the roof with ease.

"Hey." He sat down next to me, not bothering to wipe away the snow. His joggers were about to get soaked, but I don't think he cared. He pulled me into him, wrapping both arms around me.

A sigh of contentment slipped from my lips. Today, I had learned Aura was created by Mom, the clan after me were basically deranged immortal demons, Chaos was an ancestral familiar, and David's training after my meeting with Priscilla and John had been more tiring than I liked to admit. David, too, looked exhausted, but I hadn't thought I had been pushing him too hard. He hadn't wanted to miss his training session with me despite the fight a few days ago.

Ender rested his head on mine. I hadn't actually expected to see him tonight, and despite not being able to learn more from the grimoire, I welcomed his intrusion. He was warm, and his arms around me ... It just felt right.

It almost warded off the haunting images of the dead flowers in the forest, and I couldn't shake that there was something wrong with me.

Was it safe for me to be touching him? Was there darkness inside me?

Chapter Forty-Nine
Selene

I had never seen the inside of this classroom until the start of the semester two weeks ago. It was triple the size of the other classrooms. A little otter swam in lazy circles through his 500-gallon glass tank. He also had a hollowed log that sat upon a rock slab and other toys for his enrichment, including an area with real grass.

I'd seen the little otter swimming in Crystal Lake out—

"Selene Thomas?" Professor Dickson's voice snapped me out of my daydream.

"Yes?" I sat straight in my chair, lowering my hands from the stone table—no doubt used in this lab to prevent workstation fires.

"Ah." He dipped his head in disapproval. "Olive is a thing of beauty," he gestured toward his familiar, "but we cannot be distracted. What can distractions lead to, class?"

Everyone's gaze fell on me, and their apprehension was almost tangible. *Great.* Instant frustrated heat crawled at the base of my neck. No one spoke because the question was correlated with *my* actions and not another student who wasn't an ether mage.

"A failed creation," I answered.

"Worse." Professor Dickson had creases forming at the corners of his brown eyes. "A travesty. A dangerous creature that will flout all the creator's intentions."

Professor Dickson finally took his assessing gaze off me and paced the front. "Now, gather the supplies in front of you. Level ones and twos, work on constructing an inanimate object. Level threes and higher, work on creating a small sentient creature." His momentary pause when he said *higher* did not slip past me. "Remember, creatures are typically short-lived, depending on the amount of magic woven into the spell and based on the creator's intentions. Emotions factor in the outcome of the temperament your creation will have."

I stared at a large bowl of water at the front of my desk and looked over at Mara next to me. She had a pile of sticks.

"Must be they don't trust her with solid objects," a girl snickered behind me.

I stiffened and did my best to brush off the comment, but anger got the better of me and I turned in my seat. The girl, whose name I didn't even know, snapped her mouth shut and sank in her chair. If she could sink any farther, she'd be lying on the ground. I took in quick breaths, letting the simmering anger show in my glare, then turned back around.

After all, I had been thinking the exact same thing.

Mara offered me a pity smile before bringing her attention back to her contents. I might not have any of my friends in this class, but at least my lab partner wasn't malicious, just quiet. The only times I truly held a conversation with her was when I was checking out a library book. Now that I had answers about Mom and her sister, I hadn't been hunting down Mr. Hastings and saw Mara less.

Bringing the bowl closer, I dipped one finger in the room temperature water. Something still didn't sit well with me, and my emotions started to bubble.

"Focus on your intention. Calm your inner voice. Use the enchantment." Professor Dickson clicked the chalkboard where the enchantment was written. He had started teaching us this enchantment on our first day and now, two weeks later, we were implementing it.

I narrowed in on the bowl, focusing on my intent to create a palm-sized water horse—something I'd done before, but in a bigger form, matching the size of a small horse that my mother had taught me using salt water. It wouldn't last more than thirty seconds but was incredible. The enchantment started flowing effortlessly from my mouth.

The water began to ripple. Sizzling warmth sparked in my chest, a fluttering that wasn't the normal heat that pooled there during enchantments. The ripples turned into miniature waves and sloshed over the sides. Someone said something to my right, but I was drawn to the vibrating bowl in front of me.

Dark edges formed around my vision, blurring out everything else around me. The bowl kicked out, clattering to the floor, the water remaining suspended in the air, aggressively revolving. The torrent began expanding, lashing out in violent whips as wind swirled around the room.

Something is wrong.

I forced my mouth closed, ceasing the enchantment, realizing the Latin words I had been saying were not the same as the words written on the board. Mara had vacated her spot next to me. All the students had abandoned their desks and stood along the far wall, their exit blocked by my creation. Professor Dickson was shouting at me from his spot ten feet away, unable to get closer without the water whipping at his face and the wind seeming to come from the water pushing him back.

Everything should have been loud, but the sounds were muffled as a quiet hum invaded the inside of my head. The sizzling heat inside my chest grew, its edges searing my insides. I muffled a cry of pain but quickly realized... *it feels so good... addicting.*

My breaths turned into pants at the thrill as the violent swirl of water grew, flipping the stone table and shoving it to the side like it was a show of strength. Someone's hand—my hand—reached out on its own accord, inches from the twisted mass of dark water. *Can water be black?* It hummed, like a sentient creature. Its—

Fire.

Fire engulfed the entirety of the dark mass of water. I used my arms to shield my face until the heat and flash of bright fire dissipated. Black water droplets floated upward, evaporating before reaching the ceiling.

Just beyond where the hydrosphere had been stood a little black dragon. The humming in my head ceased and the gasps of the students vibrated throughout the still room.

What did I just do?

Chaos's chest raised in slow, soft breaths in his sleep, his body sprawled across the stone office desk. Aura curled herself against the little dragon, whose tail wrapped around her soft fur. I sat in the chair and watched the familiars sleep, taking up the entirety of the desk. They seemed to have taken to each other and had moved beyond the hissing and growling.

John's office door opened but I didn't look, expecting it to be him until I felt a very familiar warmth tug at me. Hazel eyes leveled with mine, worried lines etching the corners. I simply stared at his beautiful face—the sharp edges, the hard flex in his jaw, smooth skin...

I looked away, staring at the arm of the chair I sat in.

"Selene." Ender's voice was soft as he knelt and cupped my cheek, tilting my face so my gaze lifted back to his eyes. He didn't ask if I was okay. He didn't need to. I had lost control with something dark, something he understood.

But his darkness had faded the moment he snapped out of it. What was left was his own emotions. I could still feel the sizzling prickling sensation sparking inside my chest, like a combustion waiting to happen. It was as if a pilot light had gone out but the gas valve was still open, waiting for a single spark. It felt foreign. Mom would have been disappointed in my lack of control.

Ender's arms wrapped around me, pulling me in. I gave in to his warmth and touch. It was inviting, grounding. His hand cupped the back of my head. "It will be okay."

We stayed like that for a while, Chaos and Aura not bothered one bit.

"Your knees," I said.

"My knees what?" Ender pulled back just enough to see my face and tucked a loose strand of hair behind my ear.

"Your knees." I pulled back, glancing down.

"There's only one person who I would ever get down on my knees for." The corner of his mouth lifted, and despite my solemn mood, I found myself half smiling with the urge to give him a good thwack on the chest.

The door opened again, and this time it was John. Food and a cup of water jostled on the tray he carried as he came to an abrupt stop.

"You two must always be near each other." He sighed. Ender hadn't startled, his grin simply growing as he stood, taking up residence behind my chair.

John went to shoo the familiars from his desk with a hand but must have thought otherwise because he stopped halfway through the motion. He set the tray down on the chair next to me.

I couldn't bring myself to speak after Professor Dickson had escorted me here. Every single gaze had been on the little dragon that crawled behind me, hunching to the ground and growling at anyone who had come close—even the professor stayed a good fifteen feet in front of me. The existence of Chaos was supposed to be kept hidden until the third week of school—next week—in case he decided to leave. Clearly, he didn't plan on leaving. Word about a dragon at the academy and how *Ether Mage Selene Thomas* had lost control would have spread across the entirety of the grounds by now.

There would be a student riot to banish me.

"You need to eat." John pointedly glanced at the food as he leaned against the less occupied portion of his desk—which was only a sliver—and crossed his arms, frowning. It was such an informal position for him, my mind took a halt for a brief moment. His expression wasn't masking his concern, and if I hadn't known better, I would have said it looked like fatherly concern.

The door flung open for a third time and Viv charged in, lacking the grace that Ender had. Sydney followed suit, not in as much of a rush.

"Vivian. Sydney." John nodded at them both, not showing any surprise that they had shown up.

"Are you okay?" Viv stood in front of me.

"Yes. I just got carried away on an enchantment. I'm a bit rusty with creatures." I shrugged, hiding my inner turmoil.

"Maybe I need to light some things on fire to get room delivery." Sydney eyed the tray of food my dad had gotten me. *Dad.* Ugh. There was that word again.

Viv studied me for a moment before stepping back, nodding, then glancing at the tray. "It doesn't have Oreos. Three stars."

"Okay." John pushed himself off the desk. "We aren't here to discuss the academy's cuisine. Selene and the other students are all unharmed.

Vivian and Sydney, the two of you need to exit. You can wait for Sal in the hallway."

Insert Headmaster. Fatherly traces had vanished.

"The two of us?" Viv asked and then pointed at Ender. "What about him?"

"He can stay," John said.

I stood, placing a hand on Viv's shoulder. "It's okay. I'll see you in the hallway."

I leveled her my best *I'll tell you later* look and she nodded, giving John the stink eye as she backed away.

Once they left, John resumed his stance against the desk, this time with his hands in his pockets. "Go over everything from the beginning of the day until now. Do not leave any details out."

I sighed when he didn't say another word and began to relive the day by explaining everything I had done. The entire time, John never mentioned why he had let Ender stay.

Chapter Fifty
Selene

January was long gone. February had come and gone. That day in Elemental Creations Lab impacted the academy more than the dark mage attack had, or at least that was how I felt. My dad checked in with me every day, Leah Murphy and Priscilla monitored me closely, and I was pulled from Elemental Creatures Lab. He had asked me to visit Nurse Adair once a week. He and Priscilla were both concerned about my health.

Professor Dickson privately tutored me outside of the class. Even creating elements had my nerves in a bundle, let alone creatures. My magic had short-circuited a few times, giving me the wrong element or nothing at all.

Chaos often popped his little head in through the outside windows of my classes, but he wasn't allowed inside the buildings. The only place he was allowed in—theoretically—was my dorm room. Other students were uneasy in his presence. Even David kept his distance from the little dragon. April had been excited to meet a dragon until he had set her flower headband on fire.

My anger was always present, and I had to work hard to control it. I had been pushing everyone away the last two months, avoiding—more than typically—general human interaction. The intrusive thoughts ran rampant, and I had to work hard to stomp them down. My short fuse blew way too many times.

Even Vivian visited me less. I didn't blame her. I had made a comment that referred to her as a coward for hiding her relationship with April. It had sent me in a guilt-ridden spiral ever since, even after apologizing. We did, however, still occasionally hang out on the roof. Sisters through and through, I supposed.

Sydney was my roommate, yet I rarely had more than a two-word conversation with her daily. I avoided talking to her. At least her nightmares had lessened.

Ender. Ender was my safe space even though something inside me felt broken. He was relentless and his presence brought a spark of light somewhere deep in my chest. Chaos had also stayed by my side, sending little fireballs my way at random times to cheer me up.

Every Tuesday and Thursday, I met with David for our sessions. His magic control had been improving, and his scent of burnt ash was growing stronger. Trainer Murphy had even approved of him removing his gloves. I had told him I shouldn't be teaching him when I apparently couldn't control my magic like I had thought I could. He protested, insisting that it made me an even better teacher. Besides that, I never hung out with any of my other friends. I ate—if I ate—in any part of the academy where I could find solitude.

Ender had convinced me to get rid of the grimoire. He physically handed it over to David and told him that he needed to turn it in to the headmaster, giving him a chance to come up with an explanation for why he had it. Ender did not want me or any other student to set foot in the basement.

I had informed my dad months ago that a student had made it into the basement over break; I never said which student. If there wasn't a 24/7 guard placed at the door, I would be surprised. Chaos was much happier with it gone.

I wasn't myself. *Something is wrong with me.*

I released a sigh, resting my head back against the bookcase. Aura slept quietly, her little fluffy body curled in my lap. I felt better around her. My dad worked at his desk, his pen moving swiftly over the paper. He never dismissed me nor had he asked me to leave and would even have food brought here.

I had learned his office was warded to keep unwanted visitors out, even if they unlocked the door. Apparently, it needed the presence of his blood to deactivate it. It explained why I was able to open the door instead of Sydney the night we snuck in. We shared the same bloodline.

The room slowly darkened as the sun set, the candles brightening the walls. Somewhere in my chest was a hard, messy, twisted knot that I couldn't get rid of. The pain radiated against my back and wrapped around to my ribs. When I was with Aura, it dissipated to an aching throb. I was waging an internal war with myself, not wanting to give in to the voice in my head that told me to see if I could cause the flame from the candle on the shelf to catch the curtains on fire. My magic felt around the heat of the flame, surprising me it wasn't phantom fire.

"What is your element?" I broke the quiet.

My dad looked up from his papers. He appeared to think for a moment before sitting up straight.

"No one I talked to seems to know," I went on, "but based on the soot marks on your palms when we were in Singapore, I would assume fire, but magic doesn't typically leave marks like that," I rambled on.

"You are correct." He surprised me when he stood and sat on the floor next to me. He reached out and stroked Aura, who purred in contentment. "When the element of fire is created, it does not leave carbon particles like a typical fire does. Utilizing non-created fire can cause a result of incomplete combustion of its hydrocarbon counterpart."

I bit my lip, intently focusing on his words and deciphering their meaning.

"Your candles are not lit with phantom fire," I said.

He watched me as I put the pieces together, neither confirming nor denying my statement. I thought back to the lighter I had found in his desk many months ago. A fire mage would only need a lighter if they couldn't create fire themselves, and if a mage were to control fire using a lighter, it could result in the soot I had seen on his hands. In case of an attack, phantom fire couldn't be used as a weapon.

The almighty headmaster—my father—of the prestigious Fives Academy was a level one fire mage.

That was kind of awesome.

Chapter Fifty-One
Ender

I woke with a jolt, sweat dripping down my back. The clock on my end table told me it was too early to be awake on a Sunday, yet, my nightmare had decided five a.m. was the time to wake me up. After a deep breath and a quick roll of my shoulders, shaking off the phantom decaying fingers of the dark mage who had paid me a visit in my dream, I lay back down.

After ten minutes, I decided I wasn't falling back asleep even if I were to lie there for two hours. I silently climbed out of bed and dressed in joggers and a T-shirt, careful not to wake Nick, though I was positive Nick would not have woken up even if Chaos was in our dorm room, ping-ponging from wall to wall. There had been a large party in the forest last night, and Nick got in a few hours ago. Selene and I had a quiet Saturday evening and played Scrabble, winning one of three matches. It was rare that I lost even one match. In her current distress, she thankfully showed bits of her old self.

I made my way to the gym, the grounds silent other than the birds singing their morning songs. As I hit it, still trying to shake off the nightmare, the punching bag became the dark mage's body from my dream. I haven't been haunted in my sleep by the dark mages since I lost control in my training match, and I wasn't going to let this one time get to me.

After a solid forty minutes of punching the bag, I decided to head to the cafeteria to grab food, expecting the doors to be locked. The main academy doors would still be locked at this hour, so I made my way to the cafeteria door from the courtyard. Peering through the glass, I could see a figure inside.

Looks like I will be getting in early today.

I knocked.

Clara, one of the cafeteria monitors, turned around. I could make out a smile before she masked it with a frown. As much as she said she detested me, it was hard love. She made her way to the door, heaving it open and leaving her hand on the glass and blocking my path. Wind blew through the threshold, tussling her wispy, short grey hair.

"The cafeteria isn't open until seven." She glanced at her watch. "Not for another hour."

"Really?" I put on my best charming smile. "But when has that stopped us before? I'm just looking for an apple."

I gestured to the table she had just come from. It was covered with an array of fresh fruit. She released a sigh and the corner of her mouth turned up.

"Fine." She waved me through. "One of these times, I should turn you away. Or what if I don't hear your knocking?"

"Then when the other students or staff arrive, they'd find me lying on the ground by the door, dead from starvation." I turned to face her, placing a hand over my stomach like it hurt.

"Sounds very much like you." She waved a hand in the air, brushing off the jokes. "Anyway, I don't see any harm with a student getting fruit early, so long they don't cause any disruptions."

"You are my favorite cafeteria monitor." I followed her over to the table, and I could almost feel her roll her eyes even though her back was to me.

She tucked a pair of tongs into her apron pocket and grabbed an empty basket. "Have a good day, Ender," she said as she made her way back into the kitchen.

Examining the fruit spread before me, I decided to actually opt for an apple—like I had said I wanted—and a pear. I turned to head out the door and was about to take a bite of the apple when I heard footsteps from the hallway. Lowering my apple, I felt my magic simmer. Something didn't feel right.

David appeared around the corner, his blond hair pushed back like he had been running all morning. Like he'd been doing recently, he wasn't wearing his gloves. Selene and Trainer Murphy's training had been helping.

"Ender." He stopped at the entrance. "I'm glad that's you. It's Sal."

He took off and I followed suit, dropping the apple and pear on a nearby table.

"What do you mean, *it's Sal*?" I yelled after him and reached for the bond, but it felt the same—distant cold surrounding a fiery spark. That was how it had been the last month, the coolness growing around the flame.

I pulled out my phone, struggling to press the buttons as I ran. There were no unread messages or missed calls. I tried to call her, but it failed. I tried Headmaster John and then Priscilla. They all failed. I took deep breaths. I needed a clear head.

"Yeah. My phone isn't functioning. I can't make any calls or send any messages." David glanced over at me as we ran. "I saw her this morning. Something seemed off, so I followed her. Once she made it past the doors in the library that headed to the basement, I knew I needed to call for help, but my phone wasn't working. I figured someone would be in the cafeteria, and then I heard voices coming from there. I'm thankful it was you."

"Why would Selene go into the basement?" I asked.

"I don't know." He shook his head. "Her eyes. They were completely black."

I pressed my lips together. It had to be whatever had been affecting her the last two months. But what would she want in the basement? Was it the dark grimoire I basically made her give back?

"It's not safe down there." I recalled the demon rats. "We need to get to her."

"I know," he agreed as we burst through the unlocked library doors.

We ran through the deserted library. Behind the checkout desk stood the large solid oak doors. I didn't waste any time and ran behind the checkout desk, opening the doors with ease. Last time, these doors had been locked and Selene had used a stolen key from Mr. Hastings to open it.

"Why didn't you go in after Selene?" I spared a glance at David, who stared at the entrance with unease. He could have easily followed her.

"I wanted to get help." He swallowed, and I had to bite back my remark about him being spineless for not following her. At least it had led him to me.

We entered. A guard lay unconscious on the floor. A bitter, sharp tang hung in the air.

The doors slammed shut behind us.

I turned to them but was stopped by a crinkling sound, like crumpled tissue paper, coming from the walls. The symbols on the walls burned black, turning into ash.

I turned, assessing the walls. Dark magic was at play here.

"David. We need to keep—" I froze as cool metal clamped around my wrists, the tungsten of the magic-nullifying cuffs glowing green.

David stepped back, his eyes obsidian black and rimmed with red. I glowered at him with a cool, hard, assessing glare.

"You're the traitor?"

Chapter Fifty-Two

Ender

At first, a part of my brain tried to reconcile why David would cuff me, voiding me of magic, why his eyes would look like the devil's, and why the symbols on the wall meant to ward off evil had turned to ash. The first theory was that he had been controlled, but my gut instincts said otherwise. I might not have been fond of David from the start, but that was how I was with everyone. He had become an acquaintance.

Ouch.

Had he made a deal with the dark mages to give him power?

"Is Selene really here?" I nodded toward the oak doors leading to the basement.

"No." He tucked his hands behind his back. "She's comfortable in her own bed. That is, until I tell her dark mages are attacking and you are lying on your deathbed."

The thought of him being near her enraged me.

"Leave her alone." I was going to paint his khakis and collared shirt with his own tainted blood.

"That would be foolish." He waved his hand over his left palm as he said an enchantment. A black circle revealed itself.

"You did take a deal with the devil," I ground out. "Your flesh will start to rot, and you'll be a walking corpse—until I put you in a grave for doing this."

His void expression turned malicious.

"I took that deal a *very* long time ago." With a flick of his wrist, the doors leading to the library opened behind him. A figure in a black cloak walked through, their pale, black-veined hands poking out of their sleeves. They bowed to him before straightening. "I would take your power myself, but it will better serve both me and my consort once she is turned. Our reigning companionship will be built off your magic."

My breathing quickened as realization struck. The other dark mage had bowed to David. *Consort? Reign?* David was the leader, and he wanted Selene by his side as a dark mage—a level five ether mage. I needed to get to her and needed to warn Headmaster John.

I strained my wrists against the cuffs, trying to break them, but it only caused them to bleed. David's gaze flitted to my bloodied wrists, the black in his eyes pulsing as he licked his lips.

"You were a pleasant surprise—one I was happy to drain, until I learned of your bond with my consort." The edges around David's eyes hardened. "It slowed my own paradigm yet quickened its advances. I couldn't let your bond strengthen over time, but it also needed to be handled delicately. Now, the dragon. That was unforeseen. However, it should be a small inconvenience." He pulled out a dagger from an unseen sheath on his back, its black and grey swirled blade the length of a book. "It took a moment to mask my scent with a smoke fragrance to deter the little nuisance. It'll soon never be allowed to procreate."

By that, I assumed he meant killing Chaos.

"Your bond is a pesky little thing." He leaned in close, his face inches from mine. "It'll soon be broken."

I held his glower, feigning pulling my face back away from his. Instead, I was rearing it back and then slammed my head against his face.

He jumped back, one hand flitting to his gushing nose and the other shooting out.

I went flying, crashing into the unforgiving oak doors behind me. Pain shot up my spine and my head throbbed.

His chest rose in a slow breath as his nostrils flared, crimson-black blood seeping from his nose. "If you weren't ether and a testimony to Selene's alliance, you'd be dead."

"The only testimony Selene is making will be when she says 'I do' at our wedding, and that's because she wants me, not you." I rose to my knees.

He glared at me, his eyes eerily unwavering for a solid minute. *Good.* My remark got to him.

"Watch him. Concuss him. Do whatever you desire to him as long as his heart still beats and you do not touch his magic," he said to the other dark mage.

The black hood moved up and down with the dark mage's nods, and David left.

I slowly stood, leaning against the doors behind me. I spared a glance at the unconscious guard, his chest slowly rising.

"So you get left with babysitting duty, huh?" I raised my hands. "Any chance you could loosen these a bit?" The shadowed face was pointed in my direction, unmoving. "Worth a shot." I shrugged and then messed with the cuffs. They wouldn't budge.

Every second I was stuck was every second David was closer to Selene. I glanced at the door handle and an idea struck me.

"Well," I proceeded to the door, "maybe these door handles will be more personable and helpful." I set the metal bar connecting the cuffs against the handle and started making a sawing motion. "Do you know what happens when tungsten goes against tungsten?" *I didn't.* "It withers away."

By the looks of it, it didn't do anything. The dark mage stepped forward, shooting out a hand, fire extending in my direction. Its searing heat melted the hair on my arms as I stepped away from the door.

At least *they* thought it did something.

I chose that moment to clutch my heart, feigning some sort of illness from his attack. The only two orders they had was to make sure my heart still beat and that my magic was off-limits. Swallowing, I dropped to my knee, forcing myself to take deep, unproductive breaths until I felt my face redden.

The dark mage took a step. *Closer.* I hunched over, slowing my movements as if I was falling to my own false ailments. Their steps grew nearer until their black boots came into view. I slowed my breaths and movements. A slight shift in their stance told me they were starting to lean down...

I struck, leaping to my feet and maneuvering the cuffs around their neck—an advantage of being tall. Pulling as hard as I could, I made sure the bar dug into their neck, causing them to gasp. Their hand flew to my arm, and I felt searing pain where they touched me, the odor of my own burning flesh striking my nose. I needed to hold on a little longer.

The dark mage's other hand came up to my opposing arm, and my grip involuntarily loosened. They took the opportunity to escape and sent a shooting flame at my midsection. I dodged the flames, barely, and landed a blow to their face, knocking their hood off.

White hair billowed out, and her dark eyes narrowed on me. The whites had yellowed, but not so much that I couldn't also make out the red veins they were full of. She had slender cheeks and a narrow nose, and her lips were the color of a dark red. She was wearing lipstick.

"Have you thought about just going all dark and natural?" I gestured toward her face. "I think we both can agree makeup is useless at this point."

The dark mage snarled, lunging toward me. I effectively worked her up. I dodged, landing a knee to her gut. She staggered, but not before getting a hand out, shooting powerful magic into me and sending me backward against those stupid, painstakingly hard doors. My body sizzled and one quick once-over told me a quarter of my body had been fried.

"I doubt *David* wanted you to cook me for dinner." I grinned as I stood, almost wondering who was the crazy one.

The doors to the library opened and Mr. Hastings stood there, wielding a sword. A librarian wearing trousers and a suit vest while wielding a sword was a sight I'd never forget. His entrance caught the dark mage's attention as well and I lurched forward, grateful for the distraction. Again, I wrapped my arms around the dark mage's neck from behind. Mr. Hastings lunged, but she sent her fire magic in his direction. He made a quick motion with his arm and an end table flew in front of him, knocking over the gold vase that had been on it. The table shielded the flames and I pulled tighter, choking the dark mage.

When the flames ceased, Mr. Hastings attacked, slashing the sword across the dark mage's body. The dark mage let out a deep cry. The air began to get warmer and heat radiated from her body. Before I could unwrap my hands and move back, a searing explosion struck me as the mage used her magic, freeing herself and sending Mr. Hastings and me to the ground.

The previous burns throbbed even more and the new ones felt like sandpaper against my skin. I hoisted myself onto my tender arms, wincing against the pain. Mr. Hastings didn't fare too well on the other side of the room, half of his face oozing and smoldering. The dark mage walked over to the sword lying on the ground and picked it up. She began advancing toward the librarian, who was still getting his bearings together. He wouldn't see her coming.

I tried to call to him, but between the ringing in my ears and my dry throat, I couldn't tell if anything came out. Mr. Hastings didn't look up. The golden vase lay in front of me, and I grabbed it before getting to my feet. I pushed myself, each stumbling step sending shooting pain up, down, every direction in my legs.

The vase was heavy and took a good amount of effort to raise it in the air and then slam it against the back of the dark mage's head. As she dropped to the floor, she used magic to send the sword flying in my direction. It embedded itself in the side of my abdomen, and I stepped backward, somehow managing to stay on my feet.

I couldn't fail Selene. I reached for the bond—it felt so distant, but it was there. The small glow was still fading as cold surrounded it, and I couldn't think about what that meant. Was she okay? Was I dying? Would Selene survive David?

No. Selene would live.

I pulled the sword out, a guttural cry echoing through the room. Trying hard not to lose my grip on the handle, I brought the blade down on the dark mage's neck. The impact jerked my elbows and shoulders as the blade struck bone, slicing through part of her neck. The dark mage's head hung at an odd angle, her dark eyes still containing deathless life as she stared at me, eyes wide.

Yanking hard, I attempted to pull the sword free to strike again, but it wouldn't budge. She wouldn't be dead until she was headless or burned.

Gentle hands covered mine, and I looked up to see Mr. Hastings. He gave me a short nod and I let go of the sword, stumbling a few steps backward. He yanked the sword free and swung, the blade finishing the job. The woman's head hit the ground as my legs gave out and I fell.

I couldn't move. The copper and cooked meat tastes and scents that permeated my senses vanished. Mr. Hastings came into view as my vision blurred. Behind him, a small shape appeared through the open doorway. It came closer and dark brown eyes came into view—or were they black?

Warmth and something soft brushed up against me and then darkness hit.

Chapter Fifty-Three

Selene

A PHANTOM SHARP PAIN pierced the side of my stomach and I sat up straight. My pajamas were soaked, my heart pounded, and I was breathless. Slowing my heart rate and reminding myself it was just another nightmare, I closed my eyes. This nightmare wasn't easily recalled like the others. The pain lingered, but the images of what the dream consisted of weren't there. I shook it off.

I grabbed my phone and saw it was almost seven a.m. I had no messages, and my phone said there wasn't any service. Sydney slept, a quiet snore rhythmically coming from her. The end of the bed was oddly free where Chaos usually slept, and a slight breeze filtered in through the window. He must've been impatient for his walk this morning. Now that the academy knew about the little dragon, we left a window open for him so he didn't feel caged. Actually, he had torn the window screen and then we decided we would leave it open if it wasn't a scheduled snow day. Our windows faced the woods and helped keep him out of sight from most students when he flew into the trees.

Sighing, I swung my legs off the bed and headed to the bathroom to wash up. My phone buzzed the moment I set it on the counter, and I glanced at it to see my dad was calling.

Huh.

Must be whatever he did when I had left made it so he could still call me with no service. But why was he calling so early?

"Hello?" I answered quietly.

There was some sort of commotion and then the line was disconnected.

A hard, frantic knock came at our dorm room door. I ran out of the bathroom, sharing a glance with Sydney, who had sat up at the noise. I opened the door while the person on the other side still pounded against it.

"David." I assessed his heavy panting and the sweat lining his forehead. "What is it?"

"Dark mages and *Demonher* rats," he breathed out. "They have Ender."

"Where is he?" Alarm set my adrenaline on fire.

"They went toward the front of the main building," he said. "I saw them snag him on his run. I came straight here when I couldn't call anyone."

"Couldn't call as in didn't have your phone or there was no service?" I glanced at my phone in my hand.

"No service," David panted.

I nodded as understanding dawned. The lack of service was most likely due to the dark mage attack, not the normal faulty signal. The person on the inside must have had something to do with it—and the dark mages getting through.

I picked up my phone and tried calling my dad again. The phone rang but there was no answer.

"It doesn't work," David said.

"Headmaster John was just able to call me, but it got disconnected." I then tried Vivian and Priscilla. The line didn't even ring. "Sydney. Go warn Vivian and then get to my father."

I immediately set foot out the door, not wasting precious time throwing shoes on. A natural habit of mine was sleeping in similar daytime clothes, so my cargo-style joggers and loose tank top were better to fight dark mages in rather than the *Let's Avocuddle* pajama set I've seen April wear.

"Father?" David faltered behind me, but I didn't slow.

"John is my father," I said, realizing that he hadn't been privy to that information.

There was a short moment of silence.

"Do you think they will be able to make it to the headmaster in time to warn him?" He caught up to me.

"I hope so." My dad would know what to do to help bring up the barrier and wards if they were down—if he was okay. The phone call had me worried. How many dark mages and *Demonher* rats were there?

Ugh. Why did this academy have to be so huge? The grass made an excellent terrain for my bare feet as we ran along the side of the academy building. We reached the front of the building and I stopped short.

"David." I stayed still, searching the surroundings. "You said they had Ender."

"I-I did," he stuttered. "They did."

Two dark mages, one completely covered in a brown cloak and another in a black cloak, stood near the fire dragon water fountain. The one in brown stood closer to my sister, whose bloodied wrists were tied to each wing of the stone dragon. Her torso was strapped to the body while her ankles were bound at the base of the statue.

Viv lifted her head, glancing at me through her soaked strands of hair. Her face was covered in different shades of purple, and heated rage boiled in my chest. Her bruises indicated they'd had her for at least a few hours. She tried to speak, but her lips barely moved as she tilted her head to her right.

"Viv—" Wind spiraled in my direction, and I threw my hands up, easily deflecting it.

The dark mage in black advanced, and I wondered if it was the one who killed Mom. If they were here, baiting me like this, chances were it was one of the three.

Anger and the unhinged energy inside me swirled and heat blasted from my hands, sending flames toward the dark mage, who threw their hands up, easily blocking my attack. Another set of fire sailed their way, and I glanced behind me to see one of David's hands outstretched.

Using the distraction, I ran at the dark mage, landing a solid kick to their face and a punch to their stomach. No shoes helped me move swiftly but also caused more of an impact on my feet that I wasn't used to. My magic felt along the ground around me until it found something useful, wrapping its tendrils around a large rock. I recoiled my magic back like a whip and slammed the rock into the dark mage's head.

"What did you do to him?" I shouted, dread filling me. Was Ender okay?

The dark mage barely staggered, and then, with a movement so quick I could barely see, it thrust its hands against my chest, knocking me down and sending me skidding across the gravel driveway.

With a groan, I propped myself up. *Why did dark magic have to be so powerful?*

A dark figure appeared through the tree line, gliding its way toward us. David shifted next to me, his face seething with anger as he glowered at the approaching dark mage. The dark mage in the brown cloak hadn't moved.

Vivian cried out, pain contorting her expression, and I got to my feet. I tried to see where the source was coming from, but there was no movement near her. Wind lashed across my side, forceful enough that it tore my shirt and left a red, oozing welt across my hip, extending over my stomach. The dark mage I had originally been fighting lowered their hands to their side, taking a step back and angling themselves toward the approaching dark mage—almost defensively?

I glanced toward the housing for the staff—it was eerily quiet. We needed support, but something told me that help wasn't coming. Sydney would have found someone by now, and the commotion should have sent guards or professors running.

My inner forearm burned, but nothing was there. It spread from inside my veins as if my blood was lava and my arm twisted on its own accord, sending a sharp pain to my shoulder and causing me to drop to my knees.

No. No. No. No.

This was blood magic, and I had no doubt that the dark mage advancing was the one who had killed Mom.

David's boots crunched the gravel in front of me, blocking the path of the advancing dark mage.

Time for support.

I had been afraid to create creatures the past few months, but that ended today. My magic reached for the fiery dragon breath coming from the fountain. Anger, hurt, and revenge seethed at my core. I began chanting and pulled the magic, severing its connection from its phantom fire spell and adding flames, hues of red, orange, and blue at its core, until a lion, its back reaching chest high, formed. Still on my knees, I took a deep breath.

David stared in wonder at the lion, then his appraising gaze assessed me. He reached out a hand to help me up, and I took it. Something dark in me swirled at the contact, and I invited it in.

No one else was going to die—not Vivian, not Ender. He had to be okay. I would find him. And I would avenge my mother's death.

After mentally commanding the lion to attack the dark mage who had air-whipped my stomach, I focused on the approaching dark mage. That one was mine. I could feel their magic crawling inside my veins, searing my arms and legs as they tried to control me. I could feel my magic snuffing theirs out, and I began to doubt this had been the mage who killed Mom—they weren't strong enough. Mom had been too powerful.

Then again, what were the coincidences? The black circle clan had killed my mom and had been actively hunting me down. The one who killed Mom could do blood magic—a rare, powerful magic.

I slowly started toward the advancing mage, trusting my lion creature to watch my back and the other mage. Each step felt like my entire body was walking through sand, but with each step, I gained more control of my limbs. The dark mage halted, its arms outstretched.

Grinning, I continued forward. David stayed back, and I would have thought fear paralyzed him, but he was watchful, studying the situation.

Viv cried out as the burning sensation in my veins dulled. I glanced toward her, the blood magic most likely being used on her. My reflexes had me shifting to the side just as a dagger landed in my shoulder.

The hood of the dark mage in front of me must have fallen when she threw the dagger, her skin a smooth pale grey as she snarled at me. Her dark eyes were rimmed by yellow whites. Her bare head and skin the color of a very old, very rotten mage told one story, but her teeth, which were yellow-tinged and not rotted, told a different one.

She lunged at me, her expression unhinged. Ignoring the stabbing pain, I pulled the dagger from my shoulder and dodged the dark mage's attack. Gripping the dagger tightly, I jammed it into her lower back, right in the location of her kidney. She screeched, but I didn't slow, the power and bloodlust rising in me.

Yanking the dagger out, I twisted her and turned her around, then pierced her chest. Using my other hand, I forced the blade in farther, bringing her to the ground and pinning her between my legs. I let go of the dagger, placing my hands on either side of her head, and let the flames roar.

There were only two ways to kill a dark mage. Decapitation or setting it ablaze.

The ear-piercing screeches of the dark mage below me faded as another guttural roar took its place. I glanced behind me just as my creature turned to ash, the black-cloaked mage standing in its place. Movement toward Viv caught my eye as the other dark mage moved toward her in a jerky motion. They pulled a knife, reaching it high in the air, aimed at her chest.

"No!" I screamed and pulled the dagger from the dark mage below me, and using magic, sent the knife toward the dark mage in the brown cloak. It struck their back before they could finish their attack. If they'd been human, the strike would've killed them in seconds.

Vivian cried out though the knife never reached her. I was about to run to her when the hood of the brown cloak fell, revealing a beautiful floral crown set upon short red hair. *April.* Tears ran down my sister's face.

April fell to her knees, the knife sticking from her back. I stood frozen... horrified... as David passed me and knelt over the dark mage behind me, I imagine making sure she was truly dead. I assessed the other dark mage, who stood unmoving.

"Dear Enid, your death is of your own betrayal." David's voice was gentle yet stern. "You took more than what you were capable of, despite my assertions."

Who in the dark magic was *Enid*?

I made my way toward Vivian in a daze. Blood flowed from my shoulder wound, and I wondered whether the combination of blood loss, fatigue from fighting, and the shock of what I had just done had caused my ears to imagine his words.

    I killed April.

Chapter Fifty-Four
Selene

I carefully watched the other dark mage as I used magic to burn away the ties holding Vivian. She was strong, and I wondered why she hadn't used her own magic to free herself. But I felt dark magic disengaging, like a spell had been broken. The last of her bindings fell and she dropped to her knees, making her way to April, who lay lifeless on the ground. Turning her partly over, Viv sobbed, her body shaking as her hands covered April's wound even though she was already gone.

My chest tightened; the emotional pain was more consuming than the open, bleeding wound on my shoulder. I was the reason for Vivian's pain. I had killed someone she loved. Yet, something else sickly and dark twisted inside me, growing like a dark vine full of power... power that felt invigorating.

I had killed an innocent.

But I didn't know it was April. I didn't know they were being controlled by... my brain buffered, puzzles of the pieces trying to fit together, but it was too focused on controlling the internal war inside. The guilt for taking April's life was being consumed by the dark inferno raging inside me, the guilt withering away.

A black shadow streaked across the sky, casting a shadow. It barreled into David, tumbling into a mess of claws and fists, fire, and spewing magic. They broke apart, Chaos on all fours, hunched and hissing, and David, his eyes as black as Chaos's scales as he casually stood with a dagger in hand—its blade silver and black.

"Selene." A hand rested on my shoulder and I turned.

"Dad," I whispered, horrified at his concerned and wary expression.

"It'll be okay, Sal. You will be okay." My dad's gaze darted from me to Vivian and April as he held up a hand, beckoning me to take it. His usual calm mask cracked for a split second before darkening. "Stay away from my girls."

"That's unlikely as much as it is impossible." A dark laugh came from behind me, and I whirled around to see David a few steps closer to me. Chaos stood off to the side, tracking his movements and ready to pounce. "I see you were able to free the dragon mutt. Smart—he is now your only chance."

I took a few steps back, everything becoming too much, all-consuming.

"Take your clan and leave the academy." My dad's voice was hard, edged with a warning that would have made most mages duck their heads.

David hovered a hand over his palm and spoke an enchantment. Less than a second later, the clan mark appeared. My stomach soured.

"Not until I have my consort by my side." His head tilted, his gaze drifting to me. An excited thrill shot up my spine at the same time I felt sick. "You're powerful, Selene. A level five ether mage. I have waited one hundred thirty-two years for an ether mage who was worthy to stand by my side. To think there once was a time when I wanted to siphon your magic and dispose of you without knowing appalls me."

"How?" That was the only word I managed to get out through clenched teeth. The books had said the leader of the clan had been a level four ether mage. He was old and powerful, and with dark magic, he may as well have been a five. Was that why he wanted me?

"How did I infiltrate the academy, or how am I over a century old and do not look like a decaying corpse?" His gaze shifted to the front door of the academy, where Priscilla helped support a blood-covered Ender down the steps. Aura ran out behind them, her white fur covered in dried dark red blood. Her little beady eyes landed on Vivian hovering over April, and she ran over to her.

"It comes with territory of being a dark ether mage." David's gaze locked back onto me when I didn't answer. "The irony of having to consume ether magic and killing its host to grow our strength, yet being a dark ether mage is the ultimate power. Healing is a part of our capabilities. The more power we siphon, the younger we look. It takes a powerful magic from an ether mage to obtain this level of preservation."

"My mom..." I whispered, realizing it had been her magic that made him like this.

"And Ender will be yours." David took a step closer, and so did my dad.

My hand shot up, using air magic to force my dad back. I pulled my hand to my chest, unsure if that had been for his protection or if it was to keep him away from David. The internal, intrusive thoughts were running rampant again.

"What. Did. You. Do. To. Me?" I ground out at David, this time taking a step toward him.

"Our training sessions proved quite beneficial, along with the dark grimoire." He eyed Chaos.

"He's been feeding you dark magic, Selene." Ender's hard voice rose across the front lawn as he and Priscilla approached. "Whenever he touched you and whenever you touched the dark grimoire, he fed you his dark magic. It's what he did to me during our training match."

I thought of that match and how Ender had lost control in a way that wasn't like him.

"Almost an accurate assumption, but what I did to you was slightly different." David raised his chin, holding Ender's glare. "I fed you dark illusions and emotions. I only transferred my dark magic to my consort."

"But... you helped kill the dark mage who attacked the academy?" I glared at him, confusion causing my ears to ring.

He had been a friend.

"They were from a different clan." He shrugged. "I had just given them some guidance to find you, confident it would help advance things and remove a nemesis of our clan, and aided by adding *Demonher* rats into the equation."

A bone-popping sound came from my hand and I glanced down. I had pulled my pointer finger out of the socket with my thumb. My jaw set, and I set my finger back in place with my opposing hand and spared a glance at Viv, still crouched by April's body. Her gaze pierced David with a promise of harm.

"I'm not sure how you evaded or broke through the enchantments," he glanced between my dad and Priscilla, "but I must say, it is not surprising in the least. You have managed to hide your family from me, John. For an inadequate level of a mage, I wouldn't classify you as subpar."

Now he was insulting my dad while also complimenting him.

Ender left the support of Priscilla and began heading in my direction, his gaze on David. Each step he took, I could feel my magic drawn to him. It wasn't the warm and fuzzy feeling I often felt when he was near, but it was a power hungry, all-consuming, visceral sensation beckoning me to consume his potent magic.

"Ender..." I shook my head at him, unable to move. "Please don't."

His head cocked to the side.

"No, Ender. Please do," David sneered, his eyes lighting with excitement, as if he knew the insatiable hunger I felt. "Do you see her obsidian eyes? She's begging you to come closer."

My eyes were black?

Dark-cloaked figures emerged from around us, *Demonher* rats with glowing red eyes trailing them. I counted at least five dark mages and *Demonher* rats. Each dark mage wore the mark of their clan on their palm.

"This morning's events were supposed to have run smoother, but one can never be ill-prepared." David nodded at his small dark army. "Casualties, I see. I had felt them." He looked at one of the advancing dark mages, who nodded in return. "It appears Miss Lee had benefited your academy after all. It brings the odds down a couple dark mages."

"Miss Lee?" Ender glanced at Priscilla, his brows furrowing.

Priscilla gave him a short nod. "We'll discuss it later."

David laughed. "That discussion won't happen."

Then the pandemonium started.

David strode toward me as the other dark mages and rats lunged toward my family. Chaos charged at David, and a powerful burst of magic flew at the little dragon. The magic surged around Chaos as if he had an invisible shield, but his claws found purchase in David's chest. They fell to the ground and the dagger in David's hand tumbled to the grass.

"Selene!" Ender reached me, his hands resting on my shoulders. His face was bruised and covered in dry blood, and I had never seen his hazel eyes so entirely dark grey. "Hey," he said, his voice soft. He gently brushed my cheek with his hand, and my eyes shuttered. His hand radiated with energy, and all I had to do was wrap my hand around his and his power would be mine.

Vivian screamed and my eyes shot open. A *Demonher* rat circled her, its dark, suction-cupped tongue retreating after a missed strike. My dad was at her side in seconds, a lighter in hand. Fire shot from his hand in a burning torrent at the rat, causing it to back away with a hiss.

Priscilla was already in combat with two dark mages, and a rat chomped at Chaos's tail, giving David enough time to reach the dagger. The same dark mage and several *Demonher* rats closed in on Ender and me.

My heart palpations rattled inside my head and the edges of my vision darkened. Prickly, searing heat radiated through my nerves and veins. I covered my head with my arms, the pulsing inside feeling like my head was going to explode. Breathing became a chore, as if my lungs couldn't get enough air, and I was entirely too aware of Ender's presence.

Ender. My soul-bound.

My sister.

My dad.

I screamed. The ear-piercing noise burst out along with a wave of dark magic, sending everyone and everything within a thirty-foot radius flying backward, including Ender.

I turned to face David, who was the first to his feet, smiling at me with admiration.

David turned to Chaos, who slowly rolled off his side and to his four feet, shaking his head. David lifted the dagger above his head—the dagger that most likely was the one Miss Lee said could kill a dragon with one slice—and aimed the tip at Chaos.

"No!" I roared and shoved my fist into the ground, it sinking a good five inches.

The ground around David collapsed. Chaos scrambled backward, barely avoiding the small crater.

I pulled my hand free and made my way over to the crater and jumped in, landing in a crouch. When I stood, the dust had settled enough to show David leering at me, not phased at all by my assault. I turned, shoving my hands into the dirt walls and imagining an impenetrable fortress overhead. Words flowed from my mouth in a language I didn't know I possessed until black vines enclosed the crater. Interwoven trails of dark glowing lava, a rich shade of red, pulsed as if the vines were alive.

The magic was so enticing, so alive.

"Addicting, isn't it?"

I pulled my hands from the dirt, turning to face him. He tucked the dagger away behind him.

I panted, unable to respond. I could feel his formidable power now and wondered if it was something I could take. I stepped toward him.

"You can't take another ether's dark magic." David assessed me with hunger and desire, like he could read my own cravings. "I have tried, though I've never came across a level five dark ether mage. That hunger you feel will abate marginally when you take your soul-bound's magic." His words lit an internal desire and he grinned, stepping closer. "Yes, my lovely. This world will be entirely ours. Free of dragons. If any ether mages rear their heads, we will consume them."

My lips turned upward into a smile, and I felt half-hinged. I clutched my family, Ender, and the fact that this was the dark mage who had taken my mother's life, boiling her from the inside out with blood magic.

David is the reason my family is broken, why Vivian's biological parents are dead, why I killed April, why we hid our entire lives, and if he continues, he will be the reason my remaining family dies... why Ender dies.

My smile turned bitter and I reached out, grabbing him by the throat. His skin thrummed with enticing, dangerous electricity and I pulled it to me, wrapping my hands around his neck. Another foreign enchantment left my mouth, and David's body went rigid before he could struggle, his eyes wide in shock. I lifted him in the air, ignoring his hands, which made a feeble attempt to remove my grasp from his neck.

"You waited over one hundred years for someone to stand by your side, and you chose me." I squeezed tighter. "You never chose better."

As my hand clenched and his power shot through me like a live wire, something else ached in my chest, threatening to burst.

Ender. He was reaching out to me.

But my decision had been made.

With each passing of David's magic into my soul, he aged, revealing the effects of dark magic on his body. Wrinkles appeared across his paling skin, his golden hair turning brittle and grey, and his clenched teeth yellowed and became rotten. All signs of his true self showed until I noticed his blue eyes turning grey—devoid of power. He hadn't been turning back into his previous appearance as a dark mage. His body was turning to his true age.

The power vanished and I let go, the man before me dropping to his knees. David was unrecognizable. His sunken eyes gazed at me as his outermost skin turned to dust and eventually, the rest of him followed suit, leaving a pile of brown dust on the ground.

I no longer felt his power and my skin no longer prickled with energy. The burning vines above me turned to ash, coating me in soot. The ache in my chest grew into a warm throb, and the insatiable hunger died. I became disorientated, my head started to feel fuzzy, and my body became light. Dark grey-blue blurred my vision. That was when I realized I had fallen and was staring at the sky.

A thump landed next to me and Ender's face came into view. Beyond him, Chaos soared across the sky like a bullet. Sounds of fighting ensued but were distant.

My body burned.

My heart was torn.

I tried to speak, to confess one final thing to Ender.
But my body didn't listen. He wouldn't know that I loved him.
Then everything disappeared and I couldn't hear anything at all.

Chapter Fifty-Five
Ender

Priscilla and the headmaster didn't let me see Selene for the first few days she was in the infirmary. An immediate reinforced infirmary room had been created just for her—complemented with the magic-nullifying glass lining the original walls, a faint green glowing from them. Tungsten cuffs locked around her wrists and ankles were a secondary precaution. It was Selene. There was nothing dark about her—I knew it in my bones. However, they couldn't chance the safety of the other students until she woke and it was certain there was no dark magic within her.

I leaned forward in the ugly green chair, rubbing the stubble along my chin. It had been seven days and Selene had still not woken up. Chaos's lanky body draped across her legs, his tail hanging off the bed and brushing the floor in small flicks as he slept. Aura curled against Selene's hip, fast asleep.

Vivian visited, understanding why Selene had done what she had, but she was hurting. David had killed April, not Selene, even though it had been Selene who controlled the blade. Aura had tried to heal April, but she was already gone, and Aura had used up her healing magic on me. If it was not for the little fox, I would have been dead.

Someone knocked at the door. Priscilla entered with a tray of food. Only five people were allowed to enter her room—the headmaster, Priscilla, Vivian, Nurse Adair, and me.

"You need to eat." Priscilla handed the tray to me, and I took it with thanks.

"What was the update from the council?" I asked, eyeing the ham sandwich and fries—no doubt the fries were specially made at Priscilla's request.

"Eat, and I will tell." Priscilla nodded at the tray and sat in the chair next to me.

A few members of the Magic Council had flown in, along with extra security, after David's attack. The council member who approved and pushed for David's enrollment at the Academy wouldn't see the light of day again. They had known David was a dark mage and had taken some sort of deal.

The council's most recent meeting was held to decide what to do with Selene. If I had my way, I would have been in attendance.

I took a large bite of the sandwich, waiting for Priscilla to start.

"They have decided to approve the request that she stays here for the time being." Priscilla's gaze darted to Selene's bed. "She has been tested and confirmed that she no longer holds dark magic. However, the extra security measures are still in effect until she wakes."

Meaning the restraints will stay on.

"When she does, she will be furious to have those on her," I said, giving a small smile of hope. I had been worried they were going to take her off campus—away from me.

"She certainly will." Priscilla grinned and then her smile dropped. "How are you holding up? Besides Selene."

If she wasn't talking about Selene, she could have been talking about my near-death experience, but I knew she was talking about the death of my last-living relative. Miss Lee had been killed while giving the headmaster and Priscilla time to get to Selene and me. The morning of the attack, the headmaster had seen Chaos fly off alone into the forest. He wanted to alert Priscilla, who had been monitoring the grounds, that the dragon was out for a morning flight. When he couldn't reach her or the other guard stationed on the opposite side of the grounds, he became suspicious.

The headmaster followed in the direction Chaos had gone, hoping to find Priscilla. Shortly after he found her, they discovered a group of dark mages who had slipped through a breach in the ward at the far end of the grounds and trapped Chaos. Miss Lee had been fighting the dark mages.

Once Priscilla and Headmaster John freed Chaos, they needed to get back to the academy. Miss Lee had offered to stay and fight alone. After David's death, all but one of the demon rats withered into ash, and the dark mages seemed volatile. Even with his burns, Mr. Hastings had been able to free the other guards and professors, and the dark mages and last rat were destroyed.

Once things calmed down, the guards had gone to the scene where the dark mages had breached. Miss Lee didn't make it.

"I'm fine," I told Priscilla, immediately following with another bite of food to fill my mouth. Miss Lee had severed any kinship we could have or would have had by attempting to off Selene. However, that didn't mean it didn't hurt. I once told Selene there was goodness in *almost* everyone and that it was just buried—I believed that held true for Miss Lee despite the disgust I held for her.

"Well, I need to go see a few of the council members off, as they prefer not to stay any longer than necessary." There was a slight eye roll as Priscilla spoke. "They weren't pleased Headmaster John and I had hidden Selene's ability and hidden the sisters' true identity. The fact that they had a mole on the council made them question our loyalty, but it also played a pivotal point in why it was important to keep their identities hidden. They will not be removing us from our positions or titles."

"That's good." I didn't see anything wrong with their decision.

"You know, Nick stopped me in the hall. He wanted me to give you a beer." She raised a brow.

"Leave it to Nick to try to give my guardian a beer for me." I laughed. "Let me guess: that beer is no longer his?"

"You would be correct." Priscilla smiled, then rested a hand on my shoulder before leaving.

Sighing, I set the tray in the empty chair, leaving the last few bites of the sandwich untouched. I stood, picking up my chair and moving it next to Selene's bed. I rested my hand on top of hers, squeezing tightly. Aura uncurled, stretching her little furry body and one eye cracking open, then curled right back into a tight ball.

I had once thought that I couldn't give part of my soul to create a familiar. Now, I understood why the desire was never there. My soul already belonged to someone else.

Chapter Fifty-Six
Selene

Dark ominous clouds above, with red rivets like horizontal lightning, made me feel insignificant as I stood in this dream world, wearing my dirty pajamas. The white-dusted ground was vast, with nothing else in sight.

Holding out my hand, I caught an ashen flake, which smeared my palm when I rubbed it with my thumb. Once the black ash touched the ground, it melted like snow on pavement but turned into white dust. I took a step, leaving behind a black, barefoot print. My body ached, and I sent out a silent prayer that I would wake up. This wasn't like any dream I'd had before.

Bright white exploded in the distance, like a silent bomb had detonated. I threw my hands up, shielding my eyes from the migraine-inducing, blinding light. The light traveled fast until it reached me, consuming me in nothingness.

Warmth enveloped my one side and across my legs, but my eyes stayed shut. My head felt like a thousand tiny needles were picking at my brain. Something rubbed the back of my hand in small circles, its warmth and touch providing comfort in such a tiny motion. I focused on it and awareness blossomed in my chest.

Ender was sitting next to me, holding my hand.

I forced my eyes open, taking the time to adjust to the light, which was much dimmer than that white blast that had left my head throbbing.

"Selene?" Ender's soft voice drifted to me, and I turned my head to the side to get a better view of him. His short black hair was more tousled than usual at the top, a five-o-clock shadow grew along his sharp jaw, his darker skin tone was a shade lighter, and his eyes were glossy like he hadn't slept in weeks.

I opened my mouth, but the sound that came out did not resemble any coherent word—it was just a croak.

"It's okay." The pad of Ender's thumb brushed my cheek. "You're okay."

A tear rolled down his cheek as he assessed me, and I couldn't hold back my own waterworks. There were three things I knew in that moment.

Ender was okay.

I was alive.

And I was not a dark mage.

The heavy pressure that had invaded my chest the last couple of months was gone. Even with what appeared to be nullifying glass encasing the room, I would have felt the darkness. My own magic felt like it had been put on the sidelines, untouchable and absent, but there was nothing dark about it.

I glanced down to see Chaos draped across my legs and Aura at my hip, both sound asleep. A short-lived smile spread across my face, and then I let my head fall back into Ender's palm, savoring his touch.

"Ender?" My voice felt rusty, like an old bicycle that sat in a falling apart wood barn for years.

"Yes?" His voice was still gentle.

"I love you," I blurted—no context, no heartwarming speech, just laid it out with how it was. I had been so worried I would never get the chance to tell him, and I wouldn't even care if he didn't say it back.

"I love you, too," he said, and my heart melted into a puddle.

Just kidding. I cared a lot.

We stayed there in comfortable silence for a while, until the door opened.

Vivian came in, followed by my dad. Her straight black hair was pulled back in a high ponytail, not hiding the shadows lining her red-rimmed eyes. Her gaze was on me, slowly looking me over.

"You're back," she said before grinning and running over to me.

Ender stood, sliding out of the way to make room in the small infirmary room. She squished me, and I went to wrap my arms around her but realized I couldn't. I glanced down to see magic nullifying cuffs around my wrists and ankles.

Huh. They really didn't trust me. Maybe that was why my natural magic hadn't stirred.

"I'm back," I whispered into her hair as she hugged me, causing Aura to make a small grumbling noise and make her way over to lie near Chaos. "How long was I out for?"

I pulled back, looking from Vivian to Ender and to my dad.

"A week." Vivian grabbed my hands with hers, my cuffs emitting a green glow. I looked at her, recalling the events that had happened. April was dead because of me. A week wasn't enough time to process the loss of someone close—there would never be enough time.

"Viv..." I couldn't help the ugly sob that left me. "I'm so sorry. I never—"

"I know." She hugged me again.

Those two little words held a much larger statement. She might not have blamed me for April's death, but I would never let myself forget it was the blade I had controlled that had killed her. I wouldn't be at peace with it, but I would have to come to terms with it... eventually.

"You can't sleep forever." Viv pulled back, giving me a smile through her tears. "You were never the lazy one. That job is for me."

"Mom always had to pull you out of bed." I laughed, my voice a little hoarse.

"It's good to have you back." She squeezed my hands, then stood, wiping away her tears. "But I suppose someone else would like to see you now. We are going to have nightly movies and endless Oreos once you're out of this bed."

She stepped aside, letting my dad take her space.

"How do you feel, Sal?" he asked.

"If you're asking if I am going to start creating black lava vines, then fantastic because I am not going to be." I adjusted myself so I sat straighter.

"No. I'm wondering how you physically feel." He glanced at the fluid bag that led to an IV catheter in my hand.

"I'm fine," I said.

"I don't think these are required any longer." My dad pulled out a key and motioned for me to hold out my arms. He started with the wrists. "You still won't be able to use magic."

I glanced at the glass box they had made the infirmary room into, complete with enforced door, and it made me wonder if they had done that around me while I was out or transferred me to the room afterward.

The cuffs slid off and I rubbed at my wrists even though they left no marks. He removed the ones on my ankles next. My dad was correct—I still couldn't feel my magic, but I had thought I would at least feel the hum of it with those off.

"Sal." He went over to the chair Ender had been in earlier and sat down. "There is something we need to discuss."

"What is it?" I glanced around the room as everyone went quiet, holding their breaths. Dread built in my stomach.

"There is a lot of information to be relayed of the recent events. However, I feel this piece of information is important for you to hear now, and then you need to rest. The other details can be shared later. When you and David were in that pit, you essentially *healed* him of his dark magic. Healing comes at a cost, especially one as dire as this." My dad grabbed my hand, which—to my surprise—I didn't pull away. "While you were asleep, we retested you. Even with the magic nullifying cuffs and room, the device will still pick up the type and level of elemental user in their blood."

If I was asleep, I couldn't deceive the test like I had in the past.

"You are a level one ether mage."

What?

Chapter Fifty-Seven

Selene

STEAM WAFTED OFF THE dark, rich delicious liquid as I poured myself a mug of French Press coffee. Despite it being the beginning of June and the majority of the human and mage population had already switched to iced coffee, I wanted an old-fashioned steaming cup. I set the carafe back down on the wooden cart in Dad's office and glanced at the beautiful black walnut urn resting on the bookshelf next to it.

"Well, now I know I get my love of French Press coffee from both parents." I held the mug in the air. "I love you, Mom. Thank you for keeping us safe."

I took a slow, cautious sip, careful not to burn my tongue. I hadn't been able to bring myself to drink coffee since Mom had died.

Between learning I had lost the majority of my magic—which was like missing a piece of myself—and the school healing and mourning from an eventful year, time had flown by. It's been nearly three months after briefly turning... transitioning... whatever it had been called... into a dark mage and Mom's murderer was finally gone. I was taking my first sip.

Warmth built in my chest, and I set the mug down before I let the feeling lead me to the door. I swung it open and Ender stood on the other side, a smile on his lips.

"I had a feeling you were in here." He leaned against the doorframe and crossed his arms over his chest.

I reached up, catching him off guard, and kissed him. He wrapped his hands around my waist, pulling me closer. After what felt like not enough time, I pulled away.

"I don't think I'm ready for you to graduate and leave," I said.

Exams ended last week and graduation was this Friday. Ender planned to follow Priscilla's path and become an agent for the council. His ether magic had evolved significantly. They were leaving for their home in Canada after graduation, but Dad didn't need to stay on campus during the majority of the summer and was going to take me and Viv to visit. *Thank goodness.* The thought of being apart from him physically hurt. Senior year was going to be rough.

"We still have most of the summer." The pad of his thumb brushed my cheek, wiping away my worries. "Would you like to walk with me to breakfast?"

I nodded and went to follow him but paused, glancing back at my coffee.

"Can you actually give me a moment?" I asked and he followed where my gaze had been: my coffee and Mom's urn.

"I'll be in the hallway." He planted a kiss on the top of my head and stepped into the hallway, the door closing behind him.

I went over and grabbed the mug, taking another sip. My magic still hummed in my veins, just at a lower resonance. A part of me felt lost without the rest of it, and the feeling that it was gone was inescapable. Ender, my family, and friends helped fill that void. Chaos stayed near my side and Aura was always around. Sydney's parents came themselves to pick her up after her last exam. Having your daughter's school attacked by dark mages and demon rats could apparently change the outlook a parent had on their *rebellious*—rather, misunderstood—daughter. We planned to stay in touch all summer, and I will plead our case for us to be roommates next year.

I glanced back at Mom. My heart was finally the lightest it had been in a while.

"I don't know what I'm doing." I sighed. "But that's okay." I took one last sip of coffee and set the mug down. The handle suddenly became hot, and as I was about to let go, three vines grew from underneath the mug and sprouted daisies. I touched the soft white petals. They were real.

I glanced around. I was still alone. Level ones were incapable of creating any element.

I checked again. The daisies were real.

Acknowledgments

Thank you to my family and friends who have supported me through the entire process—from my husband, parents, grandparents, aunts and uncles, cousins, friends...the list goes on and on. Dad, thank you for inspiring me to use my imagination since I was little. Mom, thank you for always being my number one fan.

To all of my wonderful beta and ARC readers—you are all incredible!

A special thank you to the professional editors and cover designer who helped piece this book together and gave me guidance.

And as always, thank you—the reader—for coming along this journey.

Hello, there!

Reviews are lifelines to authors, and we love hearing your thoughts! Please feel free to leave one on Amazon or Goodreads. I would also love to say hi and meet you. You can drop in on any of my social medias.

www.authorlwood.com

The Hybrian Series

ABOUT THE AUTHOR

Hi, there. I assume that if you've made it this far, you've either finished reading the book—or just skipped to the end. Either way, I'm happy you're here!

My name is L., and I enjoy living in the countryside of the Great Lakes Region with my family. When I'm not writing or compassionately working as a Registered Veterinary Technician, I love spending time with my family, playing volleyball, hiking, and swimming. I also *really* love ice cream... especially when paired with a warm, soft chocolate chip cookie. I'm also a huge fan of Star Wars, Marvel, and DC. If you ever see me out and about, please feel free to say hi!

Please visit **authorlwood.com** for more.

www.ingramcontent.com/pod-product-compliance
Ingram Content Group UK Ltd.
Pitfield, Milton Keynes, MK11 3LW, UK
UKHW042003230426
12048UKWH00009B/515